The Limpopo
Academy of
Private Detection

Also by Alexander McCall Smith

The Limpopo
Academy of
Private Detection

ALEXANDER McCALL SMITH

Little, Brown

LITTLE, BROWN

First published in 2012 by Little, Brown

Copyright © Alexander McCall Smith 2012

The moral right of the author has been asserted.

*All characters and events in this publication, other than those
clearly in the public domain, are fictitious and any resemblance
to real persons, living or dead, is purely coincidental.*

All rights reserved.
No part of this publication may be reproduced, stored in a
retrieval system, or transmitted, in any form or by any means, without
the prior permission in writing of the publisher, nor be otherwise circulated
in any form of binding or cover other than that in which it is published
and without a similar condition including this condition being
imposed on the subsequent purchaser.

A CIP catalogue record for this book
is available from the British Library.

Hardback ISBN: 978-1-4087-0260-4
C-format ISBN: 978-1-4087-0261-1

Typeset in Galliard by M Rules
Printed and bound in Great Britain by
Clays Ltd, St Ives plc

Papers used by Little, Brown are from well-managed forests
and other responsible sources.

MIX
Paper from
responsible sources
FSC
www.fsc.org FSC® C104740

Little, Brown
An imprint of
Little, Brown Book Group
100 Victoria Embankment
London EC4Y 0DY

An Hachette UK Company
www.hachette.co.uk

www.littlebrown.co.uk

This book is for Hilary Neville-Towle, with gratitude.

Chapter One

On a Hot Day We Dream of Tea

In Botswana, home to the No. 1 Ladies' Detective Agency for the problems of ladies, and others, it is customary – one might say *very customary* – to enquire of the people whom you meet whether they have slept well. The answer to that question is almost inevitably that they have indeed slept well, even if they have not, and have spent the night tossing and turning as a result of the nocturnal barking of dogs, the activity of mosquitoes or the prickings of a bad conscience. Of course, mosquitoes may be defeated by nets or sprays, just as dogs may be roundly scolded; a bad conscience, though, is not so easily stifled. If somebody were to invent a spray capable of dealing with an uncomfortable conscience, that person would undoubtedly do rather well – but perhaps might not sleep as soundly as before, were he to reflect on the consequences of his invention. Bad consciences, it would appear, are there for a purpose: to make us feel regret over our failings. Should they be silenced, then our entirely human weaknesses, our manifold omissions, would become all the greater – and that, as Mma Ramotswe would certainly say, is not a good thing.

Mma Ramotswe was fortunate in having an untroubled conscience, and therefore generally enjoyed undisturbed sleep. It was her habit to take to her bed after a final cup of redbush tea at around ten o'clock at night. Mr J. L. B. Matekoni, her husband and by common consent the finest mechanic in all Botswana, would often retire before her, particularly if he had had a tiring day at work. Mechanics in general sleep well, as do many others whose day is taken up with physically demanding labour. So by the time that Mma Ramotswe went to bed, he might already be lost to this world, his breathing deep and regular, his eyes firmly closed to the bedside light that he would leave for his wife to extinguish.

She would not take long to go to sleep, drifting off to thoughts of what had happened that day; to images of herself drinking tea in the office or driving her van on an errand; to the picture of Mma Makutsi sitting upright at her desk, her large glasses catching the light as she held forth on some issue or other. Or to some memory of a long time ago, of her father walking down a dusty road, holding her hand and explaining to her about the ways of cattle – a subject that he knew so well. When a wise man dies, there is so much history that is lost: that is what they said, and Mma Ramotswe knew it to be true. Her own father, the late Obed Ramotswe, had taken so much with him, but had also left much behind, so many memories and sayings and observations, that she, his daughter, could now call up and cherish as she waited for the soft arms of sleep to embrace her.

Mma Ramotswe did not remember her dreams for very long once she had woken up. Occasionally, though, an egregiously vivid dream might make such an impression that it lodged in her memory, and that is what happened that morning. It was not in any way a bad dream; nor was it a particularly good dream, the sort of dream that makes one feel as if one has been vouchsafed some great mystical insight; it was, rather, one of those dreams that seems to be a clear warning that something special is about to happen. If a dream involves lottery tickets and numbers, then its meaning is clear enough. This dream was not like that, and yet it left Mma Ramotswe feeling that she had somehow been given advance notice of something out of the ordinary, something important.

In this dream she was walking along a path in the stretch of bush immediately behind Tlokweng Road Speedy Motors, the building that the No. 1 Ladies' Detective Agency shared with Mr J. L. B. Matekoni's garage. She was not sure where she was going, but this did not seem to matter as Mma Ramotswe felt happy just to be walking along it with no great sense of having to reach a destination. And why should one not walk along a path, particularly a comfortable path, without any idea of getting any-where?

She turned a corner and found herself faced with a large acacia tree, its foliage extending out like the canopy of a commodious umbrella. To dream of trees is to ... to long for trees, and find-ing herself under the shade of this tree would have been enough to make the dream a satisfactory one. But there was more to it. Underneath the tree, standing in such a position that the mottled shade of the leaves all but obscured his face, was a tall, well-built man. He now stepped forward, held out a hand and said, 'I have come at last, Mma Ramotswe.'

And that was the point at which Mma Ramotswe awoke. The

encounter with this stranger had not been threatening in any way; there had been nothing in his demeanour that was suggestive of hostility, and she had not felt in the slightest bit anxious. As for what he said, she had simply thought, even if she had not had the time to say it, *Yes, it has been a long time.*

For a few minutes after waking, she had lain still in bed, mulling over the dream. Had the man been her father, then the dream would have been easy to understand. She knew that she dreamed of her father from time to time, which was only to be expected, given that not a day went past, not one day, when she did not think of that great and good man, the late Obed Ramotswe. If you think of somebody every day, then you can be sure you will dream of him at night; but it was not him whom she encountered under that acacia tree – that was very clear. It was somebody quite different, somebody she sensed was from a long way away. But who could that be? Mma Ramotswe did not really know anybody from a long way away, unless one counted Francistown or Maun, where she knew a number of people. But those towns, although several hundred miles from Gaborone, are both in Botswana, and nowhere in Botswana was the abode of strangers. That was because Botswana, to those who lived there, was home, and familiar, and comfortable, and no place in such a country will seem far away. No, this man under the tree was from somewhere outside the country, and that was unusual and puzzling and would have to be thought about at some length.

'I had a very unusual dream,' she said to Mma Makutsi as they attended to the morning's mail in the office.

Mma Makutsi looked up from the envelope that she was in the process of slitting open. 'Dreams are always unusual,' she said. 'In fact, it is unusual to have a usual dream.'

Mma Ramotswe frowned. She thought that she understood what Mma Makutsi meant but was not quite sure. Her assistant

4

had a habit of making enigmatic remarks, and this, she suspected, was one such remark.

'Phuti,' Mma Makutsi continued, referring to her new husband, Phuti Radiphuti, 'Phuti has many dreams, every night. He tells me about them and I explain what they mean.' She paused. 'He often dreams about furniture.'

'That is because he has a furniture shop,' Mma Ramotswe said. 'So perhaps it is not surprising.'

'That is so, Mma,' agreed Mma Makutsi. 'But he can dream about different pieces of furniture.' She paused, fixing Mma Ramotswe on the other side of the room with the cautious look of one about to reveal sensitive information. She lowered her voice. 'Some nights he dreams about beds; other nights he dreams about dining-room tables. It is very strange.'

Mma Ramotswe looked down at her desk. She did not like to discuss the intimate side of anybody's marriage – particularly when the marriage was as recent as Mma Makutsi's. She thought of new marriages as being rather like those shy, delicate flowers one sees on the edge of the Kalahari; so small that one might miss them altogether, so vulnerable that a careless step might crush their beauty. Of course, people talked about their dreams without too much embarrassment – most dreams, after all, sound inconsequential and silly in the cold light of day – but it was different when a wife talked about a husband's dreams, or a husband about a wife's. Dreams occurred in beds, and what occurred in marital beds was not a subject for debate in the office – especially if the dream *related to* beds, as it appeared that some of Phuti Radiphuti's dreams did.

But if Mma Ramotswe was reluctant to probe Phuti's dreams too closely, the same was not true of her assistant. The topic had now been broached, and Mma Makutsi pursued it enthusiastically.

'There is no doubt about a dream about beds,' she continued. 'The meaning of that dream is very clear, Mma. It should be very obvious, even to a person who does not know much about dreams, or other things, for that matter.'

Mma Ramotswe said nothing.

'Yes,' said Mma Makutsi, 'if a person says *I have been dreaming about beds*, then you know straight away what the dream means. You can say to them, *I know what that dream means. It is very clear.*'

Mma Ramotswe looked out of the window, which was high, and gave a view from that angle only of a slice of blue; empty blue; blue with no white of cloud; nothingness. 'Is the meaning of dreams clear, Mma? Do any dreams make sense, or are they just like ... like clouds in the sky, composed of nothing very much? Maybe they are clouds in our mind, Mma; maybe that is what they are.'

Mma Makutsi was having none of this. 'The meaning is often clear,' she retorted. 'I have no difficulty, Mma, in understanding a dream about beds.'

Mma Ramotswe sighed. 'Well, they do say, don't they, Mma, that men have such things on their minds most of the time. They say that men think only of that, all day. Listen to the way Charlie speaks when he thinks you can't hear him. That shows you what men think about – or at least, young men. I do not think that Mr J. L. B. Matekoni has thoughts like that in his head all day. I do not think that, Mma.'

It was as if Mma Makutsi had not heard her. 'Yes, Mma. The meaning of a dream about beds is very simple. It means that you are tired. It means that you need more sleep.'

Mma Ramotswe stared at her assistant for a few moments. Then, with some degree of relief, she smiled. 'Well, there you have it, Mma. That must be what such a dream means.'

'On the other hand,' went on Mma Makutsi, 'a dream about a dining-room table is different. That does not mean that you are tired.'

'No.'

'No, it does not mean that, Mma. A dream about a dining-room table means that you are hungry. I think that is very obvious.'

Mma Ramotswe looked first at the teapot, and then at the clock. She would wait, she decided; if one kept bringing forward the time at which one had tea, then the period after teatime would become far too long. Tea had to be taken at the right time; if anything was clear, it was that.

She decided to steer the conversation back to her own dream. But just as she was about to do so, Mma Makutsi came up with a further observation on Phuti's dreams. 'When he said to me one morning that he had dreamed of dining-room tables, I was worried. Was I giving him enough to eat, I wondered?'

'And what did you decide, Mma?'

'I think I'm giving him enough food. I believe in demand feeding. I think that is what it's called. I always leave some food out in the kitchen so that Phuti can pick up a snack if he feels hungry. There are other women who believe that you should only feed your husband at set times, so that he gets used to it. But I am not one of those women, Mma. I leave food out.'

Mma Ramotswe suppressed a grin at the thought of demand feeding for husbands. The conversation, although potentially sensitive, had proved to be more amusing than anything else, and she knew that it could drift on indefinitely. It was her own dream that had started it, and it was to her dream that she now returned.

'I had a very strange dream last night, Mma,' she said. 'As I was saying.'

7

'Please tell me what it was, Mma,' said Mma Makutsi. 'I cannot guarantee that I will be able to tell you what it means, but we shall see.'

'I dreamed that I was walking along a path,' Mma Ramotswe began. 'And—'

Mma Makutsi interrupted her. 'That means you are going on a journey, Mma. There can be no doubt about that.'

Mma Ramotswe acknowledged this. 'Possibly. But then the path came to a place—'

'That is your destination,' announced Mma Makutsi. 'That place that you saw in your dream was your destination in life. That is very clear indeed. What was it like, Mma? Was it a very good place?'

'There was an acacia tree—'

Again there was an interjection. 'Then that means you are going to end up under a tree, Mma. That is where you will find yourself, under a tree.' She looked at Mma Ramotswe sympathetically. 'That is not too bad, Mma. There are many worse places to end up.'

'But the tree was not all that important,' said Mma Ramotswe, raising her voice slightly to prevent further interruption. 'There was a man standing under the tree. It was as if he was waiting for me.'

'That will be Mr J. L. B. Matekoni.'

Mma Ramotswe shook her head. 'It was not him. It was a man I had never seen before. And he did not come from here. He was a stranger.'

Mma Makutsi's glasses flashed in a slanting band of sunlight. 'Not from Gaborone?' she asked. 'Not from Botswana?'

'No. He was from somewhere else. He was not an African at all.'

Mma Makutsi was silent. Then she delivered her judgement.

'You are going to meet a stranger,' she said, with an air of gravity. 'You are going to meet a stranger under an acacia tree.'

'I thought it might mean something like that,' said Mma Ramotswe. 'But then I thought that it probably didn't mean anything at all. That it was just a dream, and I would forget about it by this afternoon.'

Mma Makutsi looked doubtful. 'I don't think you should forget it, Mma Ramotswe. I think that you should remember it, so that when it happens, when you meet that stranger under the acacia tree, you will be prepared.'

She said nothing more, but gave Mma Ramotswe an oblique look; a look that Mma Ramotswe interpreted as a warning. But she had not understood – for all her claims to understanding dreams, Mma Makutsi had missed the point. This stranger was not threatening; this stranger, for whom Mma Makutsi said she should be prepared, was not somebody to be dreaded or guarded against. On the contrary, this stranger was a good man, a kind man, and his arrival – if he were ever to come, which was highly unlikely – was something to be welcomed, something to be celebrated. And there was something else – something that was hard to put into words. The man in the dream might have been a stranger in that she had never seen him before, but somehow she felt that she knew him. *She knew him but did not know him.*

She glanced at her watch again. Resolve can be weakened by time, and by talk about dreams and by heat.

'I know it's a bit early, but I think that we should have tea now,' she said to Mma Makutsi. And Mma Makutsi, who had removed her glasses to clean them, looked up, finished her task of polishing the lenses and said that she completely agreed.

'On a hot day,' she said, 'we dream of tea.'

9

Chapter Two

Food Cooked with Love
Tastes Better

It was shortly after this conversation about dreams, or after the tea that followed this conversation, that an unknown car drew up outside the offices of the No. 1 Ladies' Detective Agency and parked beneath the acacia tree. Had this been followed by the emergence of a tall man similar in appearance to the one who had appeared in Mma Ramotswe's dream, then Mma Makutsi's belief in the prescience of dreams would have been dramatically confirmed. But this did not happen, as the person who opened the car door and stepped out – watched with bated breath by Mma Makutsi – was none other than Mma Silvia Potokwani, matron not only of the orphan farm but also, in a sense, of all she surveyed.

Mma Makutsi let her disappointment be known. 'It's nobody,' she said. 'Just her.'

Mma Ramotswe, who had not been looking out of the window, now did so. 'But it's Mma Potokwani, Mma. She is not nobody.' The reproach in her voice was evident and was picked up by Mma Makutsi.

'I'm sorry, Mma,' she said. 'I didn't mean to be rude about Mma Potokwani. It's just that I thought that it might be the man you saw in your dream. One never knows.'

Mma Ramotswe let it pass. Mma Makutsi had never enjoyed a particularly good relationship with Mma Potokwani – the natural rivalry, Mma Ramotswe thought, that results from the juxtaposition of two strong personalities. That had changed more recently, though, and in particular there had been what amounted to a cordial truce when Mma Potokwani had offered to apply her undoubted organisational skills to the planning of Mma Makutsi's wedding. This offer of help had been gratefully accepted, and had relieved Mma Makutsi of much of the anxiety that accompanies a wedding. Mma Ramotswe hoped that this cordiality would persist: she did not like conflict in any form, and it pleased her to think that these two women, who had so much to offer, might now cooperate rather than seek to undermine each other. Perhaps Mma Makutsi might help the orphan farm in its fundraising activities, now that she was Mrs Phuti Radiphuti and the occupant, therefore, of a reasonably elevated position in the town. Phuti was a man of substance, with the resources of the Double Comfort Furniture Store behind him and a large herd of cattle at the Radiphuti cattle post off to the west of Mahalapye. The size of that herd could only be guessed at – 'A very large number of cattle, all of them quite fat,' was all that Mma Makutsi had said on the subject – but whatever its dimensions, it meant that Mma Makutsi would now surely have the resources to help the orphan farm in some way.

Mma Potokwani herself was not unaware of the change in

Mma Makutsi's fortunes, and it was possible, Mma Ramotswe thought, that this visit was connected with precisely that awareness. The matron of the orphan farm was famous for the vigour of her support for her charges, with every meeting, every encounter being seen as an opportunity to solicit support for the orphan cause. But as Mma Potokwani settled herself into the client's chair in the office that morning, it became clear that it was business of a very different sort that was on the matron's mind. Immediately after the normal greetings, Mma Potokwani cleared her throat and fixed first Mma Ramotswe and then Mma Makutsi with a baleful stare.

'I have come to see you about a very difficult matter,' she said. 'In all my years as a matron, I have never come across something as difficult as this.'

'You must have seen many things,' said Mma Ramotswe.

'Many very heartbreaking things,' added Mma Makutsi from the other side of the room.

Mma Potokwani turned her head to glance briefly at Mma Makutsi. 'You're right about that, Mma Makutsi,' she said. 'Or should I be calling you Mma Radiphuti now?'

Mma Makutsi beamed with pleasure at the recognition. 'That is very kind of you, Mma Potokwani. I shall be Mma Radiphuti when I am in my house – and when I go to the shops.' That last qualification was important, as Mma Potokwani and Mma Ramotswe were quick to acknowledge. The Radiphuti name would certainly bring respect – and all necessary credit – when bandied about in shops.

'However,' went on Mma Makutsi, 'my professional name remains Makutsi. That is quite common these days, you know. Professional people – doctors and lawyers and detectives – often keep their maiden name when they marry. That is because their clients and patients, and so on, all know them by that name.'

Mma Ramotswe thought it a bit presumptuous for Mma Makutsi to include herself in the company of doctors and lawyers, but did not say anything.

'It is also the name on my diploma from the Botswana Secretarial College,' Mma Makutsi said. 'That is it, framed, up there. See it? It reads *Grace Makutsi,* just above the place where it says *ninety-seven per cent.* Right there.'

'I have seen it before,' said Mma Potokwani, slightly shortly. 'You have drawn my attention to it, Mma. More than once, I think.' She paused, waiting for her pointed remark to be absorbed, but Mma Makutsi merely smiled encouragingly.

'So, Mma Ramotswe,' Mma Potokwani continued. 'I have a rather complicated story to tell you.'

'I am used to such things,' Mma Ramotswe assured her. 'Do I need to take notes? Is it that complicated?'

'I can write it all down in shorthand,' Mma Makutsi volunteered. 'That way, not a word will be lost.'

'That will not be necessary,' snapped Mma Potokwani. 'It is complicated and simple, all at the same time. You do not need to take notes. Have you heard of a man called Mr Ditso Ditso? He is a well-known businessman.'

Mma Ramotswe nodded. She had not met Ditso Ditso, but had seen his name in the papers on numerous occasions. And she knew people who knew him; that was always the case in Botswana – you inevitably knew somebody who knew somebody.

'Rra Ditso is quite a good man, I think,' said Mma Potokwani. 'Sometimes people like that – rich people – are very selfish and forget where they have come from and who their people are. He is not like that.'

Mma Ramotswe felt able to agree with these remarks on the newly rich. The growing prosperity of Botswana meant that there were many who had come a long way, and it was not uncommon to find people who seemed to forget the claims of friends and family once their fortunes were established. Recently there had been a case reported in the newspapers of a wealthy bottle-store owner whose elderly parents were discovered to be living in extreme poverty in a remote village. They had not even heard of their son's success, but were still proud of it when it was revealed to them and declined to express any bitterness over the difference in their circumstances. Mma Ramotswe had been astonished by their response, but then had thought: no, these are the real Botswana values. The son might not have them, but the parents did. And parents – whether they were in Botswana or anywhere else – almost always forgave, whatever happened; or at least, mothers did. Whatever a son or daughter did, a mother forgave.

'It is good that he remembers other people,' said Mma Ramotswe. 'Sometimes I think that rich people live in a country in which they are the only people. It is called the Rich People's Place, I think.'

Mma Potokwani smiled. 'I think that's right, Mma. But this Ditso – he's not like that at all. He has been very generous to everybody.' She paused. 'Including ourselves. He has been very, very generous with his time.'

'That's good,' said Mma Ramotswe. 'You must be pleased with that, Mma Potokwani. You're always asking people . . .' She stopped herself. It was Mma Potokwani's job to ask people to help the orphan farm, and she should not mention it as if it might be a fault.

Mma Potokwani raised a hand. 'I should be pleased, Mma, but . . .'

For a few moments there was silence. Then Mma Makutsi said: 'You are not pleased, Mma Potokwani?'

Again Mma Potokwani shifted in her chair and glanced at

Mma Makutsi. 'No, I'm not pleased, Mma Makutsi. Do I look pleased?'

Mma Makutsi shook her head. 'I do not think you are pleased.'

'You are right, Mma. You are a very good detective. I am not pleased.'

There was a further brief silence. This time it was broken by Mma Ramotswe, who said: 'So . . .' It was not much to say, but it moved the conversation on.

'The problem,' Mma Potokwani explained, 'is that this Ditso is on the orphan-farm board. I have a board, you see, and they are the people who make the big decisions for the orphan farm. They are good people, and they like the orphans. They work very hard.'

'Of course they do,' said Mma Ramotswe. 'I know some of those people on your board. They are on many boards – working very hard for their causes.'

Mma Potokwani agreed that this was so. She very rarely had any disagreement with her board, she said, but unfortunately a major disagreement had emerged over a decision that Mr Ditso Ditso had talked the board into making. 'We were given a very big grant by a diamond company recently,' said Mma Potokwani. 'The board had to decide what to do with all the money. Rra Ditso came up with a project, although he did not consult me – not once. He said the money should be used for building purposes. I had no objection to that: we could do with a few more houses for the children to live in. But then he decided that it would be something quite different, and that was when everything began to be not quite so good.'

'He has chosen something unsuitable?' asked Mma Ramotswe.

Mma Potokwani raised her eyebrows. 'Unsuitable is not a strong enough word, Mma. His choice is a disaster – a very big disaster.'

Mr Ditso Ditso, Mma Potokwani went on to reveal, had decided that the orphan farm needed a dining hall and a modern kitchen to serve it. This would mean that all the food could be cooked in one place, and that would mean a considerable saving could be made. 'It is always cheaper to do everything in one place,' he said to the board. 'I have always done that in my business, and it has made me a rich man. Do everything at the same time, in the same place, and your costs go down. If your costs go down, then your profits go up.'

These words, reported verbatim by Mma Potokwani, hung in the air. There was something wrong with them, thought Mma Ramotswe; they might apply to a business, but ... but was an orphan farm a *business*?

Mma Potokwani sensed the reservation. 'If you're wondering whether that's the right way to run an orphan farm, Mma, then you are right to think that. We are not a business.'

'You are a home,' said Mma Makutsi.

'That is exactly right,' said Mma Potokwani. 'We are a home, and although we like to keep our costs down, there are other things to consider.'

'The house-mothers ...' began Mma Ramotswe.

'Yes, Mma,' said Mma Potokwani. 'As you know, we have little houses where the children live. They are not big – just eight to ten children in each, and one house-mother for each.'

'They are very good ladies,' said Mma Ramotswe.

'Yes, they are. I choose them very carefully. Not everybody can be a house-mother. A lady must be kind if she is to be a house-mother. She must also be able to control the children. She must know what it is like to have no parents, and she must make allowances. There are many things for a good house-mother to keep in mind. It is not easy.'

'But it works,' said Mma Ramotswe. 'I have seen those ladies and they are very fine people. The children love them.' She frowned. 'Surely the board doesn't want to do away with your house-mothers. Who would there be to love the children?'

Mma Potokwani assured her that the board had no intention of getting rid of house-mothers; there would still be plenty of work for them to do. 'They keep the houses clean. They mend the children's clothes. There are many things. But the big thing, Mma, the big thing they do is they cook the children's food and they eat it together, round a table, like a real family.'

'And if there is a new hall and a kitchen—'

Mma Potokwani became animated. 'That will all go, Mma Ramotswe! That will go! And if that happens, then the heart of our place will be ...' She searched for the right words. 'It will stop beating. There will be no heart any more.'

Mma Ramotswe looked down at her hands. Of course Mma Potokwani was right: your family was made up of the people you ate with as a child. Everybody knew that. And how could the people who sat on the board not understand it as well? Had they themselves no people to eat with?

She put that to Mma Potokwani, who thought for a moment before she replied. 'I think that maybe they know that, but they are dazzled by all the money that they are being offered. That is what money does, Mma Ramotswe – you must have seen that. Sometimes we need to look the other way when people put money in front of our noses. We have to look at the other things we can see so that the money doesn't hide them.' She sighed. 'And they are very pleased at the thought of savings. They are always saying to me that we must look for ways to save money. And here is one. They tell me that it will cost only half as much to make the same amount of food in one kitchen. They say that we cannot ignore that.'

Mma Ramotswe listened to this gravely. She understood the

point that Mma Potokwani was making; she had seen the children eating in their houses with their house-mother; she had smelled the rich stews bubbling away in the tiny kitchens of the individual houses; she knew what all of that meant. And now they were planning to have the children sit all together in one great dining hall, served by a kitchen into which they would never be allowed to wander. What chance would a child have of sticking a finger into some dish to taste what was being made? Or of standing beside a house-mother while she made a meal and sang, as some of those women did? Who would teach the children the cooking songs? Not some anonymous chef, she thought, hired to produce large quantities of food with efficiency rather than love. And food made with love, she thought, tasted better – everybody knew that. It just did.

'I'm very sorry to hear all this, Mma Potokwani,' she said. 'But I'm not sure if we can do anything to help. If you haven't been able to persuade your board to change its mind, then I can't see what any of us can do. They will just say, "You mind your own business, Mma Ramotswe." That is what I fear they will say, Mma.'

'I know that, Mma,' said Mma Potokwani. 'I have tried, and I have failed. I cannot expect you to do any better. But ...'

I should have known she would not be so easily defeated, thought Mma Ramotswe. *Not Mma Potokwani* ... 'But?'

Mma Potokwani leaned forward in her chair. Mma Makutsi did so too. 'I have had an idea, Mma Ramotswe. It's just an idea. I have no proof of anything.'

Mma Ramotswe waited. 'An idea?'

'More of a suspicion.' She paused. 'What if we found out that Mr Ditso was in favour of this project for the wrong reason?'

'I do not think the board would accept it.'

Mma Potokwani was triumphant. 'Exactly!'

Mma Ramotswe brought her down to earth. 'But is there any reason to think that he is behaving dishonestly?'

Mma Potokwani shrugged. 'How do you get as much money as he has? By working? I really don't see, Mma, how one man could do so much work that he would end up with so much money. No, there's something else there – something that we don't know about but that must be there, Mma – it must.'

That evening, Mma Ramotswe fed the children early so that they could both tackle homework that had taken second place to more attractive afternoon activities – to football, in Puso's case, and to talking to friends in Motholeli's. Both of the foster-children were bright, although Puso showed a tendency to be easily distracted.

'It says here,' said Mma Ramotswe patiently as she sat with Puso at the table that Mr J. L. B. Matekoni had made for the boy's bedroom, 'that it takes one man one hour to dig a ditch.'

Puso looked up at her. 'That is very quick, Mma. One hour? Could anybody dig a ditch in one hour?'

'It's just for this sum,' said Mma Ramotswe. 'And we shouldn't worry about that just now. What else does it say?' She looked at the crumpled sheet of paper on which the homework exercises had been printed out. 'It says that if it takes one man one hour to dig the ditch, then how long would it take for three men to dig the same ditch? What do you think is the answer to that, Puso?'

Puso frowned. 'It would be very hard for three men to dig one ditch, Mma. They would always be getting in each other's way. So it would probably take longer than it would take one man to do it. Maybe two hours?'

Mma Ramotswe smiled. 'We don't have to worry about practical things when we're doing sums,' she said. 'You can forget about things like that. What you must do is to divide one by three. That will tell you.' She paused. She was not sure whether he had learned about fractions yet, and the trouble, anyway, was that everything was different these days. Children did not learn to count in the same way as they used to. And she was not even sure whether fractions had been abolished altogether.

'Let's think of it in minutes,' she said at last. 'One hour is sixty minutes. So if you divide sixty by three, what do you get? That is how long it would take three men to do the work done by one.'

Puso closed his eyes. Opening them, he pursed his lips with effort before he replied, 'Ten minutes? No, maybe five.'

Mma Ramotswe shook her head. 'No, that's not right. The answer is twenty minutes, Puso. And do you know how I got that answer?'

The boy shrugged. 'They could do it much more quickly if they had somebody like Mma Potokwani ordering them about. She'd make them dig faster, wouldn't she, Mma?'

She did not reply to this, even if what Puso said was quite true. There was nobody like Mma Potokwani to get things done, and that applied, she suspected, as much to ditches as it did to anything else.

'I think you should try to do this by yourself,' she said. 'If you can't do these sums, then ask the teacher to help you. I am not sure how you do these things these days – it is all rather different.'

And it *was* different, as she discussed with Mr J. L. B. Matekoni when, an hour or so later, they had their own rather delayed dinner. He said that he was not at all sure if schools taught mental arithmetic any more. 'Take Charlie,' he said, referring to the older of his two apprentices. 'If you ask him to do some simple calculation – such as what the capacity of a fuel tank might be if you take a bit of it off – he looks blank and reaches for his pocket calculator. We can do those things in our head, can't we, Mma?'

Mma Ramotswe thought about this. It was true that she could work out how much change was due at the supermarket till, but when it came to fuel tanks and their capacity, she was not so confident. But the general point that Mr J. L. B. Matekoni was making certainly stood: there were some things that just had to be learned through effort, and she was not sure how popular effort currently was. 'It is all different, Rra,' she said. 'The world is all different. But people like Charlie can do other things, you know. These people who cannot add up can do other things very well.'

Mr J. L. B. Matekoni looked doubtful. 'I'm keen to hear what those things are,' he said.

'They are good at . . . ' began Mma Ramotswe, quickly searching her mind. 'They are good at computers and things like that.'

'Maybe,' he said. 'But there are things other than computers, Mma. There are proper machines with cogs and grease. Are they good at those? Are they good at fixing ploughs?'

The mention of ploughs reminded Mma Ramotswe of Mma Potokwani, who had recently asked Mr J. L. B. Matekoni to fix the small plough that they used to till the fields at the orphan farm. He had done it, of course, as he always did, and charged no fee, again as he always did. Now she told him about the visit the matron had paid to the No. 1 Ladies' Detective Agency that morning.

'She came in an unknown car,' she said. 'She told us that it had been given to the orphan farm by a big donor. Mr Ditso Ditso.'

'Ow!' said Mr J. L. B. Matekoni. 'That man is very big.'

'Yes. But the car is only the beginning. He has said that he will give a whole lot more in future.'

'He is very kind as well.'

'Yes,' agreed Mma Ramotswe. 'But the trouble is, Mma Potokwani doesn't like a new scheme he has cooked up.'

21

Mr J. L. B. Matekoni listened gravely as Mma Ramotswe told him about the reservations that Mma Potokwani had expressed as to the effect that the proposed changes at the orphan farm would have. 'And then,' she went on, 'Mma Potokwani wondered about whether his money was honestly acquired. Do you think it is, Rra?'

He did not hesitate. 'I don't think so.'

She greeted this with interest. 'Really, Rra? Have you heard something?'

Mr J. L. B. Matekoni shook his head. 'No, I have not heard anything. I have heard nothing, in fact.'

'Then how can you say that his money was not honestly earned?'

Mr J. L. B. Matekoni looked slightly uneasy. 'You will laugh at me, I think.'

'I will never laugh at you, Rra.'

'In that case, I can tell you. I know this because of his car. He drives a dishonest car.'

Mma Ramotswe tried to control herself. She made a supreme effort, but it did not work, and she burst into a peal of laughter.

'There,' said Mr J. L. B Matekoni. 'You laughed at me! You said that you wouldn't, but you did.'

'I'm sorry, Rra. I did not mean it. It's just that . . . it's just that I can't see how a car can be dishonest.'

'But it can,' he protested. 'There are certain cars that are always chosen by dishonest people, just as there are cars that only the honest will drive. When you're a mechanic for many years, you become able to notice these things.'

'And he drives a dishonest one?'

'Very,' said Mr J. L. B Matekoni. 'Have you seen? It's covered with chrome and flashy bits and pieces. Any mechanic – any mechanic at all, Mma – will say when he sees such a car: "There goes a bad man." A mechanic knows these things, Mma. He just does.'

Later that night, as she lay awake in the darkness, Mma Ramotswe considered these words. *A mechanic knows these things* ... It sounded very general, very *unscientific*, but it was, she thought, probably true. Mr J. L. B. Matekoni had always been a very good judge of character, and if he said that there was something about Mr Ditso Ditso that was suspect, then he was probably right. But the difficulty for her was that it was one thing for somebody to say that another person was bad; it was quite another thing to prove it. And that was what Mma Potokwani had asked her to do: to provide proof that could be shown to the board of the orphan farm that one of their most influential members was bad, and so was his money. It would not be easy; it is never easy to provide proof even when we feel, in our very bones, that we know something to be the case. She was sorry that Mma Potokwani had asked her to do this, but, as always, when Mma Potokwani asked you to do something, whether it was to dig a ditch or to find out information about a rich man, it was impossible to say no. Completely impossible.

Chapter Three

Your House Has Got My Name on it

Mma Makutsi had informed Mma Ramotswe that she would not be coming into the office until mid-morning the next day. It was an announcement rather than a request, and reflected a subtle change in the internal arrangements of the No. 1 Ladies' Detective Agency. This change was not threatening in any way: Mma Ramotswe and Mma Makutsi had always got along together very well, even if it occasionally had to be made clear – in the gentlest way – that Mma Ramotswe was the head of the agency and Mma Makutsi was not. There had also been a disparity in status. Not that this was anything upon which Mma Ramotswe would ever be inclined to founder, but in the past there had been no escaping the fact that while Mma Ramotswe was the wife of a prominent mechanic and garage owner, the daughter of a highly regarded man who knew a great deal about cattle, and a pioneering – indeed the only – private detective in Botswana, Mma Makutsi was none of these things. She had not exactly come from nowhere – Bobonong was not nowhere, even if it could hardly be described as somewhere – but her place, her family, her village all seemed a very long way from Gaborone. And her material circumstances had been very different, too. When she emerged from the Botswana Secretarial College she had very little: a couple of dresses and one and a half pairs of shoes, one shoe having been lost in a move from one rented room to another. And to have one and a half pairs of shoes is effectively to have only one pair, unless, of course, the single shoe could in some way be considered a potential substitute for one shoe of the complete pair. This, however, would require that they match, which is rarely the case.

Mma Makutsi had borne her straitened circumstances with dignity. Mma Ramotswe had never heard her complain – not once, not even when, towards the end of the month in those last, trying days before payday, she knew that Mma Makutsi's purse was empty, or close to empty. Mma Makutsi would never ask for an advance on next month's pay, and had declined such offers when Mma Ramotswe had made them.

'If there's one thing they taught us at the Botswana Secretarial College,' she explained, 'then it is this: never take from next month what belongs to next month. That is a good rule, Mma, and if more people paid attention to it, then we would not be in the trouble we are in today.'

Mma Ramotswe was not sure that they were in trouble. Some people were undoubtedly in trouble, but not everyone; yet she knew what Mma Makutsi meant in a general sense, and was ready to agree.

Now, of course, it was all quite different. Mma Makutsi's marriage to Phuti Radiphuti meant that she had become a member of a family that was not only financially comfortable, but actually rather well off. Phuti's father, the elder Mr Radiphuti, had by dint of hard work built up a very successful business, the Double Comfort Furniture Store. This store was now probably the largest furniture business in Botswana, and employed well over sixty people. Phuti, his anointed successor, had shown a real aptitude for the selling of furniture, and had steered the business to even greater prosperity. The profits had been ploughed back into the concern, and also into the acquisition of a large herd of cattle. Phuti did not even know the number of head of cattle he possessed, having only a rough idea; this was unusual in a country where people not only knew how many cattle they had, but also who each beast's parents and grandparents were. On this, the late Obed Ramotswe had once observed that in Botswana there were families of cattle, just as there were families of people; and that within these families there were members who spelled trouble and those who did not, just as there were such differences within human families. A recalcitrant, troublesome bullock was easier to understand if one knew, as Obed Ramotswe always would, that this bullock came from a cattle family in which the young males had a tendency to such behaviour.

There were some who whispered that Mma Makutsi had chosen Phuti Radiphuti because of what he had, rather than what he was. Such remarks were not only uncharitable but quite unfounded. Those who were aware of the truth of the matter – and Mma Ramotswe was one such – knew that Mma Makutsi had had no inkling of Phuti's situation when she first set eyes on him on that fateful night at the ballroom-dancing lesson. She had danced with him in spite of his clumsiness and inability to get the steps right; she had listened patiently to him notwithstanding his speech impediment, the stammer which at that stage had made him virtually unintelligible. That had gone, of course, as his confidence had grown and she had gently coached him in the ways of less troubled speech. All of that was done out of love and affection, with not a thought to what their engagement and subsequent marriage would bring. And observing all this on the sidelines was that shameless gold-digger Violet Sephotho, who seethed with envy at the unfolding of Mma Makutsi's good fortune.

Mma Ramotswe had been immensely relieved when Mma Makutsi had indicated that she wanted to continue working after her marriage.

'It is much better to do something rather than do nothing, Mma,' Mma Makutsi announced. 'And when you have professional training, as I do, it is a shame not to use it.'

'You are very wise, Mma,' said Mma Ramotswe. 'You are wise, and I am grateful.'

'No, Mma, I am the grateful one,' said Mma Makutsi. 'You are the person who has given me everything. You gave me a job when I was finding it difficult to get one – in spite of getting—'

'Ninety-seven per cent,' supplied Mma Ramotswe helpfully.

'Exactly, Mma. Ninety-seven per cent, and it was still impossible to find anything. When some of those girls who got barely fifty per cent at the Botswana Secretarial College, girls such as—'

'Violet Sephotho,' Mma Ramotswe contributed.

'Precisely, Mma. She is the big example. Anyway, you are the one who took me on and made me into a detective. You are the one, Mma, and I shall be grateful to you until the day I die. Right up to that day and beyond, Mma.'

For a moment Mma Ramotswe imagined Mma Makutsi in heaven, dressed in white, as people were thought to be clad there, her large glasses somehow more luminous, more reflecting, than in the mere light of this earth ... Mma Makutsi sitting, perhaps ready to take dictation from the Lord himself . . . It was a ridiculous thought, but she could not help herself from thinking it, and it made her smile.

The advent of Phuti had certainly changed Mma Makutsi's fortunes, but those had improved slightly anyway by the time of their first meeting. This improvement had come from two sources: the giving by Mma Makutsi of typing lessons to men, and the gradual growth in the revenues of the No. 1 Ladies' Detective Agency, which had resulted in a number of pay rises. This had led to her moving to rather better accommodation, and to the eventual overhaul of her wardrobe, particularly in that department dearest to her, the department of shoes.

There were a number of possible reasons for Mma Makutsi's attachment to shoes. One of these was profound: as a young girl, she had had none, and she remembered looking with envy at those so placed as to afford them. At the age of eight she was still unshod – which was not unusual in a remote village in that rather hard part of the country. But over the next year or so, shoes started to appear on the feet of other members of her class at school, and her heart ached, *ached*, for a pair. The other children's shoes tended to be hand-me-downs – nobody had new shoes then – and Grace Makutsi would have been content even with handed-down hand-me-downs. But she had to wait, though a sympathetic friend lent her a pair of shoes for the duration of her birthday – blissful, remembered hours, even if the shoes in question were slightly too small and pinched her feet in places.

With such memories, what could one do but love shoes, long for them, dream of the day when one might have several pairs safely stacked away; comfortable shoes, shoes that fitted one's feet, shoes with no history of other owners, of other feet? That day dawned for her, of course, and it brought its expected pleasure. But then something rather extraordinary happened – Mma

28

Makutsi began to imagine that her shoes talked to her. It happened quite unexpectedly, and at first she assumed that the voice had come from some passer-by; some person who had perhaps passed by and not been seen, but who had for some reason chosen to mutter *Hallo there, boss*. But then it had happened once more, again unexpectedly, when the shoes had said to her: *Watch out, boss, rough ground ahead*.

She had felt none of the alarm that one might normally be expected to feel on hearing voices: a worrying development for some. Rather, she had dismissed it as a mere figment of her imagination, similar to those snatches of melody that we sometimes hear – the memory of music; those half-formed sentences – the memory of conversation; in short, nothing to worry about. Our heads are full of such things, Mma Ramotswe had once pointed out to Mma Makutsi, and she had agreed. If, then, one heard one's shoes talking, it was really coming from oneself, and was nothing more alarming than that.

So she came to accept that the shoes would occasionally express an opinion. And she also accepted that this view might sometimes contradict what she was thinking, or even be slightly rude, or hectoring, perhaps. One cannot expect complete compliance from one's shoes, or unqualified admiration – although that would certainly be nice. One must be prepared, she thought, for at least *some* criticism from one's footwear, the occasional sharp comment, the odd note of jealousy sounded by working shoes of party shoes – that sort of thing.

Now that she was married to Phuti Radiphuti there would be plenty of opportunities to purchase new shoes, but only in good time. Mma Makutsi was very aware that there were people watching her behaviour to see whether her newly acquired position would go to her head. She was determined to deny such people the chance to crow and to make remarks such as: *Give money to a person from Bobonong and that's what you get – every time!* She would not have that; she would be discreet and would not surround herself with the trappings of prosperity.

Except for a house ... And that was the reason she would be late in to work that morning: she and Phuti Radiphuti were due to meet the man whom Phuti had selected to build the house that they were planning to live in and where, both he and Mma Makutsi fervently hoped, they would raise their children. For this task he had chosen a man to whom he had recently sold two large sofas: Mr Clarkson Putumelo, the holder of a diploma in building from the Botswana School of Construction and Allied Trades, and proprietor and managing director of the This Way Up Building Company. The sale of the sofas had been an easy and satisfying transaction. Phuti had come across Mr Putumelo browsing through the soft-furnishings section of the store and had asked if he could help him. Mr Putumelo had enquired about sofas and had been shown several. He had selected a very large one, in bright green leather, and had gone off to fetch his wife, a woman whose dimensions were almost as generous as those of the sofa. Mr Putumelo had suggested that his wife try the sofa, which she did, expressing immediate satisfaction with its comfort in a voluble and high-pitched voice. But then, when she had attempted to get up, she had been so embraced by the padding that she had been unable to do so, and both Phuti and Mr Putumelo had been obliged to pull hard at her outstretched arms to bring her back to her feet. Mr Putumelo had not been in the slightest bit embarrassed, and had simply said, 'This is always happening with this woman.' Phuti might have suggested a less commodious option – there were several sofas that had clearly been designed with this issue in mind – but this proved not to be necessary. Mr Putumelo asked about a possible discount for two, was offered ten per cent off and immediately committed himself. This painless transaction had put the idea into Phuti's mind that this might be the man to undertake the building of his house. He had heard that building a house could be a traumatic and distressing task: if the builder you chose was as affable as Mr Putumelo, then presumably that difficult process would be all the easier. He asked, and Mr Putumelo readily agreed. 'I am the man to build you a house,' he said, with a smile. 'I can tell that a mile off. Your house has got my name on it.'

The plot that Phuti Radiphuti had chosen for their marital home was well placed from more than one point of view. Gaborone had grown, with the result that many people now had a long journey into work each day, making their way into the city in swaying, crowded minibuses. It would have been easy for Phuti to find a plot of land in one of these new suburbs, but neither he nor Mma Makutsi wanted to spend hours on the roads. So when Mma Makutsi noticed that there was a small parcel of building land not far from Tlokweng Road Speedy Motors and the contiguous office of the No. 1 Ladies' Detective Agency, Phuti was quick to inspect it – and equally quick to snap it up.

'It's perfect,' he said, when he reported back to her. 'It will take you five or ten minutes to get to work – no more. And I will need fifteen minutes to drive to the store. It could not be better.'

The plot was at the end of an untarred road, a cul-de-sac that led nowhere and down which few cars would venture. There were one or two houses not far away, but nothing close by, and on at least two sides of what would become their garden, there was acacia scrub – thorn trees, low-lying bushes with twisted brown leaves, tussocks of hardy grass that would miraculously become green within hours of the arrival of the first rains. It looked like poor earth – dusty and unwelcoming – but it was enough to keep cattle happy and they could be seen wandering across this landscape, picking at what nourishment they could find, the soft sound of their bells filling the air.

Negotiations for the purchase of the plot were swift and uncomplicated, and within days of Phuti's seeing the plot it was theirs. Now came the task of designing the house that would be erected on the newly acquired land. Phuti Radiphuti, it transpired, had a friend who was a draughtsman. 'You do not need to pay an architect for this,' he announced to Mma Makutsi. 'My friend can do all the drawings for nothing.'

Mma Makutsi was slightly concerned over this. She was not sure that it was a good idea to get a friend to design one's house, even if that friend happened to be a draughtsman. There were many technical issues, were there not? Did you not need to take into account the weight of the roof and the size of the doors? And had there not been a house up in Francistown that had collapsed because these things had been ignored and the walls built far too thin? There had been a picture of it in the paper, she recalled. A woman had been captured standing outside what looked like a pile of rubble, and above it the paper had printed, *Poor lady sees her house fall down*. Mma Makutsi had been struck by the poignancy of this photograph; it must be devastating, she felt, to see one's house collapse. Presumably everything inside was covered by tumbled bricks and pieces of shattered timber: all the poor lady's pots and pans, all her clothing, all her shoes . . .

She did not feel that she could argue with Phuti. It was his money, after all, even if their wedding vows had made reference to sharing everything, and she had to accept that he knew all about how to deal with builders and suppliers and the like. If he decided that his draughtsman friend should design the house, then she would not question his judgement, no matter what private reservations she might harbour. And this view, she thought, would be approved of by Mma Ramotswe herself, who had once remarked to her, 'Men are very sensitive, Mma Makutsi. You would not always think it to look at them, but they are. They do not like you to point out that they are wrong, even when they are. That is the way things are, Mma – it just is.'

Now Mma Makutsi was gazing at the plot with Phuti Radiphuti beside her, waiting for the arrival of their builder who was coming to discuss the project.

'It is ours now,' said Phuti. 'Look at it. That is where our house will be, and over there will be your vegetable garden – if you want one, that is. You do not have to have a vegetable garden if you do not want to have it.' He looked at her anxiously, almost as if he were concerned that he might be taken to be the sort to impose vegetable gardens on people.

'I will be very happy to have a vegetable garden,' she said. 'We will start it as soon as the house is built.'

'Oh, I am so excited,' said Phuti. 'I have never built a house before.'

Mma Makutsi tried not to look concerned. 'I don't think you will find it hard,' she said.

'I think there is nothing to it,' said Phuti. 'As long as everything is straight. You have to get things level, and not like this.' He made an up-and-down movement with his hands. 'If you do that, then the house will be a good one.'

Mma Makutsi nodded. That sounded perfectly reasonable to her. She could hardly believe her good fortune: to be standing here with her husband, her real, legal husband, surveying a small square of Botswana soil that actually *belonged* to them. To own earth was a great and awe-inspiring thing; to be able to run through one's hands the very soil that was yours and nobody else's; that you could stand upon not under sufferance, but as of right; land that you could turn to your own purpose and plant

33

with your own crops, or allow your own cattle to graze – not that they were planning to run cattle in the garden, but if by some whim they chose to do so, then they could. Such things, such freedoms, such privileges were grave things, and might turn the head, unless you were careful to remind yourself of who you were – Grace Makutsi, from Bobonong, daughter of a very humble man and woman who never had much more than a few goats and scrawny cattle, but who had nursed hopes for their children and had encouraged them to make the best of their lives. She had done that, of course, and through hard work and the inspiration provided by a particular teacher, a slight man with spectacles who rode to school each day on an ancient black bicycle and who believed with all his heart in the power of education, she had somehow got herself to Gaborone and become a trained secretary. That powerful word, *secretary:* she was so proud of it; she rolled it about her mouth and uttered it as one might pronounce a shibboleth: *secretary, secretary.* That would have been enough, she now thought; to have achieved that would have been sufficient, but she had gone further and become an *assistant detective*, and then an *associate detective*, which was where she now was. What heights lay beyond? She had not really thought about it, but now, as she surveyed the plot with Phuti Radiphuti, it suddenly occurred to her that she should become a *principal detective*, if not a *chief detective*. No, that last description was perhaps going too far; Mma Ramotswe was a chief detective, she assumed, and no matter what improvements there might be in her own status, it was definitely not appropriate for her to claim equality in that field with Mma Ramotswe. That would be … it would be *pushy:* yes, there was only one word for it – pushy.

They stood for a few moments in complete silence, and around them, too, there were no sounds, beyond the faint screech of the insects that provided that wallpaper of whirring that was always there but one did not notice unless one stopped and listened. There was nothing to say, really; there were no words Mma Makutsi could use to describe the sense of fulfilment that she felt. So nothing was said until they heard the sound of a vehicle making its way up the road and Phuti turned and announced, 'That will be Mr Putumelo now, Grace.'

The vehicle was one of those ubiquitous pick-up trucks favoured by people who had things to do: carpenters, gardening contractors, electricians. It was dark brown and bore the legend on its side *This Way Up Building Co. (Pty) Ltd*. In the back were a workman's toolbox, a stepladder and several rough-hewn planks.

Clarkson Putumelo got out of the van and walked briskly towards Phuti Radiphuti. 'Very good land,' he said, even before greetings were exchanged. 'Good building land.'

He did not address Mma Makutsi. He did not greet her in the proper, approved way. He did not even appear to see her.

Phuti smiled at the builder. 'I chose it carefully,' he said. 'Or rather, my wife and I chose it.' He turned to Mma Makutsi and smiled as he spoke. *My wife.*

Clarkson Putumelo half-turned his head towards Mma Makutsi, but did not look at her. For a moment it seemed as if he was going to greet her, but that moment passed and he turned away again. 'Good building land,' he repeated. 'No problems here. You'll want to put the house over there, in the middle, right? Then you can make a drive which goes from there to there.' He pointed out the proposed route of the drive. 'There will be no problem with that. Simple as one, two, three.'

Mma Makutsi seethed. Nothing was as simple as one, two, three – even one, two, three itself was rarely that straightfor-ward – you could miss something when counting things, even a child understood that. And who was this ill-behaved Putumelo, anyway? Who was he to arrive like this and pay no attention to the wife – the *wife* – of his client? It was a breathtaking display of arrogance, she thought, and she could just imagine what Mma Ramotswe would say when she told her about it. Or Mma Potokwani ... Mma Potokwani might have her faults, but she would know how to deal with a man like this with a few well-chosen words, such that he would be decisively and deftly put in his place.

'I'll walk around with you, Rra,' said Mr Putumelo. 'We can see how it looks close up.'

'And me,' said Mma Makutsi. 'And me too.'

Clarkson Putumelo frowned, as if he had suddenly heard something quite unexpected. He looked at Phuti Radiphuti for confirmation. 'Everybody can come,' he said briskly.

They began their inspection. Mma Makutsi said nothing, but glowered with resentment. She had rarely come across so ill-mannered a man as this Clarkson Putumelo, and she wondered how Phuti Radiphuti could possibly have selected him. But then men do not see things the same way we do, she thought. They have different eyes. *Men have different eyes.* It was a very appropriate observation, she decided, and she would write it down and pass it on to Mma Ramotswe for future use, perhaps, when sayings of this nature would be required, which she knew from experience could be at any time.

Chapter Four

I Shall Simply Look Up in the Sky

Mma Makutsi gave Mma Ramotswe a full account of her meeting with Mr Clarkson Putumelo, sparing no detail of the insulting way in which he had treated her.

'He was very attentive to Phuti,' she said. 'All the time, he looked at Phuti and not at me. He never noticed nor spoke to me. I am not exaggerating this, Mma Ramotswe – it is as if I wasn't there.' She paused, her anger mounting at the recollection of the humiliating encounter. 'It was as if I was . . . some nothing, just some nothing.'

Mma Ramotswe looked sympathetic. 'There have always been men like that, Mma. Fortunately, there are fewer of them than there used to be. But there are still some, and this Putumelo must be one of them.'

Mma Makutsi now asked what made these men behave in

such a way. Were they like that because they had been badly treated by a woman at some point? Or were they like that because . . . She tried to think of another explanation, but could not. How could anybody ignore the other half of humanity? And did they behave like that to their wives? she asked Mma Ramotswe. Phuti had met Mma Putumelo when she had come into the furniture store to test the sofa, so she knew that Mr Putumelo was married. Did the poor woman have to put up with being ignored in that astonishingly rude manner? What would it be like to sit down for breakfast with a man who never spoke to you but instead looked over your shoulder as if you were not even there?

'He will be a small man inside,' said Mma Ramotswe. 'He will feel small and unimportant. That is why he needs to put ladies down, Mma. Men who are big inside never feel the need to do that.'

She was right, thought Mma Makutsi. Mr J. L. B. Matekoni was one of those men who were large inside – kind and generous, and strong too – and he was never anything but courteous in his dealings with women, and with men too, for that matter.

'So what I suggest, Mma,' Mma Ramotswe continued, 'is that you don't let this man annoy you. Just ignore his bad manners.'

Mma Makutsi nodded enthusiastically. 'I shall ignore him altogether,' she said. 'It will be as if he is not there. When he talks I shall simply look up in the sky – like this – as if I can hear something but am not sure what it is.'

Mma Ramotswe gently explained that this was not what she had in mind. 'Don't repay rudeness with rudeness, Mma. It is much better to show a rude person how to behave. Have you not seen how well that works?'

'I have not seen that, Mma.'

Mma Ramotswe knew she would not persuade Mma Makutsi, but she continued nonetheless. 'Well, it does work. A rude person wants you to be rude back to him. He really likes that. But if you just smile and are very polite, then he will realise that his rudeness has not hurt you. He has achieved nothing.'

This was greeted with silence, and Mma Ramotswe decided that it would be best to move on to another subject. There was work to do: a report to be typed up and sent off to a client, which would keep them busy for the hour or so before lunchtime. Both she and Mma Makutsi went home for lunch now – Mma Ramotswe in her van and Mma Makutsi in the car sent for her by Phuti. This car, which had *The Double Comfort Furniture Store* emblazoned on its side, had been the subject of some remark by the two junior mechanics. 'She is very grand now,' Charlie had said. 'Too grand to go on public transport, like the rest of us. You may have to sit next to some poor person in a minibus. She is now too big for that.'

Fanwell, who had at last qualified – though Charlie had not done so, and was still an apprentice – was more charitable. 'It must be very nice to have a car with a driver,' he said. 'Maybe if I marry a girl who has a furniture store that will happen to me.'

'That will never happen,' said Charlie. 'Girls with furniture stores are looking for someone more exciting than you, Fanwell. Sorry about that.'

The inference was clear: these furniture-store girls, whoever they were, would be more satisfied with Charlie than they would be with Fanwell. That was probably true, thought Mma Ramotswe, who had overheard this conversation, but the fact that something was true was not always justification for saying it.

Now there was the report to compile, and she and Mma Makutsi began to busy themselves with the task of writing it. The matter to be reported was a routine one: the bread-and-butter, or bread-and-gravy as Mma Makutsi put it, of a detective agency: marital infidelity. This case, however, was rather more sensitive than the usual run-of-the-mill investigation, as the client was a prominent politician, Mma Helen Olesitsi, a former government minister in charge of the police. She had developed suspicions about the conduct of her husband, Kholisani, who was a businessman. She was sure that he was having an affair, but had been unable to find out the identity of her rival; could Mma Ramotswe help?

Mma Ramotswe, assisted by Mma Makutsi, had done her best. Long hours had been spent parked outside houses and in the lobbies of hotels; and more than one evening wasted in bars known to be popular with married men on the lookout for a mistress. Mma Ramotswe disapproved of these bars, which, she said, knew exactly what they were doing. One, in particular, was the object of her derision, a bar that called itself The Second Home – a name that she felt was deliberately and cynically inflammatory to women. This bar advertised itself as a place where 'those in need of entertainment they cannot find at home will be given a warm welcome'.

'Those words make it very clear, don't you think, Mma Makutsi?' said Mma Ramotswe, pointing an angry finger at the offending newspaper advertisement. 'Why don't they just come out in the open and say, "Married men: you come here to meet other ladies"? That's what it should say, Mma, if they were being honest.'

Mma Makutsi was in complete agreement. 'As a married woman, I can only say that I agree one hundred per cent. Even if I know that Phuti would never go to a place like that, I know that there are many men who are far weaker and will do that. Shame on them, Mma Ramotswe! Shame on them!'

It was not clear to Mma Ramotswe whether the shame should

be heaped on the weak married men or on the bar, or on both, but she nodded her head. Their one trip to The Second Home had been an eye-opener, but had not resulted in any information on Mr Kholisani Olesitsi. They had shown photographs to the barman, who had been perfectly obliging but who had shaken his head. 'Never here, Mma Ramotswe. I have never seen this man. Not once. Are you sure that he has been here?'

Mma Makutsi had been doubtful about the truthfulness of this barman. 'I think he probably says that about anybody,' she said. 'That is why he is the barman in a place like that. He is discreet. If you showed him a photograph of ... of the Mayor of Gaborone himself, he would deny knowing who it was.'

'But the Mayor does not go into bars like that,' said Mma Ramotswe.

'You know what I mean, Mma. I did not say that the Mayor goes to bars. I do not think that he does. All I am saying is—'

Mma Ramotswe raised a hand. 'It's all right, Mma Makutsi. I know what you're saying. But we have drawn a blank: that is the important thing. Perhaps this man is not having an affair at all. Perhaps it is just another case of a wife who is too suspicious for her own good.'

'Perhaps, Mma. But what now?'

Mma Ramotswe had been unable to come up with any ideas for further investigation – at least not at that point – and had explained to Mma Makutsi that it was time for a report. 'A report lets the client know what we are doing,' she said. 'It shows that we are not just sitting around talking about a case; it shows that we are busy looking into possibilities.'

'Leaving no stone unturned,' offered Mma Makutsi.

'Yes, Mma. That is a good way of putting it.'

Sitting at her desk that morning, with Mma Makutsi's shorthand pencil poised above her dictation pad, Mma Ramotswe

41

cleared her throat. 'Mr Kholisani Olesitsi,' she began, 'hereafter referred to as "the husband"—'

'"The said husband",' interjected Mma Makutsi.

'If you wish, Mma Makutsi, although I think that "the husband" is clear enough.'

Mma Makutsi stared across the room at Mma Ramotswe, her glasses catching the sunlight from the window and reflecting it in little dancing specks on to the wall. If she sat in direct sunlight, thought Mma Ramotswe, there might be a danger that she could involuntarily start a fire, in the same way as one risked starting a bush fire if one left a bottle in the grass; the glass could act as a lens and focus the sun's rays down to a point of white incendiary heat. 'It is more official to say "the said husband",' Mma Makutsi intoned. 'It means that you are talking about a husband you have already mentioned, rather than any other husband.'

'"As the said husband", then,' continued Mma Ramotswe.

Mma Makutsi's pencil darted across the paper. She looked up. 'I am ready, Mma.'

'We have carried out exhaustive enquiries—'

Again Mma Makutsi looked up from her pad. 'Exhausting,' she said.

Mma Ramotswe sighed. Mma Makutsi did tend to interrupt dictation with the occasional suggestion, but not usually as frequently as she was now doing. Could it be, she wondered, that her new status as Mrs Phuti Radiphuti was going to her head? 'No, Mma Makutsi, exhaustive means many. It means doing everything you can. Exhausting means tiring.'

Mma Makutsi bit her lip. 'I know that, Mma,' she muttered. 'I am not some ignorant lady who has never been to a college ...'

Mma Ramotswe said nothing. By one interpretation, this was a dig at her; she had never been to a college of any sort, even the

Botswana Secretarial College, which was not all that academically distinguished, she thought; not that she would ever say so.

'Let's continue,' said Mma Ramotswe. 'We have carried out exhaustive ... no, say, extensive enquiries throughout Gaborone. We have interviewed relevant persons in the list of locations set out below—'

She was interrupted again, but this time not by Mma Makutsi with some suggested improvement to the text of the report, but by Charlie's appearance at the door.

'It is not teatime,' said Mma Makutsi.

Charlie smiled unconcernedly. 'I am not looking for tea. I have come to tell you that there is a man sitting in a car outside. He's staring at this building.'

Mma Makutsi put down her dictation pad and crossed the room to look out of the window, standing to one side so as not to be seen from outside. 'You're right,' she said. 'How long has he been there, Charlie?'

Charlie joined her in staring out of the window. 'Maybe about half an hour,' he said. 'I wasn't really paying attention until Fanwell said something about it. Then I looked and I thought, *That man is staring.* That's when I came in to tell you.'

Mma Makutsi screwed up her eyes. 'I cannot see him very well,' she said. 'He is wearing a hat.'

'He is a white man,' said Charlie. 'I've noticed that they like to wear hats.'

'The sun can be unkind to them,' said Mma Ramotswe.

'He's getting out,' said Mma Makutsi. 'I think he's coming in.'

'He will be a client then,' said Mma Ramotswe. 'Thank you, Charlie. You go back to work and we will get ready to welcome our visitor.'

Mma Makutsi knew what this meant. Mma Ramotswe had never liked it when clients arrived to find them unoccupied, staring out of the window, perhaps, or drinking tea. It was far better, she said, if the client came upon a scene of reassuring activity.

'I am ready,' said Mma Makutsi, regaining her seat. '"... in the list of locations set out below" ...'

'Yes,' said Mma Ramotswe. 'Location number one, the office of the said husband ...'

The knock, which came at the half-open door, was timid – barely audible. Mma Makutsi flipped her dictation pad shut and rose to her feet. 'I shall deal with this, Mma,' she said in a voice loud enough to be heard by the visitor. 'The important report can wait.'

She pushed the door fully open. Standing outside was a tall, solidly built man in middle age, rather square-faced, his blond hair in a crew cut. He was dressed entirely in khaki and wore sand-coloured desert boots – the standard outfit of the safari visitor. In his hands was a freshly purchased bush hat with wide brim.

'Please come in, Rra,' said Mma Makutsi, gesturing for the visitor to enter. 'Do you have an appointment?'

Stepping into the room, the visitor shook his head. 'No, I don't have an appointment, but I was passing by and ...'

Mma Ramotswe rose to greet him. 'An appointment is not always necessary,' she said warmly. 'My door is always open.'

'Until five o'clock,' chipped in Mma Makutsi. 'The office closes at five o'clock.'

Mma Ramotswe smiled. 'I meant that I am always happy to see people.' She gestured to the client chair. 'Please sit down, Rra. And Mma Makutsi, perhaps you could take this gentleman's hat.'

The visitor handed the hat over somewhat awkwardly. Noticing this, Mma Ramotswe said, 'It is a very beautiful hat, Rra. Very beautiful.'

He looked up and bashfully returned her smile. 'You think so? I had it with me up north, in the Delta, and I must say there were days when I was very happy I bought it.'

'It can get very hot up there,' said Mma Makutsi.

Mma Ramotswe thought it time for introductions. 'This is my assistant, Mma Makutsi.'

'Associate detective,' said Mma Makutsi.

'Yes. Associate detective. And my own name is Precious Ramotswe. I am the owner of this agency.' She paused. 'And what is your name, Rra?'

The visitor, who had been about to sit down, straightened up and offered his hand. 'My name is Andersen.'

'You are very welcome, Rra Andersen.'

The visitor seemed to relax. Reaching into one of the copious pockets in his khaki safari shirt, he extracted a card and passed it over to Mma Ramotswe. 'This is my card, Mma. You will see it states my profession.'

Mma Ramotswe took the card and began to examine it. She stopped, her eyes wide in astonishment. 'You are ...' she stuttered. 'You are Clovis Andersen?'

'Yes, that is my name. I am Clovis Andersen.'

There was complete silence. Mma Ramotswe looked across the room at Mma Makutsi, who was sitting bolt upright, the lenses of her glasses flashing signals of amazement.

Mma Ramotswe could barely speak. Her voice, when it came, was faltering. 'Clovis Andersen? Who wrote the ... the ...'

Now it was the visitor's turn to be surprised. 'My book? You know my book? *The Principles of Private Detection*?'

Mma Makutsi could not contain herself. 'We know that book very well, Rra!' she exclaimed. 'It is here on my desk. Right here. Look.'

She picked up the now battered copy of the book and waved it

45

in the air exultantly. A slip of paper marking a place fell out of the pages and fluttered down to the ground. Clovis Andersen watched it fall. 'This is an extraordinary coincidence,' he said. 'I had no idea that the book was read in Africa.'

'But we are always reading it,' shouted Mma Makutsi. 'Mma Ramotswe was the first, and then I read it, and then she read it again. It is always in use. Every day.'

Clovis Andersen looked down at the floor. 'Well, I must say I'm very pleased by that. And I hope you find it useful. You never know when you write a book – often you don't hear from the folks who have read it, and then ... ' He shrugged. 'Then you think: "Well, I guess nobody's read it after all."'

Mma Ramotswe shook her head vigorously. 'But of course people have read your book, Rra,' she said. 'All over the world. That book is read all over the world. There are many detectives who have read it – I'm sure of that.'

'You're very kind,' muttered Clovis Andersen.

Mma Makutsi now made another intervention. 'God brought you here,' she said.

He turned round in his chair to look at her. 'I beg your pardon, Mma?'

'God brought you here,' she repeated. 'You have been brought to see us by God himself. That is very clear.'

Clovis Andersen looked nonplussed. 'Well, actually, I was driving past and I saw your sign. I have a rental car, you see, and when I saw the sign I thought that as a matter of professional courtesy I might call in and introduce myself – since we are all in the same profession.'

'That is a very good thought,' said Mma Ramotswe. 'And we are very glad that you did.' She looked over the room towards Mma Makutsi. 'I think you should put on the kettle, Mma. Mr Andersen is thirsty and would like some tea, I think.'

Mma Makutsi rose to her feet and picked up the kettle. She would not raise the subject now, since they had a visitor, and such an important visitor too, but it occurred to her that she was always the one to make the tea. That had been her lot, in a sense – to make the tea for other people; but why should it always be the case? She was now Mrs Phuti Radiphuti, and it was about time that people started making tea for her. *Time for tea, Mma Ramotswe: would you mind putting the kettle on?* It was a delicious, delicious thought, but not one to be expressed just yet.

They talked for almost an hour, well into the lunch break. Most of the talking was done by Mma Ramotswe and Mma Makutsi, with Clovis Andersen making only the occasional intervention, nodding in agreement at some points, expressing surprise at others. From time to time Mma Makutsi picked up the copy of *The Principles of Private Detection* and read out a sentence to illustrate a point; Clovis Andersen, although he seemed flattered at these references to his work, was also reticent, making self-effacing gestures as if it embarrassed him to be considered an authority. Mma Ramotswe told him of the times they had relied on his advice and how his pithy comments had proved to be exactly the guidance needed, and Mma Makutsi added to this with examples of her own.

'You ladies are very kind,' Clovis Andersen muttered. 'I had no idea that my rather ordinary thoughts on investigation should be taken so seriously. I never imagined . . .'

'We are not kind,' Mma Makutsi protested. 'You are the kind one, Rra, to have given us all this . . . all this . . .'

'Inspiration,' prompted Mma Ramotswe.

'Exactly,' said Mma Makutsi.

Clovis Andersen looked down at the floor. He did not say anything. From the garage on the other side of the wall there drifted the sound of metal on metal; something being knocked into place, or loosened; the clanging of a spanner allowed to fall to the floor; the nagging whine of a reluctant starter motor.

'They are busy through there,' commented Mma Ramotswe.

Clovis Andersen said nothing.

Mma Ramotswe glanced at Mma Makutsi, and then back at Clovis Andersen. 'Is there something wrong, Rra?'

He looked up. His hands were folded in his lap; large, chapped hands, the skin made angry and reddened by exposure to the sun. He moved his head almost imperceptibly. A nod.

Chapter Five

I Am Your Friend, and I Am Asking

That evening, Fanwell left the garage at his usual time, which was five minutes past five. Work ended officially at five o'clock, and Fanwell, being conscientious, insisted on working until the very last moment; Charlie, by contrast, took the view that an eight-to-five day entitled him to leave the building at five o'clock exactly. This meant that work itself should stop a good fifteen minutes earlier, to give him time to put tools away, wash his hands and spend a vital few moments in front of the mirror in the washroom. Charlie had installed that mirror himself, after the denial of his request that one be provided. 'That is a washroom for the use of men,' said Mr J. L. B. Matekoni. 'It is a place to wash your hands and attend to other necessary matters. It is not a grooming parlour or a beauty salon. Men do not need mirrors, Charlie.'

Charlie had shaken his head. 'Oh, boss, that is a very old-fashioned thing to say. I do not expect to hear that sort of thing in this modern Botswana.'

The effect of this remark was to cause entirely understandable irritation. 'What is this nonsense?' asked Mr J. L. B. Matekoni, his voice rising slightly. He was the most temperate of men, but there were occasions when Charlie tested even him. 'Men do not need mirrors. Most men know what they look like. I do not need to look into a piece of shiny glass and say, "Oh, look, there's Mr J. L. B. Matekoni." What other use is there for a mirror?'

Charlie grinned. 'These days there are new men, boss. They are more like their sisters.' As he spoke, he watched Mr J. L. B. Matekoni, assessing his reaction. 'Boys and girls, Rra – they are all the same today.'

Mr J. L. B. Matekoni was unmoved. 'If you think that, Charlie, you're in for a big surprise.'

'Hah!' said Fanwell, who had been following this exchange with interest. 'A very big surprise! Maybe you need to tell him about some things, boss. Maybe Charlie doesn't know yet!'

Charlie had been bettered, and he left the subject at that. But the following day, armed with a screwdriver and drill, he had installed a cheap wall mirror directly above the washbasin. *For the use of modern men*, he had written underneath. Some time later that day, Mr J. L. B. Matekoni had taken a pen to the notice and altered the wording to read, *NOT For the use of modernest men*. Fanwell particularly appreciated this: 'That will show him, Rra,' he said. 'That will teach him to think he's so big and handsome!'

The mirror remained, though, and was regularly used by Charlie, even if neither Fanwell nor Mr J. L. B. Matekoni made any use of it – or admitted to doing so. Vanity was one of

Charlie's shortcomings, but it had always been tolerated by Mr J. L. B. Matekoni, who also put up with Charlie's early stopping of work and unseemly dash for the door, while Fanwell continued at his post until five and then took five minutes to put away his tools and tidy up. Then it was time for him to board one of the swaying, overloaded minibuses that plied the Old Naledi route. If he was lucky, he would not have to wait long before one of these minibuses arrived, and then the journey never took more than fifteen minutes, depending on traffic. Jumping off at his stop, he would cross the road, leap across the storm drain and walk down the unpaved road that disappeared into the heart of the informal suburb.

Old Naledi was the one scar on the neat landscape of Gaborone. While there were other places that had cheap housing, none was as cheap as this, with its rickety houses made half of breeze-block, half of mud daub, their roofs consisting of tarpaulins, odd sheets of corrugated tin and such other bits of building material as could be scavenged from here and there. It was not quite a shanty town, but at times it seemed to be not far off that, so great was the contrast between its evident poverty and the well-found prosperity of the other parts of the town.

The people who lived there did so because they had no choice. As often as not it was the only place that new arrivals could find – people who came into Gaborone from remote villages, lured by the promise of work and payment they could never find at home. Then there were people from over the border, from countries less fortunate – people for whom the small comforts that Old Naledi afforded, and its comparative safety, were paradise found. These people took what jobs they could, and were often exploited. They painted houses, fixed pipes, patched up roofs. They worked without complaint, and at the end of each month sent home what money they could spare, aware of the fact that every *pula*, every *thebe* they wired back to Bulawayo or beyond might be the crucial one that separated a full stomach from an empty one; that meant that a child could stay in school rather than be excluded for non-payment of the tiny fee the schools required.

Fanwell lived in this place, but his lot was infinitely better than that of the migrants. He was a Motswana, a citizen, and thus enti-tled to the benefits that came with citizenship. He had been well schooled and had – eventually – completed his apprenticeship. He had a trade; he could get a job anywhere now, as there was always a call for qualified mechanics, even for those who did not have a great deal of experience. If he chose to continue working with cars, the fact that he had trained with Mr J. L. B. Matekoni would stand him in good stead; already he had had an indirect, some-what veiled offer from one of the big garages. 'Ever wondered what it would be like to work in a *proper* garage?' they had asked. 'Think about it, Fanwell. Good conditions. Big pay cheque. Latest tools. The lot.'

He had turned this approach down, resenting the implication that working at Tlokweng Road Speedy Motors was somehow inferior. 'I'm working with the finest mechanic in Botswana,' he said. 'That is enough.' And it was – at least in the professional sense. From the monetary point of view, though, it was true that he could be earning more elsewhere, although Mr J. L. B. Matekoni had raised his salary as much as he could. And it would certainly be useful for Fanwell to have more money at his disposal, given his family obligations.

Fanwell lived with his grandmother, an aunt and four siblings. His father, from whom the family had not heard in a long time, was now believed to be dead, and his mother was working in South Africa. She sent money home, but it was sporadic and could not be relied on. For the day-to-day needs of the family, it was effectively Fanwell's pay that kept the household afloat, eked out by the grandmother with such tiny amounts as she could earn through her skills with crochet or as a potter. Fanwell never complained about this – not once – accepting that this was the way things were. 'When they grow up,' he said, referring to the younger siblings, 'then they will earn money too. Things will get better.'

Now, approaching the street corner on which their house stood, Fanwell noticed that there was somebody occupying the stool that his grandmother normally used when she sat out in the yard, working on her crochet. As he crossed the road to the house, the figure stood up and approached him, his hand extended in greeting.

'So, Fanwell, how goes it?'

It took Fanwell a moment or two to place the visitor. Then came the prompt: 'Chobie, man. You remember me. Chobie, your friend.'

He did remember him. 'Of course. Yes, Chobie.'

Fanwell took his friend's hand and shook it.

'So,' said Chobie. 'I've been waiting, man. I've been sitting here for two hours thinking, when's my old friend Fanwell going to come home? That's what I've been thinking. True as God.'

Fanwell smiled, but he felt nervous. He and Chobie had been at school together, and he remembered him as frequently being in trouble. There had been some row about something or other – he could not recollect what it was – and this had led to Chobie's being sent away. It was a long time ago, of course, and one could not be expected to remember everything that happened.

Fanwell gestured for Chobie to follow him to the room that served as the kitchen – and as sleeping quarters for three of the children.

'You've got lots of children already,' Chobie said, gesturing to the sleeping mats stacked together in a corner.

Fanwell laughed. 'Brothers and sisters, Chobie.'

Chobie winked. 'Myself, I've got some sons. Don't know how many, but more than two. Big boys.'

Fanwell acknowledged this confidence with a polite nod of his head. He looked at the shelf; there was very little food, but he could give Chobie a plain slice of bread and jam and some tea. He offered this, and Chobie accepted readily.

'That old lady . . . '

'My grandmother,' said Fanwell.

'Yes, her. She said to tell you she's gone somewhere until seven o'clock. Then she'll come back.' Chobie paused. 'You look after her, Fanwell?'

'Yes.'

'That costs money, man.'

Fanwell admitted that it did. 'But there's nobody else, you see.'

'Tough,' said Chobie. 'These grandmothers eat a lot of food. But I've got the answer for you, my friend.'

Fanwell was busy lighting the paraffin stove on which the family cooked and boiled water for tea. His grandmother ate very little, saving as much as she could for the children; he had seen her holding back, had seen how thin she was. He said nothing.

Undeterred, Chobie continued: 'This is a business proposition, Fanwell.'

'I have a job. I'm a mechanic at Tlokweng Road Speedy Motors.'

Chobie made a dismissive gesture. 'That's day work. You never make money doing day work. I can give you night work – big money.'

Fanwell glanced at Chobie and then looked away again quickly. 'I am very busy,' he said. 'I can't do more work.'

'Everybody's busy,' said Chobie. 'But not too busy if the money's good enough – and it is, Fanwell. It's very good.'

'No,' said Fanwell.

Chobie got up and came to stand beside him. 'I'm not asking you very much, Fanwell. All I want is for you to help me fix some cars. Three or four to begin with – then you can decide whether you want to carry on.'

'What is wrong with these cars?' asked Fanwell. 'And why can't you take them to a garage?'

Chobie became animated. 'And be charged hundreds and hundreds of *pula*? Thousands, maybe? No, not me. These are cars I'm selling – that is how I make my living these days. All I want is a little help to get them ready to be sold. Little things. New exhaust pipes, maybe. Fixing lights. That sort of thing. Hard for me, but easy for you. You're a mechanic.'

Fanwell remembered now: Chobie had the reputation of being persuasive. It had always been difficult to say no to him.

'I don't have much spare time,' he said weakly.

Chobie put a hand on his shoulder. 'Thank you,' he said. 'I am your friend, and I am asking you a favour. I knew that you would say yes.' He paused. 'Don't bother with the tea, Fanwell. Let's go. I have this car over at my place that needs a new fan belt, and maybe there's something wrong with the brakes – I can't tell. You'll know straight away. Then, *smack-smack*, it's fixed!'

Chobie had a car parked round the corner. He had paid a small boy to watch it for him while he was waiting for Fanwell, and now he gave the child the rest of the fee – a few coins pressed into an outstretched palm.

55

'See this car?' Chobie said proudly, patting the side of the vehicle. 'You got a car like this, Fanwell? No chance. You could have one, though. Easy, easy. You come in with me and you could have one of these. Turbo-charged. V-8. You name it. It's there for the taking, Fanwell.' He paused, looking bemusedly at the young mechanic. 'Of course, I forgot: you work at Tlokweng Road Something-or-other Motors.'

'Speedy Motors,' muttered Fanwell.

'Speedy not,' said Chobie. 'Ha ha. Speedy not. Tlokweng Road Old-fashioned Manual Transmission Motors. That's what that place should be called.'

Fanwell laughed weakly. Even a half-hearted laugh, though, felt like a betrayal. 'It is a good garage.'

'Oh, I'm sure it's a good garage. Good for old ladies and their rubbish, one-horse-power cars. You fix donkey carts in that place, Fanwell?'

Fanwell looked away. 'They do not bring them. They do not bring any donkey carts.'

Chobie patted him playfully on the shoulder. 'Only joking, Fanwell. Anyway, let's get in and go over to my place. I've got this yard, see, and the car I want you to fix up is there. Get in, my friend, get in.'

It was getting dark now. To the west, over the Kalahari, the sky was copper red, fading into pink and then into a colour that was somewhere between blue and white, the colour of emptiness; the lights of the town, bright pinpoints, were beginning to punctuate the dusk. Fanwell felt empty. He did not like Chobie; he had never really liked him. But he found it hard to resist the other young man's enthusiastic banter, and there could be no harm, surely, in helping out with this business of his. The second-hand car trade was a notoriously tricky one, and Fanwell had no doubt that Chobie was at the questionable end of it. But if Chobie chose to mislead – and possibly even cheat – his customers, it was not really any of Fanwell's business. Indeed, one might argue – and this line of argument was just occurring to Fanwell – that it would be positively better for him to work on Chobie's cars; that way, the customers would have fewer problems and would get cars in better condition than would otherwise be the case. This work for Chobie, then, was virtually charitable, even if there was payment attached; that is how Fanwell looked at it, and that was how he was looking at things when Chobie turned the car into the gateway of a fenced-off storage yard. On the wall of this yard there was the wording, painted in high letters: *Reliable Autos. We get you there.*

'Get you where?' asked Fanwell.

Chobie smiled. 'Where you want to get. That's where everybody's heading, after all. To where they want to get.'

Fanwell did not say anything. Chobie switched off the engine and gestured to the single car that the yard contained. 'Isn't that a beauty?' he asked.

Fanwell was non-committal. 'They can give a lot of trouble, those cars,' he muttered. 'Mr J. L. B. Matekoni says—'

He did not finish. Mr J. L. B. Matekoni took a poor view of cars in which styling played a more important role that mechanical reliability, but Fanwell did not have the chance to relate these views before Chobie interrupted him. 'Mr J. L. B. Rubbish. Of course he doesn't like cars like these. These cars are for successful people, not for people called J. L. B. Rubbish. Come on, let's get going.'

Chobie had rigged up a lamp on the end of a long extension cord. This was plugged into the lean-to building at one side of the yard. Fanwell could not help but notice that from this structure there ran another wire, which snaked back to disappear over the wall. Such electricity as the site had, he realised, was drawn from elsewhere – stolen power. Chobie saw him looking at this. 'You've got a problem with that, Fanwell? Him over the wall – he's got much more power than he needs. I'm just taking a little bit – just this much.' He made a gesture with two barely separated fingers – a gesture that signified inconsequential smallness.

'Where did you get this car?' asked Fanwell, as they approached it across the yard.

Chobie was ready with an answer. 'I bought it from a man. Paid good money.'

'Where did he get it?'

Chobie shrugged. 'How do I know? Do you think you have to know every car's mother? Do you think you have to know its father? Cars are cars, man. They come, they go. You can't ask them all the details.'

Fanwell faltered, but only for a moment. He had his suspicions about Chobie, but he did not see what further enquiry he should be expected to make. It might be that Chobie had obtained the car in an underhand way but it might equally be that he had come by it quite legitimately. Was it his business to find out? No, he thought; not on balance, and he would ask Mr J. L. B. Matekoni the next day, to see what he said. If he told him that it was wrong to fix cars when there was a doubt about their past, then he would refuse to help Chobie. If, however, he considered it to be all right, then he would help him. After all, the extra money would be useful.

The new fan belt was soon installed, and he then turned his attention to the brakes. This was a comparatively minor problem, and he was able to fix it in spite of the complexity of the braking system installed in that particular make of car. After an hour or so, everything was done, and Fanwell was wiping his hands on the small hand towel that Chobie had thoughtfully provided. As he did so, he glanced at the lettering on the towel: *SUN HOTEL.*

Noticing this, Chobie laughed. 'They gave that to me,' he said. 'I know somebody who works there. Big time. He gave me that towel as a souvenir.'

Fanwell finished wiping his hands. 'I should get home now,' he said.

Chobie held up a hand. 'Not so fast, Fanwell. I owe you.' He reached into his pocket and took out a number of folded bank-notes. Counting out three hundred *pula*, he pressed these into Fanwell's hand. 'Fee for service,' he said. 'See? Good money for good work. And there'll be plenty more – plenty more. Tax-free, too, ha!'

They began to walk back towards the car in which they had come. As they did so, a nondescript black van drew up at the gate and a man emerged. Chobie looked at the man and frowned. 'Yes, Rra? You want something?'

The man nodded. 'I need to buy a car, Rra. I need to buy a car for my wife. I saw your sign.'

Chobie, who had been tense at the beginning of this encounter, now visibly relaxed. 'Well, you're in the right place, my friend. But unfortunately I'm a bit low on stock now – we only have that big car over there. But have you got a mobile? You give me the number and I'll fix you up with something good. No rubbish – something good. And my mechanic here . . .' he gestured to Fanwell, 'my mechanic is top-class. He'll make sure that it's in A1 order when you get it. You won't see your wife for dust. *Bang, bang.* She'll overtake all the other women. *Bang, bang.*'

The man laughed. 'My wife would like that,' he said. 'So, here's my number. You'll call me?'

'Of course I will,' said Chobie. 'Give me four, maybe five days and I'll call. And I'll get my mechanic . . .'

The man turned to Fanwell and greeted him formally. 'And your name, Rra?'

Fanwell gave the man his name.

'He trained at Tlokweng Road Speedy Motors,' boasted Chobie. 'They have top-rate mechanics out there. Do all the big cars.'

The man nodded. 'I know the place,' he said.

Chapter Six

The Things of which a Mechanic Might Speak

Mr J. L. B. Matekoni had been in Lobatse and was late home. By the time he arrived, Mma Ramotswe had fed the children and was chatting with Motholeli in her room. The young girl had been in an argument with another girl in school and had been on the verge of tears over dinner. Now it was all coming out and the story, punctuated by copious weeping, was being pieced together by Mma Ramotswe. *This is what I do*, she thought. *During the day I sort out the problems of adults; at night I sort out the problems of children.*

Mma Ramotswe dabbed at Motholeli's tears. 'Oh, my darling,' she said, 'you mustn't cry. Who is this girl, anyway? How can I help you if I don't know her name?'

'She's a girl in my class,' said Motholeli. 'She's called Kagiso.'

'There are many Kagisos,' said Mma Ramotswe. 'What is her other name?'

'It is Nnunu. Kagiso Nnunu. She's horrid and I hate her. I hate her more than snakes.'

Mma Ramotswe put an arm around Motholeli's shoulder. It is so small, she thought, and fragile, as if too great a hug might break it: *the shoulder of a small person.* And there was the illness, too; the illness that confined her to the wheelchair took its toll elsewhere – made it difficult for the body to grow at the rate that it should.

'It doesn't help to hate somebody,' she said quietly. 'I understand why you want to, but it doesn't help. Not really.'

Motholeli looked at her incredulously. 'But it does, Mma. If you hate somebody hard enough, then they can die.'

Mma Ramotswe caught her breath. Where had the child learned that? Was that the sort of thing that was being peddled around the playground?

'Who said that?' she asked. 'Did somebody tell you that?'

Motholeli's answer came quickly. 'The teacher told us. She said that if you hate somebody hard enough then they can die. She said that it can happen.'

Mma Ramotswe shook her head. 'But Motholeli, that is just not true. That is not true. And . . . ' She was about to say that no teacher would express such a thought, but then she stopped herself. Teachers seemed a different breed these days, more like everybody else; when she had been a pupil at the government school in Mochudi, the teacher had been a figure of authority in the village. People respected teachers and listened to what they had to say. She remembered walking with her late father on the road to Pilane when a cart had gone past, a donkey cart, and there had been a man sitting on the back holding a case of some sort and her father had raised his hat as the man passed. She had asked why he had done this, and he had replied that the man was a teacher and he would always raise his hat to a teacher. She did not think that happened today.

'Are you sure?'

'Yes, I am sure, Mma. She said that if you hate somebody then they can die. She told us that. I'm sure about that, Mma.'

Mma Ramotswe hesitated. She did not want further to undermine the authority of a teacher – there were enough people doing that anyway – and so she decided to say no more, at least about that side of it.

'But why do you hate this girl, this Kagiso?'

'Because she said I should stay outside in the parking place – in the place for cars. She said I should have my lessons out there.'

Mma Ramotswe was accustomed to receiving shocking confidences, and to receiving them with equanimity; now, however, she gasped. 'But why ... why would she say something like that, Motholeli? What did she mean?'

'She said that my wheelchair is like a car and that it should not be brought inside the school. She said there is no place for cars inside the school. She said I am just like a car.'

Mma Ramotswe closed her eyes. It was only too easy to imagine a child saying such a thing; children showed endless inventiveness when it came to devising torment for other children. She opened her eyes and made an effort to smile. 'That is the silliest thing I have ever heard, Motholeli. It is so silly that ... well, I think you should just laugh at that girl. Laugh, and say how silly she is.'

Motholeli remained silent.

'Well?' prompted Mma Ramotswe. 'Don't you think that's the best thing to do? Don't you think that would be better than hating her?'

'No. I think it would be better to hate her. Then she might die, and she wouldn't be able to say these things about me.'

Mma Ramotswe tried another tack. 'Would you like me to have a word with the teacher?'

This brought an immediate reaction. 'No, Mma. It is not the teacher's business.'

Mma Ramotswe sighed. There was a limit to the extent to which you could fight the battles of children. Down among the children, in the jungle they inhabited, the word of adults could count for very little. An adult's reprimand, or punishment, might get a wrongdoer's attention, but would not necessarily change attitudes, which would revert to their natural state the moment the adult disappeared. No, Motholeli was right: it might not help to take it up with the authorities.

'Well, you think about what I have told you,' Mma Ramotswe said. 'And here's something you can remember. It's a thing you can say to a person like Kagiso. "Sticks and stones may break my bones, but words will never hurt me." You remember that.'

Motholeli muttered something.

'What was that?' asked Mma Ramotswe.

'I was practising it, Mma. "Sticks and stones may . . ."'

'May break my bones,' prompted Mma Ramotswe. 'But words will never hurt me.'

Watching the child's reaction, her solemn contemplation of what had been said, Mma Ramotswe felt some satisfaction that she seemed to be getting through to her. That was the beauty, she thought, of those little sayings, those proverbs that children could learn and use to help them through life. That one came from somewhere else – she had read about it when she was a child her-self – but there were plenty of old Botswana sayings that did the same thing, that gave you little rules for getting through life, for coping with its disappointments and sorrows. And did it matter, she wondered, whether they were true or not? Words *could* hurt you, and hurt you every bit as badly as sticks and stones. So that saying was wrong; but that was not the point. The point was that if it made you better, made you braver, then it was doing its work. The same thing was true, Mma Ramotswe thought, of believing in God. There were plenty of people who did not really believe in God, but who wanted to believe in him, and said that they did. Some people said that these people were foolish, that they were hypocritical, but Mma Ramotswe was not so sure about that. If something, or somebody, could help you to get through life, to lead a life that was good and purposeful, did it matter all that much if that thing or that person did not exist? She thought it did not – not in the slightest bit.

By the time Mr J. L. B. Matekoni's truck drew into the driveway of the house on Zebra Drive, its headlights describing a wide arc across Mma Ramotswe's garden, illuminating the mopipi tree and the flourish of bougainvillea, the children were asleep and Mma Ramotswe was herself sprawled dozing on the sofa, her feet up on a cushion, a newspaper spread across her stomach. The sound of the truck dispelled tiredness, and she rapidly sat up, folded the newspaper neatly and slipped back into her comfortable, flat-heeled house shoes. Mr J. L. B. Matekoni's dinner, a mutton stew rich in grease and lentils, sat warm and secure in the lower drawer of the oven. It was her dinner too, as she had held back from eating with the children so that she could sit down with Mr J. L. B. Matekoni and recount to him the momentous events of that day. She had planned exactly what she would say, starting with an invitation to guess who had walked in the door that morning. He would never guess, of course, and so she would tantalise him with snippets of information until, almost casually, she would let drop the name of Clovis Andersen. And then she would tell him everything: Mr Andersen's plans; what he had said to her and Mma Makutsi; what Mma Makutsi had said to him; what she had said to Mma Makutsi after Mr Andersen had gone and what Mma Makutsi had said to her. No detail would be spared.

Mr J. L. B. Matekoni came into the house and tossed the keys of his truck on to a table. 'There are some people,' he began, 'who should not be allowed on the road. Maybe they shouldn't even be allowed to walk anywhere, either. Maybe we should hang a large sign around their neck saying *Very Dangerous*, or *No Sense*, or something like that.'

Mma Ramotswe spoke soothingly. 'You have been on the Lobatse Road, Rra. It always makes you cross.'

'The road itself is not the problem,' said Mr J. L. B. Matekoni, stretching out his arms to dispel an incipient cramp. 'It is the people who use the road. There was one man, you know, who came up behind me, and although he couldn't possibly see what was coming – we were right on the brow of a hill and there were lines on the road warning you not to overtake – in spite of that, he just pulled past me. And then there was this big Botswana Defence Force lorry coming the other way and it was full of soldiers, I think, and the driver of that had to go right over on to the verge and kicked up a big cloud of dust and little stones flying all over the place, and one of those stones comes – *zing* – and makes a little crack in my windscreen. And this stupid man just drives on like a . . . like a . . . like an ostrich.'

'Like an ostrich?'

'You know what I mean, Mma. You know how ostriches run, and how they go this way and that, swerving around. Anyway, he was lucky that he didn't make that Defence Force driver go right off the road because that would have put him in big trouble. It would be like declaring war, Mma. You don't declare war on the Botswana Defence Force.'

Mma Ramotswe agreed that such a thing would be unwise. 'I'm very sorry to hear about these stupid people on the road,' she said. 'I'm sorry that we still have such people in these modern days.'

'Yes,' said Mr J. L. B. Matekoni. 'And so am I.' He sniffed at the air. 'Is that mutton stew, Mma? Is that what I can smell?'

'It is, Rra. There is a big pot waiting for you – for us – in the oven. It will be ready after you have washed your hands. And while we are eating, I can tell you of a very strange thing that happened to me today. Or happened to both of us, should I say. To Mma Makutsi and me.'

He went through to the bathroom to wash his hands, but they continued their conversation down the corridor. The children were never disturbed by the sound of voices and would sleep through even the most animated conversation elsewhere in the house.

'So something happened,' he called out. 'You found out some big important bit of information? You won a big prize – ten thousand *pula*? You saw a lion under your desk?'

She laughed. 'These are all quite possible developments, Rra.' For a moment she imagined Mma Makutsi suddenly whispering across the office, 'Don't make any sudden movements, Mma, but I think there is a lion under your desk. I think I can see its tail.' And she would reply, 'I shall take what action is necessary, Mma Makutsi, but we really should finish dictation first ...'

There came the sound of splashing water, and then the gurgle of the basin draining. 'So what was it?' Mr J. L. B. Matekoni asked. 'You had a visitor?'

'Yes,' she replied.

'What did you say, Mma?'

She raised her voice. 'I said yes, Rra. We had a visitor, but you will never, never guess who it was. Not in a year of guessing. Not even then, with twenty, fifty guesses a day; even then you would never get it.'

There was a momentary silence at the other end of the corridor. A tap was run again, and then there came the sound of the towel roller turning. 'Well, Rra,' Mma Ramotswe went on. 'Try to guess. I'll give you one clue: he is very important.'

'That man who wrote that book of yours. What is his name? That Chlorine Andersen, or whatever he's called.'

'Clovis, not Chlorine.'

'Him?'

She sounded crestfallen. 'Yes, Rra. How did you know?'

He came back into the room, wiping his hands on the sides of his khaki trousers. 'I guessed. You said that I would never guess, and so I chose the most unlikely name I could think of. And that was that man, Clovis Andersen. That's how I did it, Mma. Simple.'

Over a large helping of mutton stew, Mma Ramotswe narrated the story of her extraordinary meeting with Clovis Andersen. It was the same story that Mma Makutsi had, just an hour or so earlier, told Phuti Radiphuti; but more accurate, perhaps, in Mma Ramotswe's telling of it than in that of her assistant. Mma Makutsi had a tendency to embellish stories for dramatic effect, or at least to tell the tale from her own perspective. In her version, then, Clovis Andersen had introduced himself first to her, rather than to Mma Ramotswe, had been facing her desk when he sat down and had addressed almost all of his remarks to her. But in this, surely, she could be forgiven; for who among us does not see the world as turning towards him or her rather than towards others? The weather is weather in so far as it affects *us*; great events are great events in that they have an impact on *our* lives; life, in short, was to be judged by what it had in store for Mma Makutsi, or for those within her immediate circle. This was neither solipsism nor selfishness – Mma Makutsi was actually quite generous; rather, it was a matter of *perspective*. It was a universe made up of several key institutions, principal among which was the Botswana Secretarial College and all that it represented (the motto of the college being *Be Accurate*). Then there was the Double Comfort Furniture Store, to which she was now firmly attached as the wife of its managing director (and the motto of that concern was *Be Comfortable*); the Government of Botswana, its ministers and permanent secretaries; and finally the No. 1 Ladies' Detective Agency and its owner and founder, Mma Ramotswe. This was her world, and these were the bodies to which she was unswervingly loyal.

Mr J. L. B. Matekoni listened with interest to the story that Mma Ramotswe told, only interrupting her occasionally for clarification of some salient point.

'Out of the blue?' he asked. 'He came out of the blue? Just like that?'

'Yes,' said Mma Ramotswe. She had not told him about her dream; there would be an opportunity to discuss that later. 'He came into the office and, believe it or not, Rra, to begin with Mma Makutsi and I had no idea of who he was. He was a stranger, obviously, but that was all we could tell. And there are so many strangers about these days, there was no reason why we should know; he could have been anyone.'

'But do they not have a photograph of him on the cover of his book?' asked Mr J. L. B. Matekoni. 'I thought that they put photos of authors on books. So that you know what you're going to get.'

Mma Ramotswe shook her head. 'There is no photograph of Mr Andersen. He is a very modest man. As you would be too, Rra, if you wrote a book. *The Principles of Car Maintenance*, for example. You would have a photograph of a car on it, not of you.'

'I have not yet written a book,' mused Mr J. L. B. Matekoni. 'I have thought of it, but I have not started one yet.'

Mma Ramotswe was eager to continue with her story, but could not let this remark go uncommented upon. 'This book of yours, Rra: would it be about car maintenance, or is it something different?'

Mr J. L. B. Matekoni looked bashful. 'It will be something different, I think.'

She looked at him expectantly. 'Well, Rra?'

He hesitated, as if deciding whether to trust her with a secret. 'I thought of writing something for ladies.'

Mma Ramotswe's eyebrows shot up. 'For ladies? That is very interesting, Mr J. L. B. Matekoni! What exactly will this book for ladies be?'

'It will be on how to fix things in the house,' he said. 'There are many things that a lady can fix herself. Washing-machine repairs, for example, are not all that difficult. Then there are things that can go wrong with cars. There is no reason why ladies should not change tyres, or do simple things like that. You do not need a man to do those things.' He paused. 'That will be my book, Mma, if I ever write it, which I do not think I shall. I thought I might call it *Mr J. L. B. Matekoni's Book of Hints for Ladies*.'

Mma Ramotswe clapped her hands together. 'It will be a first-class book, Rra! They will sell it at that bookshop at Riverwalk. It will be in the window and take up all the space. Everybody will be buying it.'

'I must write it first,' said Mr J. L. B Matekoni. 'And the problem is that I do not know how to do that. I am just a mechanic, Mma Ramotswe – as you well know. I am not a person who can write a book. You need a BA for that, and I do not have a BA.'

They returned to the subject of Clovis Andersen.

'What did he want?' asked Mr J. L. B. Matekoni.

'He did not want anything,' said Mma Ramotswe. 'He was passing by and he thought he would call in and say hello. It was just because he is a detective too. It is called a professional courtesy call, I think.'

Mr J. L. B. Matekoni took a forkful of his mutton stew. 'Passing by? How is it that a famous person like that is just *passing by* the Tlokweng Road? How many famous people do you see on the Tlokweng Road, Mma Ramotswe? I have never seen one – not one. It is not a place where famous people like to go.'

'Those were my thoughts too,' said Mma Ramotswe. 'So I asked him, and he told me.'

She waited while Mr J. L. B. Matekoni dealt with his mutton stew. Then she resumed. 'He said that he was in Botswana because he was invited here to visit some lady.'

'Some Motswana lady?'

She shook her head. 'No, an American lady who has lived here for a few years. This lady is working here on a scheme that the American government has to build libraries in schools. They are building a library in Serowe, I think, and another one at Selebi-Phikwe. There will be many libraries all over the place, and it will be very nice for the children. That is what she is doing.'

Mr J. L. B. Matekoni nodded. 'It sounds like good work. And so Mr Andersen knows this lady, and she asked him to come to see her. Has he not got a wife back wherever he comes from? Is there no wife to say, "You must not go off and visit library ladies"?'

Mma Ramotswe raised a finger in the air. 'No, Rra, that is the point. There was a wife – there was a Mrs Andersen, but she is late now.'

Mr J. L. B. Matekoni lowered his head, as was polite to do,

even if one did not know the late person. 'I am very sorry to hear that.'

'Yes, it is very sad. So he has no wife now . . . '

'And he is hoping that the library lady . . . '

'No, he is not hoping that. But I think the library lady is hoping that she will be the new Mrs Andersen.'

'You mean she's keener than he is?'

'That is exactly what I mean. He did not use those precise words, of course, but that is the impression I formed. I think that she is keen to marry him, but he has different ideas. I think he wants her just as a friend.'

'But what is the problem?' asked Mr J. L. B. Matekoni. 'Do they not like one another? Is that not the most important thing?'

'I think they do like one another. In fact, he said to me, "I am very fond of this lady, but I do not love her." That is what he said, Rra.'

He shrugged. 'There are many people who marry one another without being in love. There are many good marriages like that. I could make you a long list, Mma.'

She looked away. Was their own marriage based on love, or was it something else that brought them together? Affection? Friendship? The comfort of sharing their lives? She knew what she felt about Mr J. L. B. Matekoni: she loved him. It was as simple as that. He was her husband, and she loved him. And she had every reason to believe, she felt, that he had loved her when he asked her to marry him and she had agreed. She was sure that he had loved her when they stood together, before Bishop Mwamba, under that tree at the orphan farm, with the sound of the children's singing rising up into that great, empty sky and the words of the marriage service – those profound words – hanging in the air, proclaimed by the Bishop and repeated by the two of them so that all might hear; she was sure that he had loved her then, and she believed that he loved her still. She would not ask him, though, because you should never ask that question of another; you should wait for him or her to say it, so that you know, then, that it comes from the heart, from that part of us that can never lie, can never conceal the truth.

She acknowledged the veracity of what he said. 'Yes, there are many such marriages, but I think that people still like to believe they are in love when they get married. I think that is important.'

Mr J. L. B. Matekoni looked thoughtful. 'So he does not love this lady? Then why did he come out to see her here? Surely that is unkind, if she thinks that he's coming out to Botswana so that he can ask her to marry him, and all the time he has no intention of doing that. Surely that is not very kind.'

She admitted that it could seem a bit like raising somebody's hopes, but would it not have been more unkind to refuse to come at all? He saw that. 'It is a very difficult situation,' he said. 'It must have been very hard for Mr Andersen.' He stopped for a moment before continuing: 'Why does he not love her, Mma? Is there a reason?'

Mma Ramotswe settled back in her seat. 'That is the point, Rra. There is a very big reason why poor Mr Andersen cannot love this lady who builds libraries. It is because he is still in love with his late wife. That is the reason.'

Mr J. L. B. Matekoni finished the last of the mutton stew on his plate and looked enquiringly at Mma Ramotswe. Sometimes he was allowed a second helping, but these days, following the discovery that a belt he had been wearing for years no longer fitted him, he was on a less calorific regime.

'No more,' she said. 'We can eat the rest tomorrow.'

He sighed, but did not argue.

'So, Mma Ramotswe, what is Mr Andersen to do?'

'I do not know, Rra. All that I know is that he is sad in his heart.' She touched her chest. 'That is the place where his sadness is. Right there. And I do not think that it is ever very easy to deal with sadness in that part of the body.'

He nodded his assent to that comment. 'You are right, Mma. It is very difficult.'

'But I shall do my best to cheer him up,' said Mma Ramotswe. 'I have invited him to come to the office tomorrow to discuss some of our cases. He was very happy to be invited – I think that he has nothing to do all day while the library lady is building libraries. And he is here for three weeks, Rra, which is a long time when you have nothing to do.' She paused. 'Except to be sad. Three weeks of sadness is a long time, I think.'

It was, reflected Mr J. L. B. Matekoni. Three weeks of sadness was a long time, by any standards, but it would be particularly long when one was far from home in a strange country, when everybody else would have their friends and family about them and would seem so occupied with their own lives. In such circumstances you might easily forget who you were, and how you once were happy. He almost expressed these thoughts to Mma Ramotswe, but did not do so, inhibited, perhaps, by the feeling that he was just a mechanic, not a poet or a philosopher, and that on the lips of mechanics such words might sound false or contrived, and certainly not as authentic as anything they might say on the subject of gearboxes, or fuel systems, or any of those other matters in respect of which he knew he stood on far firmer ground.

Chapter Seven

The This Way Up Building Company

Grace Makutsi, Dip. Sec. (97%), did not accompany her husband, Mr Phuti Radiphuti (of the Double Comfort Furniture Store) to his next meeting with Mr Clarkson Putumelo, the proprietor of the This Way Up Building Company. This was not because she was indifferent to the design of the house that Mr Putumelo was to build for them – she was extremely interested in that – but because she felt that she had not forgiven the builder his rudeness towards her and would avoid being in his presence until such time as he changed his attitude. That, she knew, was unlikely; in Mma Makutsi's opinion, attitudes were qualities with which one was born, and the likelihood of their being changed was, sadly, remote.

That is not to say it was impossible, as in her time she had witnessed a number of marked changes in attitude so profound, in fact, as to be quite astonishing. There was a man in northern Botswana, for instance, who was a known cattle thief; and yet while he was visiting a relative up near Kasane, he had come under the influence of a charismatic preacher and had been baptised in the waters of the Zambezi River. The change in that man had been so remarkable that there was talk of its being attributable to the special qualities of the Zambezi River. People said that as far as washing away sin was concerned, there was nothing to beat Zambezi water and that the religious zeal of those immersed in lesser waters – the Notwane River, to name just one river readily on hand for baptism ceremonies – was far less impressive than those of Zambezi converts. Of course it would be difficult to measure something as elusive as inner virtue, but in the case of this man there had certainly been a dramatic change. Far from stealing the cattle of others, he now actively sought out those that had been stolen, identified the thieves and then reported the matter to the owners and the authorities. In all of this he was conspicuously successful, owing to his intimate knowledge of the ways of cattle thieves, his having been one in the first place. *Set a thief to catch a thief.* Mma Makutsi had read that somewhere and it had struck her as containing a valuable insight – almost worthy of elevation into one of Clovis Andersen's famous rules in *The Principles of Private Detection*.

Mma Makutsi did not imagine that Mr Clarkson Putumelo would change, and she therefore reconciled herself to having to watch the building of the house from a distance, making only irregular visits to the site. She had full confidence in Phuti, though, as she took the view that if you could manage a large furniture store, as Phuti did so successfully, then you could manage just about anything. She had nonetheless been careful to explain to Phuti exactly what she wanted in the kitchen. That would be her domain, and she wanted everything to be perfect. 'The fridge,' she said, 'must not be too close to the door, or you will find that you cannot have the kitchen door open at the same time as you have the fridge door open.'

'Very wise,' said Phuti. 'I would never have thought of that.'

'That is because you're ...' Mma Makutsi stopped herself in time. She had been about to say, 'That's because you're a man,' but then she thought that this was perhaps a bit unkind, even if it was true. You should not make people feel guilty about things that are beyond their control, and the fact that Phuti was a man was not something he could do anything about. So she completed the observation by saying instead, ' ... because you're too busy thinking about so many other important things. How can you be expected to think about fridge doors when your mind is full of big decisions on things like ordering furniture, and so on and so forth?'

Phuti nodded. It was true that he had many such decisions to make, but he also felt that he should concern himself with minutiae. He called this *micromanagement*, and he had learned about it from a correspondence course he had taken called 'Managing the Details in Retail and Related Industries'.

'Is there anything else?' he had asked. 'Do you need one cooker or two?'

Mma Makutsi was unprepared for this question. Never in her wildest dreams had she imagined that she would be in a position to have two cookers; indeed, it was achievement enough, she felt, to have had the single-plate cooker-cum-oven that she had successfully used for the last few years. Two cookers!

'Oh, I think now that you mention it, we should perhaps have two,' she said, trying to sound as casual as possible, as if the choice between one or two cookers was a decision of little weight – the sort of decision one might easily make without giving it much thought at all.

'So you will have two cookers then,' said Phuti, proud that he was able to offer his new bride two cookers. 'It is best to be prepared.'

Mma Makutsi nodded gravely. She was not sure what eventuality they were planning for; indeed, she could not think of any reason why one would need two cookers, but they were now committed to a two-cooker kitchen, and she was happy enough with that.

There were several other minor matters to be settled.

'The floor must be easy to clean,' said Phuti. 'So I'll tell Mr Putumelo to lay special tiles that can be easily washed.'

Mma Makutsi thought this very wise. 'But they must not be not too slippery,' she said. 'Some of these modern tiles . . . ' She shook her head, as might one who had only too frequently been wrong-footed on unsuitable tiles. In reality, for Mma Makutsi the thought of any tiles at all was almost intoxicating in its implications; her floors, until now, had been – at best – red-painted concrete, and not all that long ago, in Bobonong, the traditional option of packed mud.

They had spent a further half-hour discussing cupboards – these were to be plentiful and deep enough to accommodate a vacuum cleaner as well as a full set of brooms and brushes. They also discussed the bedroom windows; these had to be of a sufficient size to let in enough light but not so large as to invite passers-by on the road to stare in at the occupants. 'I cannot stand people staring in through your windows,' said Mma Makutsi. 'What happens in a house is none of the business of people outside that house. Inside is inside; outside is outside. That is what I always say.' It was true that she did not like to be looked in on from outside, but what she did not mention was the fact that she herself frequently yielded to the temptation to glance through another's window if the opportunity presented itself. But she was a private detective, and such glances were not prompted by mere idle curiosity, or even nosiness; they were … a *professional* matter, an assessment – akin perhaps to the surreptitious clinical glance a doctor cannot help himself but give at a manifestly unhealthy person he passes on the street.

Armed with these requirements, Phuti met the builder at the headquarters of the This Way Up Building Company. He had stipulated that the meeting should be there, turning down Mr Putumelo's offer to come to the furniture shop, so that he could cast an eye over the builder's office before he signed the contract. In doing this he was following advice imparted to him by his father, who had always recommended doing business on the home ground of the other side. 'If they are no good,' he had said, 'you will be able to tell that immediately. Look at their furniture. A man who has a rickety chair is a rickety businessman. A man whose table is not straight is himself not straight. These signs will never let you down, Phuti.' It was an experienced furniture-seller's view of the world, but it had proved an accurate guide and had on more than one occasion prevented the signing of contracts that would have led to trouble and loss.

Mr Clarkson Putumelo's office passed the Radiphuti test with no difficulty at all. The company had an impressive office on its own lot, not far from a cluster of prosperous shops off the old Francistown Road. There was an office building on which the company name was painted in large lettering, a garage in which several vehicles, working and otherwise, were parked, and a large yard in which piles of brick and timber were neatly stored under tarpaulins or standing corrugated-iron covers. There was nothing sloppy about the scene, and Phuti was immediately reassured.

'So, here you are, my friend,' said Mr Putumelo, welcoming Phuti into his office. 'This is the headquarters of my little enterprise, as you see. It is from here that we go out every morning and build the new Botswana.'

Phuti smiled. 'And you build it the right way up,' he said.

Mr Putumelo did not appear to see the joke. 'We are always building,' he said solemnly. 'That's the building trade for you. One building goes up, and you start the next.'

'It's the same in the furniture trade,' said Phuti. 'You sell one bed and then you sell the next one.'

Mr Putumelo considered this for a moment before nodding in agreement. 'That's business, isn't it? And who would have it otherwise?'

This exchange completed, they sat down to the business of agreeing the terms of the contract. 'I have an offer for you,' said Mr Putumelo. 'As you know, Rra, there are many people in this business who are bad men. They give the building trade a bad name because they are unscrupulous.'

Phuti said that he had heard this.

'You see it in the newspapers,' went on Mr Putumelo. 'You read about Mr So-and-so or Mrs What's-her-name having a big argument with a builder over some contract that went wrong. He says one thing and the builder says another. Blah, blah. And you know what, Mr Radiphuti? In ninety-nine per cent of these cases it's because of the sort of contract they've signed. The builder has given a price for the job in order to get it, then he spends the rest of the time trying to do the thing on the cheap so that he ends up with a bit of profit. It's always the same. Agree a low price, then try to cut corners.'

'I can see how that happens,' said Phuti. 'Sometimes with our suppliers we agree on a specification for, let's say, a set of chairs, and then—'

Mr Putumelo cut him short. 'Exactly, Rra. You hit the nail on the head.'

'That's for a builder to do,' said Phuti.

Again Mr Putumelo did not appear to grasp the reference.

'But,' he said, raising a hand to emphasise his point, 'I have a way round this problem. If you have a contract with the client that says *I will erect the building for cost plus twenty per cent*, then you can't go wrong. You get a good building; you don't get rubbish. I know that I'm going to make a profit, and so I don't try to cut any corners: what's the point of doing that?'

Phuti thought about this. He did not want his builder to cut corners; he wanted a solid house that would last them a lifetime. It seemed to him a very good idea, but he was a businessman and an opening percentage was always just that: the point at which negotiations could begin. 'It seems a good approach,' he said, 'but the percentage . . .'

'Oh, that,' said Mr Putumelo. 'That nineteen per cent margin . . .'

'Seventeen,' said Phuti.

Mr Putumelo shook his head. 'Nineteen.'

'Eighteen?'

'Done,' said Mr Putumelo, extending a hand. 'You will not regret this, Rra: I can assure you of that.'

Phuti took the builder's hand and shook it. 'This is very good,' he said.

The builder laughed. 'Very good? It's excellent. First class.' He reached for a piece of paper that had been lying face down on the desk. 'Now all that we have to do is write in the relevant percentage here.' He fumbled in the breast pocket of his shirt for a pair of horn-rimmed spectacles. The effect of these glasses was to make him look erudite; like a teacher, thought Phuti, remembering, with a sudden pang, the teacher whom he had idolised at Gaborone Senior School and who had been killed one weekend by a drunken driver on the Lobatse Road, the young Radiphuti's first real encounter with death and with the realisation, so hard at that age, that immortals, too, can die.

81

A few scribbles of the pen and the contract was duly executed 'according to the laws of Botswana', as its final clause attested. Phuti was pleased, and sealed the bargain again with a handshake, while continuing to fold and tuck the piece of paper with his free hand. That done, Mr Putumelo reached for a brochure from a shelf behind his head and leafed through it to find an illustration to show his client.

'In my opinion,' he said, 'we should go for brick rather than for these concrete blocks that everybody is using these days. You can't go wrong with brick.'

Phuti looked momentarily confused. 'I thought that most houses were built with brick, except for low-cost housing.' He pointed out of the window in the direction of the fields of neat, two-room, flat-roofed houses that the Government had built.

Mr Putumelo shook his head. 'No, Rra, you are wrong. Well, you are wrong and right, both at the same time. You see, you are right about that low-cost housing: it is very good for people who do not have much money, and they are happy with the concrete-block construction. And those houses are strong, too! They will not fall down for many years, I can tell you. But when it comes to big houses – the sort of house that a man like you wants to build, then you would think that good materials would be used. You would think that, wouldn't you?'

He waited for Phuti to answer.

'Yes, Rra. You would think that they would use—'

'Good-quality brick,' interjected Mr Putumelo. 'Or even stone. You've seen those houses out at Mokolodi? You've seen those good stone walls? Those houses will last for ever, my friend. One hundred years – easy. Maybe two hundred years. Who knows how long? How long is a piece of string? That is what I always say.'

Phuti began to say something, but was again silenced by Mr Putumelo.

'Now you'd think that a good-quality house would be built of brick or stone, but is that what is happening today? I can tell you, Rra Radiphuti, that there are builders in this town who are making those high-class houses with concrete blocks and then just putting lots of fancy plaster on the outside and making people think there are solid things inside. That's what they are doing, those people, but we are not. We are still making good houses out of good building materials.' He paused. 'So you see this brochure, Rra? You see these bricks? They are top-quality bricks. I would recommend one outer layer and one inner layer, with good metal ties in between. Then we will put ventilation grilles to allow the house to breathe. That will keep you cool in the hot months. That is very important.'

Phuti studied the picture of the brick. It seemed like an ordinary brick to him, but it had several lines of explanation printed below, setting out its superior properties. He handed the brochure back to the builder. 'That is very good,' he said. 'I think that we should have those bricks, Rra.'

Mr Putumelo took off his glasses and deftly folded in the arms. 'Done,' he said. 'I will order everything we need and then we can start ...' He looked at an annotated calendar on the wall. 'We can start in four days. Maybe three.' Then he added: 'Payment for work done will be due every ten days, for work done during those ten days, until completion of the contract. Agreed? Good.'

Phuti had not been prepared for this: beginning a house was a major step, he thought, and it seemed now to be happening so quickly.

'There are some details that my wife has raised with me,' he said. 'I think that perhaps we might ...'

Mr Putumelo fixed him with an intense stare. 'Your wife? She knows about houses?'

For a few moments, Phuti was at a loss. 'She thinks that ...'

Mr Putumelo frowned. 'Building a house is a very complicated matter, Rra. There are not many women in the building trade.'

'But women know about houses, Rra,' Phuti protested. 'They are the ones who look after them.'

Mr Putumelo burst out laughing. 'That is not the point, Rra. Women are very good at cleaning houses, but that does not mean that they know how to make them.' He reached for a handkerchief from his pocket and dabbed at the corner of his mouth; a curious, rather fussy gesture. 'But I must not stop you from telling me what your wife thinks, Rra. I am sure it is very interesting.' The last remark was heavy with sarcasm.

Phuti told the builder of Grace's requirements. Mr Putumelo reached for a pen and made a few notes; he looked sceptical as he wrote, as an unhelpful bank manager might look as he entertained a risky client's request for a loan. 'I have written that down,' he said, once Phuti had finished. 'We shall see what can be done.' He examined his own note. 'There are some requests here that are not very practical, of course. And this business of two cookers: where does that nonsense come from? Has your wife seen some picture in a magazine? Two cookers! Have we each got two mouths, Rra, so that we need to have two dinners at the same time?'

Phuti winced. It had been his suggestion, even if Grace had readily agreed to it, and he should have the courage to say as much to Mr Putumelo. He should say: 'No, that was not my wife's idea, Rra – it was mine, and I am the client. If I want two cookers, then I can have them. You are only the builder and I am paying you to do what *I* want. Understand?' That is what he should have said, he knew; but he did not say it. Instead, he said, 'Two cookers are not an important element of the design, Rra. One will do quite well.'

Mr Putumelo appeared to take no notice of the concession.

'And as for this business about floor tiles,' the builder said. 'All floor tiles are of much the same composition. I shall choose the right ones, and do not need to be reminded of what is necessary.'

Again, Phuti did not protest. Mr Putumelo knew what he was talking about – the horn-rimmed spectacles spoke to that, as did the pile of brochures and the certificate on the wall informing the public at large that Mr Clarkson Putumelo was a member in good standing of the Botswana Federation of Master Builders. One could not argue with that, and if such a person said that one only needed one cooker, and that any floor tile he chose would most certainly not be too slippery, then such assurances should be accepted. Phuti realised that Mr Putumelo was not perhaps the most charming of men, but did one necessarily want a charming builder? What one needed of a builder was an understanding of technical matters – it was clear that Mr Putumelo had that. One expected, too, a sense of organisation and logistical skill – and it was equally clear from his orderly yard that Mr Putumelo was endowed with these qualities. If he was also arrogant and dismissive of women, then these failings were to be regretted, but did not necessarily affect his ability as a builder. Or so Phuti told himself as he left the premises of the This Way Up Building Company, although he somehow felt guilty about this concession. It was as if he had failed in some way to stand up for his wife, as if he had been cowardly. *Perhaps I am a coward, perhaps that is what I am.* The bitter thought brought back something that had not troubled him for many months – his stammer. *C . . . c . . . c . . . coward*, he muttered in unhappy self-reproach. *F . . . f . . . frightened of a b . . . b . . . builder. You should be a . . . a . . . ashamed of yourself, Ph . . . ph . . . ph . . . uti R . . . r . . . r . . . r . . . adiphuti.*

Chapter Eight

Mma Ramotswe Drives Clovis Andersen to Mochudi, and Thinks

M r Clovis Andersen, author of *The Principles of Private Detection*, the great work of detection theory that had guided the No. 1 Ladies' Detective Agency since that momentous day on which it had opened its doors – the book now so familiar to Mma Ramotswe and Mma Makutsi that they could quote whole paragraphs without reference to the text itself – that same Clovis Andersen, who had so unexpectedly and impossibly stepped through the front door of the agency, was now due to meet Mma Ramotswe on the veranda of the President Hotel. It was mid-morning on the day following their first encounter, and Mma Ramotswe had arranged the meeting there because she was due to go out to Mochudi that morning and she wanted to show him the village where she was born and where she went to school. It would also be an opportunity for her to talk to the great detective without Mma Makutsi interrupting every second minute. It was clear to Mma Ramotswe that her assistant was star-struck, as she had gone on for some time about Clovis Andersen after he had left the office, her eyes flashing with excitement behind those large round glasses of hers. No, Mma Makutsi should not be allowed to monopolise Clovis Andersen just yet; she would have her fair share of the distinguished visitor's time, but it would be important not to create the impression at this early stage that *everybody* in Botswana wore large round glasses, made rather firm pronouncements on a wide range of subjects and reminded others of the marks they had achieved in their final examinations in whatever it was they had studied. But even as she thought this, even as she heard Mma Makutsi's voice say *ninety-seven per cent*, she stopped herself. That was unkind, and she should not think it; that ninety-seven per cent was important to Mma Makutsi because she had started off with so little and had worked so hard to escape from a life of poverty and drudgery. She had worked hard to make something of her life when there were so many who simply sat about and took what life offered them. No, she would make sure that Mma Makutsi had ample time to spend in the company of Clovis Andersen, but not just yet . . .

The veranda of the President Hotel is not a place in which a great deal happens. This is not in any way to disparage it: it is important that there should be places where not a great deal happens because such places remind us that life is not entirely and exclusively made up of exciting or significant events. Every life needs spells of calm, every life needs expanses of time when nothing much occurs, when one may sit for several hours in the same place and gaze upon static things, upon some waxen-leafed desert plant, perhaps, or a patch of dry grass. Or a group of cattle standing under a tree for the shade, the slow, flicking movement of their tails the only indication that they are animate beasts, not rocks; or a sky across which no clouds, or perhaps only the merest wisp of white, move. Now, seated at her table on the veranda of the President Hotel, Mma Ramotswe had nothing much to look at while she waited. Down below, beyond the parapet, there were people in the square: sellers of clothes and dried herbs, carvers of wooden ornaments, sunglasses merchants, purveyors of potions to put on one's hair. All these were there, as were their customers, but Mma Ramotswe chose not to watch this market scene; rather she looked up at the sky and wondered what it would be like not to have a sky above one's head; to be a prisoner, perhaps, or one who could not take the sun and had to remain indoors. She had known one such person when she was at school in Mochudi; a girl afflicted by albinism, whose pale, patchy skin, as brittle and translucent, it seemed, as the bark of what they called the paper tree, was so sensitive to the rays of the sun that she would burn painfully if she spent more than a few minutes outside. And that poor girl had been unable to go to school as she could not walk those miles from the family's village outside Mochudi, and they could not afford the creams that could protect her skin from the sun. And the other children had stared at her on the occasions that they saw her and had whispered among themselves. Mma Ramotswe felt the shame still that she had not done anything for that girl, and now she had heard that she was late, having died giving birth to her first child, and there had been no husband. There were so many lives, she thought, that could only be led with difficulty, with pain, and because we were so bound up in our own lives so many of these were invisible to us until suddenly we saw, and knew, and felt that sudden pang of human sympathy that comes with knowing.

It was strange that the girl should come into her mind, the memory triggered by no more than looking up at the sky. But that, she told herself, was how memory worked; one would see something and then it would make one think of one thing and then of another; snatches of conversation would come back, images of things one had seen, memories that one thought one had forgotten, but that had been filed away in the back of the head, in those recesses where such things are tucked away. Clovis Andersen and his *Principles of Private Detection* ... When had she first seen that book? Right at the beginning of her life as a private detective; and she had held it in her hand and opened it at the title page with all the excitement that you feel when opening a new book and there are the words on the page, ready for you, as if the author himself is standing in front of you, clearing his throat, ready to engage you in conversation. And she had seen the name Clovis Andersen little thinking that years later, after so much had happened, she would be meeting the very man, that he would address her as Mma Ramotswe; that she would, for a short time, have the attention of the world's greatest authority on private detection ... Such a miracle, such an extraordinary development ... such a privilege.

'Mma Ramotswe?'

She gave a start, and turned in her seat to see Clovis Andersen standing behind her. He was dressed in rather baggy khaki trousers with an olive-green shirt on to which far too many pockets had been stitched – the sort of outfit that people thought was standard dress for Botswana but was really only worn by visitors. It was a practical enough outfit, she supposed, but she wondered what people could possibly do with so many pockets. Did they imagine that one needed to carry penknives and compasses and the like, even when going to Mochudi?

89

'This is a very fine view you get from here,' said Clovis Andersen as he sat down.

Mma Ramotswe glanced at the square and remembered how, long ago, she had once asked the dress-seller down below for information because she knew that such people missed very little of what happened around them. And Clovis Andersen himself had said . . .

'You see that woman,' said Mma Ramotswe as Clovis Andersen settled himself into his chair. 'I asked her for information once. She knows everything, I think. And you say in your book *Always ask somebody who knows*. That is what you wrote, Rra, and I have always followed that advice.'

Clovis Andersen smiled. 'I remember writing that. And I suppose it's true, isn't it? If you ask somebody who doesn't know anything, then you won't get much of an answer. At least, that's the way I look at it.'

'But you're so right, Rra,' said Mma Ramotswe. 'And I have always wondered how you know all these things. It must be experience, I think.'

Clovis Andersen looked away. 'Experience and common sense,' he said. 'There are so many jobs that are just a matter of common sense. Most jobs, in fact. They look complicated, but when you look closely you'll see that all you really need is common sense.'

Mma Ramotswe considered this. It was true that private detection involved a great deal of common sense, and undoubtedly there were many other professions in which common sense would get you by, but surely there were those where the limits of common sense would very soon be revealed – being a dentist, for example, or an airline pilot . . .

She toyed with the idea of pointing this out to him, but decided not to. The traditional ways of Botswana were clear about correcting a person who was senior to you, or a stranger, and on both of these counts she should not directly contradict Clovis Andersen. You did not have to remain silent, of course, if such a person was wrong, but you should be careful how you voiced your disagreement. So she simply said, 'Common sense is very useful. Yes.'

There was a brief silence. Then she said, 'You must have seen so many things, Rra. In your career as a detective, you must have seen so many things.'

Clovis Andersen nodded. 'There are many things to be seen in this life, Mma. All one has to do is keep one's eyes open.'

Mma Ramotswe voiced her agreement. 'Oh, you are so right, Rra. The big mistake is to close your eyes. There are so many who have closed eyes. You look at them, of course, and you think that they have open eyes, but then you look more closely and you realise that although their eyes are open, there is nothing going in.'

'That's because they aren't looking,' said Clovis Andersen. 'If you do not look, you do not see.'

'That is so true, Rra,' enthused Mma Ramotswe. 'That is so true.'

He went on. 'There are some people who have their eyes open and are looking, but do not see anything because they are looking for something that is not there. That can happen, I believe.'

'Oh, I believe that too, Rra,' said Mma Ramotswe. 'I have always believed that – all along.'

'That is not to say there's nothing there,' continued Clovis Andersen. 'There may be something there, but because nobody's looking for it, it won't be seen. So we should always ask ourselves: are we looking for the right thing?'

Mma Ramotswe agreed again. 'That is definitely the thing to do,' she said.

The waitress appeared, notebook at the ready, to take their order. Clovis Andersen ordered coffee, which made Mma Ramotswe smile; she had heard about the American weakness for coffee, but again she said nothing; people cannot help liking the things that are liked where they are born. At some point in the future she would introduce him to the pleasures of tea; there would be plenty of time for that.

The waitress moved off, and their conversation continued.

'Your cases must be much bigger ones than mine,' said Mma Ramotswe. 'I am always dealing with very small things. Is that man cheating on this woman; is that woman cheating on this man? Who is stealing cattle here, or taking money there? Who is using the company truck for private business when the rule is that it must not be used for such things? That sort of thing – very different from the big cases you must have every day. Who has shot this person? Who has shot that person? Who has taken the million-dollar necklace from the neck of this big film star? Big things like that.'

Clovis Andersen looked at the floor. 'Not really,' he muttered.

'And one day I can see them making a big film about your life,' Mma Ramotswe continued. 'It will be very popular throughout the world, and I will say to Mma Makutsi, "That is our friend, Mma – that is all about our friend."'

Clovis Andersen shook his head. 'Oh, I don't think so, Mma Ramotswe. I don't think I'll be of sufficient interest for that.'

Sensing his reluctance to talk about it – an admirable modesty, she thought – she changed the subject. She asked him about his plans to see the country, and he told her that he had organised a trip to Ghanzi over the next few days. For now, though, he was keen to see the area around Gaborone. 'Mochudi, then,' said Mma Ramotswe. 'That is the place, Rra.' They should start the drive up to the village immediately after their tea – or tea and coffee – as it would be better to arrive there before the noonday heat made it uncomfortable to sit in the van, in spite of its ancient, if valiant, fan.

'I am looking forward to seeing it, Mma Ramotswe,' said Clovis Andersen. 'I come from a similar place, you know – a small town in the Midwest. And my wife too, she comes . . . came from such a place. She always said . . . '

He faltered, and she watched him.

'It is good to talk about late people, Rra,' she said quietly. 'It is what they want us to do. Late people would be happy if they knew we were talking about them.'

He looked up, as if he had heard some important piece of news.

'Do you think that's true, Mma Ramotswe? Do you think they can hear us?'

She wanted to say yes. She wanted to reassure this man who was obviously still so full of grief. But could she? She did not know – not in her heart of hearts – whether her father, the late Obed Ramotswe, could hear her. She addressed him often enough, drawing his attention to some unusual sight she encountered along the road; she addressed him as if he were sitting there in the van with her, but she thought that it was just wishful thinking, nothing more than that. She did not think that he had altogether ceased to exist, but of where exactly he was, where that place to which he had gone was located, she had no idea, other than it was somewhere above Botswana, or on the same level as Botswana but around some corner that one day we all must turn. Beyond that, she could not be certain. All she knew was that it would be a place of cattle bells and gentle, life-giving rain; a place in which all our tears would be wiped tenderly away.

'I am not sure about these things, Rra,' she said quietly. 'But I think that they are watching over us somehow – the people who have gone before.' She fixed him with a gaze; the poor man in his sorrow. 'Your late wife will know that you still love her, Rra. She will know that.'

Chapter Nine

The Government Does Not Own the Air

Mma Ramotswe had planned to spend the following day carrying out a number of minor tasks that for one reason or another she had been putting off. There were bills to be paid – a painful process for both her and Mma Makutsi, who had a special expression she adopted as she folded the cheques and placed them in their envelopes. 'You have your bill-paying face on,' Mma Ramotswe remarked. 'It is as if you were swallowing some bitter medicine, Mma. Or eating an aloe, maybe.'

Mma Makutsi acknowledged that she found the whole business of paying bills a difficult one. 'There are just too many bills,' she complained. 'If there were only one or two, then I could pay them without looking as if I had vinegar on my tongue. But look at them, Mma ... electricity bills, the book-keeper's bill, the stationery bill, the water bill ... How much water do we use here,

Mma? How can they charge us this much when all we do is take a little bit of water to make tea? And a little bit of water for the bathroom? That is all. But they charge us as if we're the Victoria Falls. Look at that bill! Just look at it.'

'Water is very precious,' said Mma Ramotswe. 'It is not cheap.'

Mma Makutsi was unimpressed. 'And soon there will be a bill for air,' said Mma Makutsi. 'They will be saying: you have used so much of the Government's oxygen this month – please pay us. Terms: thirty days net.'

Mma Ramotswe laughed. 'I do not think so, Mma—'

Mma Makutsi, sticking down an envelope flap with perhaps slightly more force than was strictly necessary, cut her short. 'And who says the air belongs to the Government, anyway?'

'I don't think the Government says that, Mma.'

'Oh, don't they? I think they do, Mma. If they didn't say that the air belongs to them, then why do they say that you need their permission to fly through it? Phuti knows a pilot, and he told him that he has to speak on the radio to some government people called Air Traffic Control and ask their permission to fly through the air above Gaborone. That means that they think they own it – as if it's their own yard, or something like that.'

Mma Ramotswe shook her head. 'They do not say they own the air, Mma. All that those people are doing is making sure that planes don't fly into one another. If you've got one plane going this way and another plane flying from the other direction and they meet, then that would not be very good, would it?'

Mma Makutsi hesitated for a moment; but no, she was not convinced. 'They are just interfering,' she said. 'The pilots can see exactly where they're going. They're not asleep.'

'It happens very quickly,' said Mma Ramotswe. 'And there are clouds, Mma. You cannot see what is happening in a cloud.'

'Then you shouldn't fly through them,' snapped Mma Makutsi. 'You see a cloud and you go round it. That is all you need to do. Phuti says that it's not a good thing to fly through clouds. You can get struck by lightning and then that will be the end.'

Mma Ramotswe was silent. She had great admiration for Mma Makutsi, but not when she was in one of these contrary moods. When that happened, she would dig in over some matter and become quite unreasonable, even if it was plain that she was arguing a lost cause. There were so many examples of her doing this, and Mma Ramotswe had learned that the best response was to change the subject.

'Lightning is very dangerous,' she said. 'Not just in the air. That poor man in Molepolole – did you read about him, Mma? He was struck by lightning when he was walking home across a field. He is late now.'

'It was very sad,' said Mma Makutsi. 'I read that the lightning hit his hat. Perhaps he should have had a lightning conductor on the top of it, with a wire going down his back to the earth. Do you think that would work, Mma?'

'I do not think so, Mma Makutsi,' said Mma Ramotswe. 'It is safer to stay indoors.'

'Oh no, it isn't,' came the quick rebuttal. 'One of the men who worked for Phuti – one of the men who loaded furniture – he fell over in his own house and broke his leg. They took him to hospital, but that stuff you have in the middle of your bones . . .'

'Bone marrow.'

'Yes, that stuff. It leaked into his blood and blocked one of his pipes . . .'

'Blood vessels.'

Mma Makutsi shook her head solemnly. 'Exactly. It blocked it up and now he is late too.'

There was a silence. Mma Ramotswe looked at the clock. She had things to do outside the office, and she thought that it was a good time, perhaps, to get out and about and leave Mma Makutsi to attend to the office tasks. By the time she got back, Mma Makutsi might be in a less difficult mood.

'I have to go and see Mma Potokwani,' Mma Ramotswe announced, rising from her chair. 'This business with Mr Ditso. I must get some more details from her.'

'That one's not going to end well,' said Mma Makutsi. 'We'll never find out anything about that man, Mma. He's far too clever for us ...' She looked across the room at Mma Ramotswe. 'I'll tell you something, Mma. You know how they say *money talks?* Well, I say the opposite is true: *money doesn't talk*. And I say that because money never tells you where it has come from. Never. So if Mma Potokwani thinks that she will find out that this rich man of hers has got his money from some bad place, she is going to be very disappointed. Money has no mouth, Mma. It cannot speak.'

Mma Ramotswe shook her head. 'Don't give up before we've started, Mma.' She paused. 'And remember: we have a secret weapon.'

Mma Makutsi frowned. 'And what would that be, Mma?'

Mma Ramotswe waited for a few moments before she answered. 'Clovis Andersen,' she said simply.

The large round glasses caught the light; flashed. The contrariness evaporated – at least to an extent. Yes. Clovis Andersen. Oh, yes!

She drove out to Tlokweng along one of the back roads – a roundabout way that gave her time to get over the tension that Mma Makutsi's odd mood had injected into the day. Driving, she found, always helped her to unwind, and as she made her way slowly along the winding dirt road she found herself smiling again. The one thing you could not say about Mma Makutsi was that she was dull; far from it – Mma Makutsi was what her friend Mma Moffat would have described as *a character*. And it was better to be a character, she felt, than to be one of those people who spoke about nothing at all, and probably thought about nothing, too; such people were soporific and could be marketed by some enterprising person as *walking sleeping pills*. Yes, that was a good idea: if you had difficulty sleeping you could phone up one of these people and, for a small charge, they would come to your house and sit and look at you, and you would gradually nod off to sleep. You would have to pay them first, though, as otherwise they would have to wake you up to collect their fee, and that would defeat the purpose of calling them in the first place ... And there could be another service for people who felt sleepy but for some reason needed to keep awake. They could phone for Mma Makutsi and she would come and talk about this and that and make the sort of remarks that would keep people on their toes, puzzling over what she meant, or getting irritated and hot under the collar because they disagreed with what she was saying. Makutsi Wake-up Services would be a good name for such a concern. There were so many possible businesses ...

She turned a corner, and there was another small business, set back from the road – one she had not seen before. The Minor Adjustment Beauty Salon. She slowed down. The premises was a tin shed – not much more than a shack – topped with a freshly painted notice announcing the name of the concern and laying claim to national pre-eminence in the field. *Famous throughout Botswana*, the notice claimed. *First consultation free. No appointment necessary.*

She stopped on impulse. Mma Ramotswe did not patronise beauty salons, although she knew many who did, including, she suspected, Mma Makutsi. There was something about this salon that intrigued her, though, and she had time on her hands. Mma Potokwani was not expecting her, and so it did not matter when she arrived at the orphan farm. If the initial consultation was free, then it would be interesting to see what they suggested. And there was another reason for stopping: as a private detective, Mma Ramotswe was acutely aware of the importance of contacts, who might provide information at some point in the future. The people who ran beauty salons were known to be repositories of gossip, and the owner of the Minor Adjustment Beauty Salon would probably be no exception to that general rule. There would be no harm, she thought, in making a new acquaintance who was so placed.

As she parked the van, she became aware of a face and then a pair of eyes peering out at her from the dark interior of the building. She stepped out of the van and closed the door behind her, which was the signal for the face and eyes to emerge too; now she saw a woman in a blue dress, rather like a nurse's tunic, standing in the doorway watching her. The woman greeted her as she approached.

'*Dumela*, Mma.' An outstretched hand.

The greetings over, the woman gave her name. 'I am Mma Soleti. I am the owner here.'

Mma Ramotswe inclined her head. 'I am Precious Ramotswe.' There was a moment's hesitation; it did not always help to say that one was a detective, but honesty, she felt, required it. 'I have a small business, the No. 1 Ladies' Detective Agency.'

Mma Soleti smiled, exposing strikingly white teeth. 'I know that place. I sometimes drive past it. There is a garage too.'

'That is Tlokweng Road Speedy Motors. The mechanic is my husband.'

Mma Soleti nodded. 'I hear he is very good.'

Mma Ramotswe beamed with pleasure. She never tired of

hearing compliments paid to her husband. 'I am very lucky to be married to such a man,' she said. 'He is kind.'

'That is very good, Mma.'

A brief silence ensued before Mma Ramotswe spoke again. 'A consultation . . . I was wondering . . .'

Mma Soleti clapped her hands together. 'And I was hoping! I said to myself, "This is a lady who will do very well with a bit of guidance and adjustment." You have made a very good decision, Mma.'

Mma Ramotswe drew back involuntarily. 'Just an initial consultation, Mma. I don't know if I want to do too much. I am traditionally built, you see, and I am not normally one who bothers too much about these matters of fashion.'

Mma Soleti considered this for a moment, turning her head slightly as if to assess Mma Ramotswe from a different angle. 'Really, Mma? But being traditionally built is a positive advantage, in my view. You see, if a lady is one of these modern . . .'

'Stick insects,' Mma Ramotswe supplied.

Mma Soleti burst out laughing. 'Yes, that is what they are, Mma. Stick insects. It's very difficult to do much with those ladies because . . . well, there's so little of them. But with a traditionally built lady like yourself, it's like painting a big wall – there's much more room for the artist.' She paused. 'And I do think of myself as an artist, Mma.'

Mma Ramotswe found herself warming to this woman. Following her into the tin building, she saw that there was a plastic-covered couch, rather like those used by doctors to examine their patients, a desk and a glass-fronted cupboard full of bottles and jars. Mma Soleti gestured for her to sit on the edge of the couch. 'There is no need to lie down, Mma. Not at this stage. I shall be mostly concerned with the face in this consultation. We can deal with the rest of you some other time.'

Mma Ramotswe perched on the edge of the couch. It was of such a height that her feet barely touched the ground, and one of her shoes, her flat walking shoes that were such a contrast to Mma Makutsi's more fashionable footwear, began to slip off. Mma Soleti paid no attention to this. She had picked up a large magnifying glass and had begun to peer closely at her new client's face. It was a disconcerting experience; the beautician's eyes, viewed from the other side of the glass, were large, like the eyes of a fish, Mma Ramotswe thought.

'Mmm,' said Mma Soleti, adding: 'Aahh.'

'You have seen something?' asked Mma Ramotswe.

'Nothing,' said Mma Soleti, moving the focus of her gaze across to the other side of Mma Ramotswe's face. 'I have seen nothing that I didn't think I'd see.'

Mma Ramotswe wondered what that meant, and was on the point of enquiring when Mma Soleti said, 'Oh.'

'Is there anything wrong, Mma?'

'There is nothing wrong. This is a very good face, Mma. There can be no arguing about that. This is a good Botswana face.'

Mma Ramotswe was not sure what to make of that. She frowned, only to provoke an immediate warning from Mma Soleti. 'Try not to frown, Mma. That makes lines on the face, and if you go on frowning, those lines will be there for ever, even when you aren't frowning inside.'

'I was just wondering about what it meant to say that I have a good Botswana face.'

'It means that you have the best sort of face,' said Mma Soleti, finishing her examination. 'Botswana faces are honest faces. There are some faces that are very different, I'm afraid. Those people have faces that are full of anger or anxiety or all those things – negative things.'

'I see.'

'Yes, Mma. That is what I meant.' She lowered the magnifying glass and sat down opposite Mma Ramotswe. 'Now, Mma,' she continued, 'we need to talk about your skin. There are some big holes in it.'

Mma Ramotswe gasped. 'Holes in my skin?'

Mma Soleti reached out and took her hand. 'Don't worry, my sister. They are just what we call enlarged pores. They are normal. Most people have some enlarged pores. They let grease out. Very greasy people have many of them; people who are not so greasy do not have so many.'

'That's a relief, Mma.'

'Yes,' said Mma Soleti. 'You need not worry. Your skin is actually very good. But we can do something to make those enlarged pores go away. There are some cleansers that we can use to get all the impurities out, and then the skin will take care of itself.'

The beautician rose from her chair and opened the cupboard behind her. Leaning forward to read the labels, after a few minutes she chose a jar with a white and silver label. 'This is very good,' she said. 'If you apply this at night before you go to bed it will do its work while you are asleep. Many of my customers have been made very happy by this cream.'

Mma Ramotswe took the open jar from Mma Soleti and sniffed at it. She liked the smell. 'I suppose there's no harm in trying ... '

'No harm at all,' said Mma Soleti, taking the jar back from her and slipping it into a paper bag. 'You are very wise, Mma. That will last you for maybe one month. Then you can get some more.'

The cream was less expensive than Mma Ramotswe had feared. She paid, and then accepted Mma Soleti's offer of a cup of tea. Her favourable impression of the beautician had grown stronger, and she did not resent the purchase she had been rather press-ganged into making. But now, she decided, she might get her share of benefit from the encounter.

'You have many clients, Mma?' she asked.

Mma Soleti nodded. 'More than ever, Mma. This month was busier than last month, and last month was busier than the month before.'

'You must see everything, Mma. In this job of yours you must see everything.'

Mma Soleti looked at her sideways. 'Are you asking me that as a private detective, Mma? Is that why you are asking?'

She's clever, thought Mma Ramotswe; this woman understands. 'As a detective,' she confessed.

'You're very honest, Mma. I like that.'

Mma Ramotswe waited for her question to be answered.

'So, I see everything? Well, yes, I think I do. I see and hear a lot.' She paused. 'Is there anything in particular you want to know, Mma?'

Mma Ramotswe was not prepared for this. She had not intended to ask any direct questions – at least not at this stage – and she was not sure what to say. But then she thought: Mr Ditso.

'There's a man we're interested in at the moment,' she said. 'He's called Ditso. You will have heard of him, Mma?'

The effect of the question was immediate, and Mma Ramotswe wondered whether she had inadvertently asked about Mma Soleti's cousin. There was a presumption in Botswana, she had discovered, that if you talked to one person about another, then the two persons in question would be cousins, or even brother and sister; she had proved that time and time again. And that meant you had to be very careful.

'Are you related to that man?' she asked Mma Soleti.

The beautician shook her head vigorously. 'I have never met

him. But I know one thing about him, Mma. I know one thing that maybe I shouldn't talk about.'

Mma Ramotswe made a sympathetic noise. 'It's generally better to talk, Mma. It's not good to bottle things up.'

Mma Soleti seemed only too ready for this advice. 'I shall tell you then, Mma. My sister is a beautician too, Mma. Actually, she is my half-sister, and she does sessions at that nail place, you know, near the post office. She is very good. She has a diploma in nail care from Durban. She went down there to get it. It was very expensive going all the way to South Africa, but she said it was worthwhile. Now she does very well.'

'Time spent on getting qualifications is never wasted,' said Mma Ramotswe.

'You have qualifications in detection, no doubt,' said Mma Soleti. 'Are they hard to get? I can imagine they would be.'

Mma Ramotswe sighed. 'I have no qualifications, Mma.'

Mma Soleti stared at her in surprise. 'You mean any old person can go and put a sign up saying that she is a private detective? Is that true, Mma?'

Mma Ramotswe nodded. 'But I have done a lot of studying,' she said. 'There is a very good book, you see. *The Principles of Private Detection.*' She paused; she was not boastful, but there were some temptations that were irresistible, and this, she decided, was one. 'I know the author, you see, Mma.' Immediately she regretted it, and added: 'Not very well, though. I could not really call him a friend.'

She need not have worried. If Mma Soleti were to be impressed, then it was not to be by the mention of a mere author. 'People write books,' she said casually. 'I have had people in here who are thinking of writing a book.'

Mma Ramotswe gently nudged the conversation back in the direction that she wanted it to follow. 'Your sister, Mma ...'

Mma Soleti remembered. 'Of course, yes, my sister: she has that nail place near the post office in town. She is very busy with people's nails, and gets many people coming in to see her. Sometimes it is almost too late to do much for them, as they have neglected their nails.' Her gaze moved to Mma Ramotswe's nails, and was noticed. Mma Ramotswe glanced down too: she did not use nail varnish, although there was a bottle of it somewhere, unless Motholeli had been playing with it, which was very likely. But there was nothing essentially wrong with her nails, she believed; they did what they were supposed to do, which was . . . What were nails meant to do?

'So all sorts of people come in,' continued Mma Soleti. 'And she says that one of the women who come in to have their nails done is the secret sweetheart of that man, that rich man you mentioned. She is secret because he has a wife, and the wife comes in to have her nails done too! My sister has to make sure that their appointments don't overlap. Can you imagine that, Mma? That would not be very good, I think.'

Mma Ramotswe nodded. She wanted to hear more of this story, but she did not want to probe too obviously; in her experience, people could suddenly dry up if you became too insistent in your questioning. 'Oh, well,' she said. 'Men are often doing that, Mma.'

'They are, my sister,' said Mma Soleti. 'But I do not always blame men, you know. They are very weak, and there are some women who are prepared to take advantage of that weakness.' She looked knowingly at Mma Ramotswe, as if to imply that should she wish it, she could provide a long list of such women.

'That is very true,' said Mma Ramotswe. 'I have known some bad women in my work.' She paused, and looked out of the tin building's small window – a patch of sky, cloudless and innocent, blue. There was no glass between her and that sky; the window must be secured by a shutter that had been opened. There had to be a shutter: you could not leave all those potions and creams unguarded, she thought; greasy people, open-pored, walking past, might seize the opportunity to help themselves to skin cleansers ...

'Who is this woman, Mma? Do you know her?'

Mma Soleti shook her head. 'She did not give my sister her name. She just calls herself by some name that my sister thinks she has invented. She actually forgot one time what she had called herself before.'

'I do not think you forget your own name,' said Mma Ramotswe. 'Not normally.'

'No.'

'Even if you are very busy ... '

'No. Not even then.'

Mma Ramotswe asked a final question. 'And you know nothing else about her, Mma?'

Mma Soleti appeared to consider this for a few moments. 'The only thing my sister said is that she is one of those women who are always looking out for men. You know the type? She is not interested in talking to women.'

Mma Ramotswe knew exactly what Mma Soleti meant. There was a certain sort of woman who was always aware of which men were in the vicinity and was always very attentive to them, but who would neither notice women nor bother to speak to them. Women like Violet Sephotho, for instance ...

Chapter Ten

She Was Like a Deflated Balloon

Mma Potokwani was not in her office when Mma Ramotswe arrived at the orphan farm. This was not unusual: the matron was often to be found in one of the outlying buildings, attending to one of the numerous minor, or sometimes major, problems that might be expected to crop up in the day-to-day life of an orphanage. Most of these she resolved herself, dispensing advice, fixing something, or simply wiping away tears; all of which she did with the same brisk confidence that she applied to any task that confronted her. Not for nothing had Mma Potokwani previously been appointed as matron of a small but well-run hospital, and the skills she had learned in the wards there – dealing with unhappy or nervous patients, keeping nurses and others on their toes – she now applied in the rather different circumstances of the orphan farm.

Mma Ramotswe, still thinking of her conversation with her new acquaintance, Mma Soleti, parked her tiny white van under the tree that always shaded it on her visits: a towering jacaranda tree on the lower limbs of which the children had climbed, rubbing the bark bare with their legs. We should all have a tree in our childhood, she thought – a tree one might explore, a tree from which one might learn how to fall. She had fallen out of just such a tree as a girl and winded herself, while the children who were with her stood in a circle about her and laughed; they were boys, of course, and found misfortune funny in a way in which girls did not. She had never forgotten the sensation of being winded: of having all the breath knocked out of you and waiting for your lungs to draw it back in – but it was as if your lungs were stunned and were waiting for instructions from you ...

She made her way to the veranda that lined the building in which Mma Potokwani had her office. The door leading off into the office was open, and she could see that nobody was within. A fan had been left on, though, and was whirring away industriously. That meant that Mma Potokwani would not be far away – a counter of *thebes* every bit as much as *pula*, she would not waste electricity for long. Many of the goods supplied to the orphan farm she begged and borrowed from businessmen in the town, but you could not do that with electricity. There was no human face to the electricity board, no manager whom one could negotiate a lower price with or sweet-talk with a promise of some future favour. The electricity board charged a set amount for electricity, and if you used it you had to pay for it. There was no way round that, as there was with other bills. *You can't be charging the poor orphans that much*, was one of Mma Potokwani's favourite lines, regularly invoked against traders who supplied the orphan farm with its needs, and it was often highly successful. But you could not say that to an electricity board that had no shame, no sense of what it was like to be an orphan.

Mma Ramotswe decided to go in search of the matron rather than stay in her office and wait for her to return. She did not like to sit unattended in another's office – even if invited, explicitly or implicity. There was always the feeling, she thought, that the person whose office it was would think that you had sneaked a look at the papers on their desk, which was what some inquisitive people did, no matter how hard it was to read upside down. And that notion reminded her of Clovis Andersen, who had written – had he not? – in *The Principles of Private Detection*, something about learning to read upside down. It came back to her now, from that section of the book that dealt with the skills that a good detective should try to master. 'Being able to read in a poor light puts one at a great advantage over those who cannot,' he wrote. 'There have been many occasions when I have been able to glean information from a document which would be too poorly lit to be legible to most. And the same ability has seen me safely through a number of tricky, not to say perilous, situations.' And what, she wondered, were those? Now she could ask him, of course, although he would only be able to tell her about them as long as disclosure on his part would not compromise the strict rules of confidentiality that he set out elsewhere in the book.

Then had come the section on reading upside down. 'Now there can be no doubt,' he wrote – and how she loved that phrase, *there can be no doubt*, how assured it was, how definitive – 'Now there can be no doubt but that being able to read upside down is extremely useful and is, in fact, a skill well worth mastering. It enables you to read a document that lies before the person on the other side of the desk from you. They may think that you cannot read it; they may think that they can tell you what is in the document without your being able to verify their version. But they reckon without your ability to read upside down!'

Indeed they do, thought Mma Ramotswe.

'And it also enables you,' Clovis Andersen continued, 'to read papers lying about on a suspect's desk. These are usually facing the wrong way and you cannot necessarily turn them round. Nor will it do to turn your head.'

Mma Ramotswe had imagined the contortions such a manoeuvre would entail and had decided that it was impossible to angle one's head and neck in such a way as to be able to read satisfactorily. It could not be done, she decided, unless one were somehow to upend oneself – to do a handstand, so to speak – which would be difficult and self-defeating, as one's dress would drop down over one's head and eyes and effectively prevent one from seeing anything, let alone reading. And it would be difficult to explain what was happening if the suspect returned to his office and found a visitor with her legs pointing up to the ceiling. Anything you might say in such circumstances would surely sound somewhat weak. 'I was practising my handstands – I hope you don't mind.' Nobody would believe that, not even the normally gullible. They would suspect that something untoward was happening – and they would be right about that.

There were few matters on which she disagreed with Clovis Andersen's advice, but this, perhaps, was one of them. She was not sure that it was ever right to read somebody else's letters or private papers unless you were certain that it was the only way of averting some very serious consequence. Or . . . and there were other exceptions. Errant husbands, for instance, could hardly complain if a wife, or somebody acting for the wife, read the letters they might write to their mistresses. That was because a wife has a right to read her husband's letters, in Mma Ramotswe's view, because he agreed to that in the marriage ceremony; not that those exact words were used, but they were surely implied. Perhaps it might be better to spell it out in the wedding service, where it might be put tactfully, along with the general promise to share. *I promise to share all my worldly goods – including letters, parcels and other items of correspondence, opened or unopened.* Perhaps that sounded a bit too formal, but no doubt there were ways of saying the same thing in a warmer, more romantic way.

No, she would not wait in Mma Potokwani's office but would go in search of her. As she stepped off the veranda into the hot sun, she saw one of the house-mothers standing at the door of one of the small buildings that served as home for eight or so children. These were busy women, who cooked and cleaned all day, and made a home that each child could regard as his or her own. They were not necessarily educated women, but that was not the point; what they had was far more valuable than any formal education, and that thing was love, vast wells of it, enough for ten children, for twenty if needs be.

This house-mother, who knew Mma Ramotswe well – having come from Mochudi – greeted her warmly as she approached.

'I am not just standing here,' she said to Mma Ramotswe after the traditional greetings had been exchanged. 'Don't think that I'm being lazy. I'm thinking about what I have to do next.'

Mma Ramotswe laughed. 'I would never think you lazy, Mma,' she said. 'I know how hard you work.'

The house-mother sighed. 'Our work is never done, Mma, but there we are. That is just one of the things that God has said must be. He said: mothers must work hard. That is a firm rule.'

Mma Ramotswe nodded. 'But he also wants mothers to have a bit of a rest sometimes. That is why he said: men must not be lazy, and must help ladies.'

The house-mother grinned. 'Were men listening when the Lord said that?'

'I think that some were,' said Mma Ramotswe. 'But others did not hear too well.'

That led to further mirth. Then Mma Ramotswe asked if the house-mother had seen Mma Potokwani. 'She has gone over to her house, Mma,' came the reply. And then, after a short pause, 'She is not happy, I think.'

Mma Ramotswe frowned. That was very unlike Mma Potokwani, who had a reputation for a certain breeziness and optimism. 'Not happy? Are you sure, Mma?'

The woman nodded. 'I spoke to her about my fridge and told her that it was not working very well. I told her that some of the meat I had for the children had turned bad, and that this was a waste. You should not waste good meat, Mma.'

'And?' pressed Mma Ramotswe.

'And she said something that was really nothing. You know how it is when a person says something but it is really nothing very much at all?'

'I do, Mma. But, tell me, why should Mma Potokwani be unhappy?'

The house-mother said that she did not know. She agreed that it was unusual; perhaps she was not feeling well – there had been a few cases of flu recently, and when you had flu you did not feel inclined to be cheerful.

'No,' said Mma Ramotswe. 'It is hard to smile when your head is splitting.'

The house-mother nodded. 'She was like a balloon with all the air taken out of it,' she said. 'You know how that looks, Mma?'

Mma Ramotswe did. She exchanged a few more comments with the house-mother, and then took her leave. Mma Poto-kwani's house was at the far end of the orphan-farm grounds, beyond the vegetable patches that the children worked, beyond the scrap of ground that the smaller boys used as their soccer pitch: a square of dusty, baked earth devoid of so much as a blade of grass, but the scene of many a tiny sporting triumph, a ball sent shooting past the goalkeeper, a clever pass – things that were in their transience quickly forgotten but for a short time meant so much in a young life that had not known much triumph or even, until now, much love.

She stood at the door of the Potokwani house and called out *Ko, ko!* Inside, somewhere within the cool interior of the house, the voice of Radio Botswana broke the silence: a discussion about a new power station and the problems of building it. Was that the sort of thing that Mma Potokwani listened to, or was she dozing somewhere, catching up on lost sleep, having left the radio on? Discussion of power stations could easily send people off to sleep, although some people – mostly men, she imagined – might be woken up by such things.

She repeated the traditional request for admission. '*Ko, ko,* Mma! *Ko, ko!*'

There was no reply. 'We must be careful that we have enough power in future,' intoned a voice on the radio. 'We cannot always buy our power from our neighbours, who have a shortage them- selves. What is it they said? Enough's enough: no more power for you, Botswana, or you, Swaziland. You go and buy candles.'

Mma Ramotswe was not interested in that. She was thinking of what the house-mother had said: *she was like a balloon with the air taken out of it.* She felt a tinge of alarm. Sometimes people had a stroke without realising what had happened, and then they became confused and could fail to reply when somebody came to their door and called *Ko, ko!* Could Mma Potokwani be lying unconscious, in the kitchen perhaps, or on the cold floor of the bathroom? Her husband was often away for days, she had said: he had cattle somewhere. If that were so, then it might be a long time before anybody thought to look for her, and by then it could be too late. A floor was no place to lie for very long, even in warm weather.

She pushed the door fully open and entered the house, calling out Mma Potokwani's name as she did so. Her voice seemed so loud; even louder that the voice of the engineer who was expressing a view on coal-fired power stations on Radio Botswana. 'These stations are much better than they used to be,' he said. 'Like so many things.'

Like so many things, thought Mma Ramotswe. Like medicines, like supplies of vegetables in the supermarkets, like electric fans, like the road to Lobatse, like ... She entered the sitting room, and there, on the couch before her, was Mma Potokwani, sitting as motionless as a figure in a painting or a photograph – clearly not dead, but not herself. *Like a balloon that has had the air taken out of it.* Yes, just like that.

Mma Potokwani's eyes registered the arrival of Mma Ramotswe and she moved slightly, as if beginning to get up to welcome her but then thinking better of it.

'Mma, are you all right? You didn't answer. I called out and ...'

Mma Potokwani raised a hand to point to a chair. 'You should sit down, Mma. Yes, I am all right, but not all right really. I'll tell you. You sit down.'

Mma Ramotswe did as she was bade. 'But you do not look very well, Mma. Are you sure you're not ill?'

Mma Potokwani shook her head. 'I'm not ill,' she said. 'No, that is not the problem.'

Mma Ramotswe waited for her to continue, and she did.

'I am shocked, Mma; that is all. I shall be better soon, I think, but now I am shocked.'

'You've had bad news?'

'Yes,' said Mma Potokwani. 'I have had bad news. Not bad news that somebody has become late – not that sort of bad news. No, the bad news is that I have been dismissed. As from the end of this month. Dismissed.'

It took Mma Ramotswe some time to absorb this. You did not dismiss Mma Potokwani. You did not tell her that she was no longer going to be the matron of the orphan farm. You did not do it because it was simply inconceivable. You did not dismiss the sun from the sky. You did not tell the Limpopo River to flow the other way. You did not say to the great Kalahari that it was not wanted; that its winds, its dry, desert winds should blow somewhere else, in another quarter, beneath another sky. You did not do that because it was against the order of things. And it was quite against the order of things that Mma Silvia Potokwani, matron, matriarch, scourge of businessmen slow to open their wallets for charity, defender of children, citizen of Botswana, should be dismissed from her position like some young and incompetent girl. You did not do that. Nobody did that. It was impossible.

'Has this thing really happened?' Mma Ramotswe stuttered.

Mma Potokwani nodded. No words were needed; just a nod was sufficient to signify the end of an era, the end of a world.

Chapter Eleven

An Innocent Man, a First Offender

It would have been bad enough if that was all that had happened that day; but there was something else. Later, when Mma Ramotswe and Mma Makutsi would survey their list of days – happily few in number – when things appeared to go seriously wrong, then this day would seem egregious.

It was while Mma Ramotswe was on her visit to the orphan farm that Mma Makutsi heard raised voices outside the office. This was not altogether unusual: the apprentices sometimes engaged in rowdy banter with one another – so much so that she had occasionally gone into the garage or the yard to ask them to bear in mind that there were at least some people in the vicinity who needed to concentrate on their work, and that was very difficult, was it not, if there were other people who insisted on shouting at the top of their voices about some matter of no interest to anybody else, namely, which girls were particularly friendly towards boys and which were not, or the prospects of the Zebras in the forthcoming football finals, or semi-finals, or whatever they were.

This time, though, it was a bit different. She recognised the voices of the apprentices but there was another voice too, a deeper, more mature voice, and a woman's voice behind that. And was that Mr J. L. B. Matekoni joining the fray, saying something about somebody making a big mistake? He at least talked calmly, unlike the others, who seemed to be becoming increasingly shrill in expressing their view about whatever it was that lay behind the argument; for it was now clear that it was an argument, and not just a disagreement about some unimportant matter of girls or soccer.

Mma Makutsi put down the document she was reading and went into the small courtyard that separated the offices of the No. 1 Ladies' Detective Agency from the premises of Tlokweng Road Speedy Motors. She stood in the doorway, quite still, in shock as she realised that the two strangers involved in the row, a man and a woman, were both police officers. As she appeared, everybody turned to look at her, and it was then that she saw the handcuffs that had been placed on Fanwell's wrists.

Mma Makutsi gasped. 'What is this? What's happening?'

Charlie pointed at the police officers. 'They have arrested Fanwell,' he said, his voice breaking with emotion. 'This is a very bad mistake.'

The male police officer, the older of the two, gave him a glance. 'We have a warrant,' he said patiently. 'It's perfectly in order. All signed. Official. We're arresting him for handling stolen goods.'

Mma Makutsi shrieked, 'No, no. You cannot do that. That is Fanwell. He is a very honest young man. He is not a thief, Rra!' She looked pleadingly at the policewoman. 'Mma, you cannot let this big mistake happen. You cannot take this young man.' She moved forward to plead with the police officers. 'Listen, Rra. Listen, Mma. I am a detective and I can tell you: this young man would never do anything like that. Guaranteed. Guaranteed. I am a detective. I'm telling you, this is not right.'

The policeman looked at her doubtfully. 'You're a detective, Mma? CID? Which office – Gaborone? Where is your card?'

'I'm not that sort of detective,' said Mma Makutsi. 'I'm a private detective. The No. 1 Ladies' Detective Agency.'

The policewoman smiled. 'Sorry, my sister, but you should keep quiet. This is proper police business. This is not play detectives.'

Mma Makutsi looked at Fanwell. 'What is all this, Fanwell? Do you know what these people are saying?'

Mr J. L. B. Matekoni answered the question. 'They say that he was repairing a stolen car for resale. Some friend of his had it. That is what they're saying.'

'I didn't know it was stolen, Mma,' said Fanwell, his voice shaking with fear. 'I just did it as a favour for Chobie. He's a friend of mine. I did not know it was stolen.'

'That friend,' muttered Charlie, and spat, 'I'm going to get him.'

The policeman threw Charlie a warning glance. 'Look, we can't stand here for ever,' he said. 'If this young man has a story, then he can make a statement at the charge office. Then he can go in front of the magistrate, who will look at that statement and decide whether it is true or whether it is all lies. I'm sorry to say this, but sometimes people tell lies, and this young man may well be doing that.'

'You cannot say that, Rra,' protested Mr J. L. B Matekoni. 'Surely he is still innocent until the magistrate has decided that he is guilty. This is Botswana, you know.'

The policeman turned to face Mr J. L. B. Matekoni. Out of deference to the mechanic's dignity and bearing, he did not speak roughly, but there was nonetheless an edge to his voice. 'Yes,' he said, 'you're right, Rra. This is Botswana. And in Botswana we do not take kindly to young men who take other people's cars and then sell them to unsuspecting members of the public. We do not like that either.'

'What are you going to do with him?' asked Mma Makutsi.

'He will stay in the cells,' said the policewoman. 'He'll be all right there. He'll get a blanket at night. You needn't worry about him, Mma. I'll see that he's all right.'

The policeman now took Fanwell by the arm and began to lead him away.

The young man stumbled, but was kept on his feet by the policeman. 'I haven't done anything wrong.'

'Did you hear that?' exploded Charlie. 'Did you hear what he said?'

'Calm down,' said the policeman. 'It doesn't help if people shout.'

'Just keep quiet, Charlie.' Mr J. L. B. Matekoni put a restraining hand on the young man. 'We'll speak to a lawyer.'

Charlie shook his head. 'These people . . . '

The policeman gave him another warning glance, and Charlie stopped.

They watched in silence as Fanwell was led to the police car parked outside. The rear door was opened and he was bundled inside; the door slammed and the car moved away. They saw his face briefly as he looked back towards them; then the car pulled out into the traffic on the Tlokweng Road and was gone. In the anxious conference that followed, Charlie said very little, but sat morosely shaking his head, muttering about what he was planning to do to Chobie.

'Do you know this Chobie?' asked Mma Makutsi.

Charlie nodded. 'I will find him.'

'But maybe the police have found him already,' said Mma Makutsi.

'Then he can tell them that Fanwell did not know,' said Mr J. L. B. Matekoni.

Charlie and Mma Makutsi exchanged glances. Mr J. L. B. Matekoni was decent by nature and the problem with people who were trusting, she had always thought, was that they assumed others were like them, and they were not. They could hope that this Chobie might explain that he alone was answerable for handling stolen property, but they could not rely on it. Nor could they rely on his being believed even if he were to say it. If two young men were standing in the dock together, why should a magistrate believe one of them if he said the other was innocent?

'This is very serious,' said Mma Makutsi.

'He's innocent,' said Charlie.

'Of course he's innocent,' snapped Mma Makutsi. 'We know that Fanwell would never do anything wrong. But we're not the ones who will be sitting there in court, are we?'

Charlie stared at her. 'If they convict him, what then?'

'They send you to prison for handling stolen property,' said Mr J. L. B. Matekoni. 'That man at the bottle store – remember him? He went to prison for two years for selling stolen beer.'

'Two years!' Charlie exclaimed.

'He's a first offender,' said Mma Makutsi.

This remark, innocently intended though it was, drew Charlie's ire. Pointing a finger at Mma Makutsi, he almost shouted. 'You think he's guilty, don't you?'

Mma Makutsi shook her head. 'I do not think that.'

'Then why do you call him an offender? Isn't an offender somebody who's guilty?'

Mma Makutsi tried to explain what she had meant; Charlie listened resentfully.

'We mustn't argue,' said Mr J. L. B. Matekoni. 'Arguing won't help Fanwell.'

'Nothing will help Fanwell,' said Mma Makutsi.

Mma Ramotswe returned to the office an hour or so after the police and a fearful, almost tearful Fanwell had left. Her heart was heavy with the upsetting encounter she had just had with Mma Potokwani, and so when she came in and saw Mma Makutsi sitting disconsolately at her desk, she assumed that her assistant was merely sharing her own distress over the injustice done to her friend. But then she realised that Mma Makutsi did not know what had happened, and whatever the explanation for her assistant's state of mind, it was not that.

'Is there something wrong, Mma?'

Mma Makutsi reached into the pocket of her blouse and took out a handkerchief. 'Oh, Mma Ramotswe, it is very bad, very bad.'

Mma Ramotswe froze. Her mind went quickly to those she loved: which one of them had had some terrible accident, was even at this moment under the surgeon's knife at the Princess Marina Hospital? Had something happened in the garage? Mr J. L. B. Matekoni had said that one of the pneumatic jacks was playing up – had it failed altogether and a car come down on him, pinning him to the ground? Puso? Motholeli? They should be safely at home from school by now, but there were always perils, even in that short walk between the house and school – only a few days ago a car driven by a young and inexperienced motorist had mounted the pavement and knocked over a fruit-seller . . .

'Fanwell . . .' Mma Makutsi began.

Mma Ramotswe gasped. 'Oh no, Mma, oh no . . .' Fanwell was dead. He had been under the car when the jack had failed.

Mma Makutsi quickly understood the conclusion that Mma Ramotswe had jumped to, and she corrected the mistake. 'No, Mma, he is not late – nothing like that. He has been . . .' She struggled with the word; it was just so unlikely, so impossible. 'He has been arrested.'

Mma Ramotswe's relief on hearing that the worst had not happened was tempered by shock. 'Arrested? Surely not, Mma? Not Fanwell . . .' She tailed off; the unspoken thought was that if Charlie had been arrested it would not be so surprising.

'Yes,' said Mma Makutsi. 'If they had arrested Charlie, then maybe it would not have been so surprising. But Fanwell? No, Mma, it is a very shocking thing.'

Mma Ramotswe nodded. 'I know, Mma, I have often thought that Charlie was asking for trouble.' She paused. 'Do you think that they made a mistake? Do you think they thought that Fanwell was Charlie?'

'It is all a big mistake,' replied Mma Makutsi. 'But it is not that mistake. No, they knew that Fanwell was Fanwell, and he was the one they were after.'

Mma Ramotswe crossed the room to her desk and sat down. 'There is other bad news too,' she said quietly. 'Mma Potokwani has been dismissed from her post. At the end of the month she will no longer be the matron.'

Mma Makutsi shrieked. 'No, Mma. That cannot be. It cannot.'

Mma Ramotswe explained what had happened. She had found Mma Potokwani in her house, she said, and had been given the news directly. Mma Potokwani told her that she had had the news given to her by the secretary to the board of directors of the orphan farm. The directors had decided, she was told, that her attitude to the proposed new buildings had been unhelpful and

123

obstructive. In the circumstances, since she had shown herself unwilling to comply with the properly determined policy of the board, it was thought that she should be replaced with somebody who could embrace the new approach to cost-effectiveness that the board had endorsed. And with that, her regime was brought to an abrupt end.

Mma Ramotswe was slightly surprised by the intensity of Mma Makutsi's reaction to this story. Although her assistant had previously not enjoyed the best of friendships with Mma Potokwani, relations between the two of them had been rather better recently. And now, hearing of Mma Potokwani's misfortune, any past disagreements seemed immediately forgotten. 'That is terrible, Mma,' wailed Mma Makutsi. 'Oh, it is so unfair, so unfair. And on the same day as Fanwell's arrest – and he is innocent, Mma, as we both know. Mma Potokwani, too. They are both the victims of some very bad things. Oh, Mma . . .'

And with that, Mma Makutsi began to sob. Mma Ramotswe immediately rose from her desk and went to put an arm around the other woman. 'It is very bad,' she said consolingly. 'It is a very bad day for everybody.'

Mma Makutsi's sobbing became louder. 'Poor Fanwell,' she spluttered. 'He is looking after that whole family, and there will be no money now. And Mma Potokwani. What will she eat? It is all so wrong, Mma.'

Mma Ramotswe felt the tears begin to roll down her own cheeks. She closed her eyes and saw Mma Potokwani sitting on her sofa, staring so blankly and hopelessly ahead. She had given her working life to those children; she had spent every waking hour, it seemed, battling to give the children a decent start. She was tireless in her efforts on their behalf. And there was her fruit cake, too, that she used as a means of ensnaring others to help the orphans; that fruit cake, that tea, those hours spent together talking about anything and everything. And the wisdom that the matron had, the understanding, the deep wells of kindness under that imposing exterior; all that, it seemed, meant nothing to the juggernaut of reform and efficiency and cost-cutting.

She wiped away the tears with the back of her wrist: salt against skin, our human tears. 'Mma Makutsi,' she managed to say.

Mma Makutsi looked up. Her voice, when she spoke, was half choked with sorrow. 'Yes, Mma?'

'I am going to make some tea. We shall drink a cup of tea.'

Mma Makutsi nodded, and sniffed. 'It is always the best thing to do, Mma.'

It was, of course. The sound of the kettle boiling was in itself the sound of normality, of reason, the sound of a fight back against the sadness of things. And the making of tea – ordinary black tea for Mma Makutsi and redbush for Mma Ramotswe – was the first step in restoring a sense of order and control into their disturbed universe. Then, sitting close together for company, nursing their mugs of tea, they began to discuss what they should do.

'Clovis Andersen,' said Mma Ramotswe.

Mma Makutsi nodded. 'We must speak to him. He will know what to do.'

It gave them both a reassuring feeling that Clovis Andersen was there to help them. If anybody would know what to do, then surely it would be the great Clovis Andersen. 'He's bound to have some ideas,' said Mma Makutsi. 'If you have written a book like that, then you will always have ideas on how to get out of a crisis.'

'That is true,' said Mma Ramotswe. 'One of his rules must surely apply here, or if it doesn't, then ...'

'Then he can make up a new one,' supplied Mma Makutsi.

'Exactly, Mma. He can make a new one. Rule 9b, or something like that.'

'That will be a very good rule,' said Mma Makutsi. 'I think you should go and see him, Mma.'

That settled, they sat in silence for a few minutes. Now the tea began to do its work – as it always did – and the world that only a few minutes previously had seemed so bleak started to seem somewhat less so. There was bound to be some solution to both of the problems they faced. As far as Fanwell was concerned, there could be character references to lay before the court; Mma Ramotswe was already beginning to draft one in her head: *This young man came from a background of poverty. He spends all his wages, every pula, on the needs of his grandmother and his brothers and sisters. He is completely honest and upright* ... Surely they would pay some heed to her if she wrote on their headed paper. And Mr J. L. B. Matekoni could write as his employer; they would have to listen to him, because everybody loved and admired him and even the magistrate might be aware of that. If he were not, though, was there anything to stop them getting a character reference from the writer of character references ...? And as for Mma Potokwani, they would just fight back. There was no doubt in Mma Ramotswe's mind who was responsible for the dismissal of Mma Potokwani: Mr Ditso. Those rich men did not like anybody to contradict them; to stand in the way of their pet schemes. Well, if that was the way he chose to conduct himself, then the gloves could come off. Not that she ever saw herself wearing boxing gloves, of course, but if she did, then now was the time to divest herself of them. Mr Ditso, she thought, you are engaging with a heavyweight; and that, she said to herself, is true. Do not take on a traditionally built person unless you are prepared for a heavyweight bout. *Do not enter the ring with an opponent above your weight.* That was a good proposition, she decided – almost worthy of Clovis Andersen himself. She would suggest it to him, in case he should ever think of a new edition. For a brief, tantalising moment the title page flashed before her eyes: *The Principles of Private Detection: a new and revised edition by Clovis Andersen, with additions by Mma Precious Ramotswe (Botswana) and* ... yes, she should be generous in such a matter ... *and Mma Grace Makutsi (Dip. Sec., Botswana Sec. Coll., 97%).*

Chapter Twelve

The Effect of Lime

The next three days were days of anxiety – and inactivity. Fanwell had been released from custody shortly after having been charged, but was told that it might be some time before his case was called in court. Until then, there was not much he could do, although Mr J. L. B. Matekoni had obtained the services of a lawyer, a rather distracted man who had described the case as 'an open and shut one'.

'That is very good news,' said Mr J. L. B. Matekoni.

The lawyer looked surprised. 'Good news?'

'Yes. You said it was open and shut . . .'

The lawyer laughed. 'Yes, open and shut from the prosecution's point of view.'

Mr J. L. B. Matekoni looked incredulous. 'But he's not guilty. They cannot convict him if he did not do it.'

The lawyer tapped the side of his nose; it was a curious gesture that Mr J. L. B. Matekoni could not quite interpret. 'Oh, Mr Mechanic, I'm afraid that they all do it. All these people who appear in court say, "I did not do it." But usually they did.' He tapped his nose again. 'I haven't had anybody come to me and say, "I did it, Rra." Not one. So I ask myself: if none of these people did it, then who did? Can you tell me? No, I didn't think you would be able to.' He sighed. 'But I'll do my best for this young man. I'll try to get them to give him a suspended sentence, although that depends on which magistrate gets the case. Some of those fellows have got very bad tempers. You never know.'

Mr J. L. B. Matekoni did not tell Fanwell of this exchange. All he did was to tell him that he had secured the services of a lawyer, and that the lawyer had assured him that he would do his best. Charlie, who was with Fanwell at the time, clapped his hands together and did one of those impromptu dances that he performed to mark pieces of good news. 'Ace!' he exclaimed. 'You hear that, Fanwell? A big-shot lawyer. Very smart.'

'Good,' said Fanwell. 'I am very lucky then.'

Mr J. L. B. Matekoni looked away. He wondered whether he should try to get another lawyer, but he had already paid a substantial amount as a retainer, and he would probably lose that if he tried to change. Perhaps it was best to have a lawyer who was realistic – after all, one would not want one who showed unfounded optimism in the face of bleak prospects.

Mma Ramotswe did her best to comfort Fanwell, telling him of the character reference she was preparing and assuring him that justice was bound to be done. For the most part, though, she left the Fanwell affair to Mr J. L. B. Matekoni; the apprentice had always been his responsibility, and it seemed that he was doing all that was required to see Fanwell through this. Her mind was more taken up with the issue of Mma Potokwani's dismissal. She made a point of going out to the orphan farm each day to speak to her friend and to encourage her to challenge the dismissal.

'I've already done that,' said Mma Potokwani. 'I have written to the board, but they say that they cannot consider my letter until the next meeting, which will be in two weeks' time. Until then, there is nothing I can do.'

Mma Ramotswe bit her lip. 'I have been making enquiries about that man,' she said. 'I have been speaking to a friend who writes articles on business matters for the *Botswana News*. I have asked him whether he has any information.'

Mma Potokwani shrugged. 'Nobody knows anything. Your friend will say the same thing.'

This was true. The journalist had promised to see if there was any helpful information on the newspaper's files but had come back with nothing to report. 'He seems to be absolutely above board,' he said. 'The money comes from straightforward businesses. A number of dry-cleaning places, a fleet of buses – that sort of thing.'

Mma Ramotswe thanked him for his efforts. She tried to keep up an appearance of cheerfulness, but she now felt quite despondent about the chance of being able to help Mma Potokwani in any way. Had she been able to provide her with ammunition, then she was sure that the redoubtable matron would have been able to stand up to Mr Ditso and his friends on the board. But without that, then Mma Potokwani, it seemed, was powerless and all that she, like any of them, could do was to wait. So all three of them – Mma Ramotswe, Mr J. L. B. Matekoni and Mma Makutsi – found themselves bound up in a shared circle of anxiety, each unable to do anything much to reassure the others or to throw anything but a bleak light on the misfortunes of Fanwell and Mma Potokwani. 'It seems as if everything has gone wrong,' said Mma Ramotswe. 'I know that we should not despair, but everything seems suddenly to have gone wrong.'

'The whole world is tumbling down,' said Mma Makutsi. 'It is surely the end.'

That, it seemed to Mma Ramotswe, was possibly overstating it, but she knew how Mma Makutsi felt. In fact, they both felt powerless, and were unable even to seek Clovis Andersen's advice, as he had take the opportunity to accompany his friend to visit a library being built at Ghanzi, on the other side of the country, and had left word that he could not be contacted for four or five days.

'I'm sure he will have something to suggest when he comes back,' said Mma Ramotswe.

'Maybe,' said Mma Makutsi, but then added gloomily: 'But maybe not.'

Phuti Radiphuti had been kept informed, and had shaken his head sadly at the news. He had met Fanwell, and he thought it highly unlikely that he had done anything dishonest, but he knew that sometimes the police could, quite reasonably, believe they had a case against an innocent man. It had happened before to one of his employees, and the poor man had spent nine months in prison for an offence that Phuti Radiphuti was convinced he had not committed. There had been evidence, though, and the conviction had been sustained on appeal, which showed, Phuti decided, that even in a well-run system of criminal justice mistakes could be made.

He was busy, though, and, although sympathetic, he had no time to brood on these matters. He had received a large order to furnish a new hotel to be built on the edge of the town, and there was a great deal of paperwork to be completed in that transaction. There was also the matter of his new house, for which the foundations had now been prepared. Concrete had been poured, and the lower parts of the walls were beginning to appear, allowing the layout of the rooms to be envisaged. Like the bones of a developing skeleton, of a creature still in formation, the structure of the house was taking shape. Soon the walls would reach the height where the window spaces could be seen, and not long after that, the first beams of the roof would begin to reach out to one another. After that, it would simply be a matter of finishing, as the tilers and the plasterers, the electricians and the plumbers set about their respective tasks. Mr Putumelo had promised to finish the whole job in two months, and it looked to Phuti as if he would easily meet that target.

Mr Putumelo had gone out of his way to discourage visits to the site during construction. 'It is best if the client doesn't go tramping about the place,' he said. 'Building sites are dangerous places, Rra. We had somebody, one of our clients, who put his hand into a cement mixer once – while it was turning.' He shook his head sadly; whether over the consequences, or whether over the whole issue of human foolishness, it was not apparent.

Phuti said nothing. He resented the implication that he was the sort of man to put his hand into a cement mixer, but his customary mildness of manner prevented his engaging in dispute with the rather arrogant builder. He thought, though, that if he wanted to visit his house, he would do so, irrespective of what Mr Putumelo had to say about it. It was his land, after all, and he was surely entitled to walk over it if he wished, taking care, of course, not to insert his hand into any cement mixer.

He decided that it would be best to go shortly after five one evening. Work would have stopped at that time of day, and he would be able to inspect the works without incurring the displeasure of Mr Putumelo. So one afternoon, a few days after Fanwell's arrest, he drove down to the road-end opposite his plot, parked his car and walked up the rough track that the builders' vehicles had made to the house.

It was that time of evening when the sun, although still in the sky, had given clear notice of its intentions. Shadows, lengthening, merged with one another; birds exchanged their late-afternoon messages, reporting food here, shelter there, or drawing noisy attention to the presence of some predator, a snake perhaps, lurking in a treetop. The soft light seemed to paint everything with warm gold, and for a moment he imagined the scene that was likely to play out in a few months' time; of him coming up the drive and seeing Mma Makutsi waiting for him on the veranda, a fine stew bubbling away in the kitchen and then, maybe a bit later – but not too late, he hoped – children running out to meet him and him holding them up to the sky, as children love to be lifted, to their squeals of delight.

As he approached the house, he felt a sudden rush of excitement. It really was happening; this really was his house – *their* house; the low brick walls were *his*, the expanses of cement, laid where the floor would be, were made up of *his* cement, bought with *his* money. He could not help smiling, and he even said, 'Well, well, well,' although there was nobody to hear him.

Or so he thought. It was as he was stepping over one of the low walls in order to stand in what would in future be a bathroom that he heard the voice.

'Yes, Rra. Can I help you?'

Phuti Radiphuti spun round. A short man in a set of blue overalls, a battered grey hat atop his head, had appeared as if from nowhere.

'I am Radiphuti,' Phuti said. 'This is my house.'

The man wiped his hands on a piece of grimy towelling. 'I have heard of you,' he said, switching to English; they had started in Setswana, but the man spoke hesitantly and with an accent. 'Mr

Putumelo has told us about you.' He folded the piece of towel and put it into his blue overalls. 'Have you come to look at the house?'

It seemed to Phuti to be a rather superfluous question. Of course he had come to look at the house. Why else would he be climbing over these little walls and standing in the middle of the future bathroom? But he checked himself and simply nodded.

'We are making good progress,' said the man. 'I am one of the carpenters, but I also do bricklaying and other things. My name is Thomas.'

Phuti reached out to shake the man's hand, which was rough to the touch, like sandpaper. That was the effect of lime; he had heard about how it pitted the skin. Lime and bricks.

'You are not from here,' said Phuti.

The man pointed. 'Up there.'

'The other side?'

'Yes.'

There was hardship on the other side of the border; people crossed over to earn a living, to survive. It was not easy for them; those who stayed, or were sent back, had little to look forward to.

The man rubbed his eyes. They were bloodshot. 'I have been here for three years now. I have managed to be in work all that time. I have worked every day.'

Phuti frowned. 'Every day for three years? Even Sundays?'

The man nodded. 'Especially Sundays. I have not had one day off. Three years.'

Phuti was silent. It was not all that surprising, he supposed. Every *thebe* this man earned would be doing some important work up there: perhaps even paying for the drugs that kept some relative alive through the illness that stalked Africa, that could be kept at bay but only if you had the money, or somebody had the money, to pay.

'This will be a very good house,' said the man. 'Lots of room. It is good to see a house with as much room as this.'

Phuti acknowledged the compliment. 'I designed it myself. There was a draughtsman who drew the plans, but I designed it.'

'You have designed it very well,' said Thomas. 'Everything will be in the right place. Perfect.'

They walked into what would be the living room. The walls there were slightly higher – two or three feet by now – and the bricklayer showed Phuti how they were constructed.

'I have asked for very good-quality bricks,' said Phuti, examining the outer layer. 'These are the ones. They come from South Africa, I think. Mr Putumelo ordered them specially.'

'They are very expensive,' said Thomas. 'Good bricks always are.'

'And I'm very pleased,' said Phuti, 'that they are being laid by a good tradesman like you, Rra. I'm very pleased.'

Thomas looked at him. There was something in his expression that disturbed Phuti, but he was unsure as to what it was. Distrust? But why should this man distrust him, or even feel uneasy? Was he working illegally? That was perfectly possible, but then if it were the case that he did not have a work permit it would have been unlikely that he would have spoken so openly. Those who worked illegally kept to the shadows, claimed to be from the north of the country, protested that they had a Motswana parent; did anything but talk too openly about their necessarily clandestine lives.

Thomas held Phuti's gaze for a few moments, and then looked away.

'Is there something wrong?' asked Phuti.

Thomas again fixed him with an intense stare. It was difficult for Phuti to look directly into his bloodshot eyes – disconcerted, he wanted to pass him something with which to wipe them.

'I cannot always say what I'm thinking,' muttered Thomas.

Phuti thought about this. 'No, it is not always easy.' He paused. A go-away bird – a grey lourie – had perched on one of the acacia trees and uttered its accusing cry; the world, for some birds, was always unfair. As it was for some people, too. 'But I think you can talk to me, Rra. You can talk to me if you are troubled in some way. I may not be able to help you, but it might help you just to say what you need to say.'

Thomas shook his head. 'There are some things I cannot speak of. I have a family, you see, Rra, and I am sending money ... '

Phuti nodded. 'I know what you people do. It is a good thing.' There was a world of difference between this man's circumstances and his own. Phuti was a citizen, and a secure one at that, of a well-ordered country; this man, he imagined, had known real fear and could not return to a place that was his, his own, the place to which he was entitled. Nobody spoke for him; nobody.

'So I cannot say anything that would put my job at risk. Do you see that?'

Phuti stiffened. There was only one way in which this could be interpreted: this man, this bricklayer from over the border, knew something about Mr Putumelo that Mr Putumelo did not want anybody to know. And that could be anything, ranging from not declaring income for tax purposes, to using stolen materials, or building unsafe structures ... He looked about the site. Was everything being built correctly, or was Mr Putumelo cutting corners in exactly the way he condemned in others?

He decided to ask directly. 'Please tell me, Rra; please tell me man to man, as one brother to another; tell me – is this house being built properly?'

Thomas seemed to be taken aback by the question. 'But of course it is, Rra. Mr Putumelo is a very good builder, and I can promise you that I am taking great care with the work I am doing. I would never build anything that was not solid.'

136

Phuti breathed a sigh of relief. So the disclosure, whatever it was, had nothing to do with his house. If Thomas did not want to make it, then he would not press him; he would not be at all surprised to learn that Mr Putumelo was up to something, but what that might be was not really his business. Phuti himself was honest – scrupulously so – but one honest man could not make the rest of the world honest, no matter how hard he tried: where would he start?

Phuti bent down to examine one of the walls. They were in a part of the building where Thomas must have been working that day; the mortar around the bricks was wet to the touch, cool against the skin, soft too. *Our house*, thought Phuti. *Our house.*

And then he thought of something that Mr Putumelo had said. *Your house has got my name on it.* That was strange, but there were many aspects of the building trade that Phuti found odd, just as he had no doubt others found aspects of the furniture business hard to fathom. He completed his examination of the incipient wall. 'This is very well made,' he said. 'This is very good work.' It was: the wall hugged the plumb line, set by a practised and conscientious eye.

He turned round. Thomas, who had been standing immediately behind him only a few moments before, had gone.

Chapter Thirteen

There Are Some Nice People
on the Road

Clovis Andersen returned from the far side of the country, exhausted by the journey, to receive the message that Mma Ramotswe had left for him. In this she gave him no news of the awful events that had occurred, but simply proposed that they meet for tea at the President Hotel, suggesting that if he telephoned her they could agree on a time. He did, and they met on the day after his return. It was a hot morning, but even though the air was heavy, it held a hint of what might come; somewhere, still far away, but building up, there were rain clouds. And the rain would bring relief from the heat and the dryness, and the earth would drink it up thirstily and suddenly be touched with the green of new growth.

'So hot,' said Clovis Andersen, as he sat down opposite Mma Ramotswe on the hotel veranda. 'So awfully hot.'

'Then we shall have tea,' said Mma Ramotswe. 'That will make you feel better.'

The tea did not take long to arrive, and as Mma Ramotswe poured it from the stout white pot she began to reveal to Clovis Andersen the troubles they were facing.

'I know these are not your problems, Rra,' she began, 'but we ... that is, Mma Makutsi and I, feel that you will have some idea of what to do.'

Clovis Andersen stopped her. 'Hold on, Mma Ramotswe. I may have written that book, but really I wouldn't hold myself out as ... as an expert.'

Mma Ramotswe could not believe that he was serious. 'But, Rra, your book is famous. You have a rule for just about every-thing. Rule No. 6, for example ...' She began to quote Rule No. 6; Clovis Andersen, barely concealing his surprise that there should be anybody who remembered that there was a Rule No. 6, let alone anybody who was capable of quoting it verbatim, listened in silence. Then: 'Yes, Mma, that is indeed Rule No. 6, but all I'm saying is that I'm not necessarily able to sort everything out.' He stared at her, as if willing her to read something into his protestations.

Mma Ramotswe was not deterred. 'Let me tell you, Rra,' she said. 'Let me tell you about a very dreadful thing that has hap-pened. We have a lady here who is the matron of an orphan farm. She is called Mma Potokwani, and she has many fine qualities. She is traditionally built, and she makes very famous fruit cake. She will do anything for those orphans – anything – and for many of them she is their mother. Mma Potokwani has more children than any other woman in Botswana – she is mother to many hundreds of children who are now grown-up. That is what she is like, Rra.'

Clovis Andersen listened politely. 'It sounds as if she must be much appreciated, Mma.'

Mma Ramotswe replied that this was true, but it seemed to her that this appreciation did not extend to some members of her board. She told him of the dismissal, and of Mr Ditso Ditso's suspected role in it. 'It must have been him, Rra,' she said. 'Nobody else would think of such a thing. People like that think they should control *everything* – just because they are a success in business.'

'Indeed,' said Clovis Andersen, looking vaguely out over the square. He had no idea who Mma Potokwani was, but it seemed to him that to dismiss a woman like that – if she was like that – was not only foolish, but perverse too. When Mma Ramotswe finished, he tapped the table thoughtfully. 'This sounds very nasty,' he said. 'I don't like that sort of thing. It's a form of bullying, isn't it? Hounding somebody out of her job because she sees things differently.' He shook his head. 'Not nice.'

Mma Ramotswe waited for him to say more, but he seemed to be thinking about something else altogether. For a few moments she felt uncertain: should she really be asking the great Clovis Andersen for advice on something as small, as local – at least in his eyes – as the dismissal of Mma Potokwani? But then he turned to her and said, 'Mma Ramotswe, I think you're going to ask me what to do. Is that right?'

She answered him with relief. 'Oh yes, Rra. That is quite right. You see, I cannot seem to think of anything that we can do to help Mma Potokwani, and I thought that since you had written that book, and we all know how—'

He held up a hand. 'You misjudge me, Mma Ramotswe. I'm not the man you think I am.'

She shrugged.

'Anybody can write a book . . . '

She brushed his objections aside. 'Rra, you are very modest – and that is good, too. But we do not have to talk about that. The real question is what I should do.'

Clovis Andersen sighed. 'Somewhere in the book I say something about going to the source of a problem. I forget ...'

'It is on page 126,' said Mma Ramotswe. 'The chapter is called "Seeing the Wood from the Trees".'

Clovis Andersen nodded. 'Yes, I think it's there. I think I said something about finding out where a problem originates and then going directly there.'

'Yes, Rra. That is what you said.' She looked at him expectantly. 'The source of the problem here is Mr Ditso.'

Clovis Andersen nodded. 'Yes. So you ask the question: why is he doing this?'

Mma Ramotswe looked up at the sky. There were so many reasons for bad behaviour, for meanness and unkindness. Sometimes the explanation of such things was very simple; people caused harm to others because they were of malevolent disposition. That was sheer human wickedness, something that had always existed and always would. Some people, it seemed, derived pleasure from inflicting suffering on others, and any enquiry as to why they did it could stop there. But then there were those other cases where the real explanation lay elsewhere, where there was some quite different motive in play – greed, ambition, a grudge ... There was so much to choose from.

'He wants to build a new hall at the orphan farm,' she said. 'He wants the children to eat in one place and save money. It's cheaper, you see, to cook all the meals in one place.'

Clovis Andersen considered this. 'Is he a frugal man, this Mr Ditso? Does he live simply?'

Mma Ramotswe smiled. Mr J. L. B. Matekoni's words were coming back to her. 'My husband could answer that, I think, Rra. He says that you can tell what a person is like by looking at his car.'

This seemed to interest Clovis Andersen. 'He's got something

141

there, Mma Ramotswe. Yes, he's certainly got something there.' He paused. 'So, what sort of car has our friend got? Something simple?'

'No, Rra. It is very fancy. Fancy and shiny.'

Clovis Andersen absorbed this. 'So maybe he doesn't want just to save money. Maybe he wants to spend it.'

Mma Ramotswe pointed out that it was not Mr Ditso's money that would be spent: it would be the orphan farm's.

'Sure,' said Clovis Andersen. 'But who's getting the money? Where's it being spent? Remember what I said in the book. *Follow the money*. It always works, Mma Ramotswe.'

She looked at him. Of course he was right. And it had never occurred to her to ask herself this question, not once in the course of all the pondering and worrying of the last few days. And now this man who was so modest, who seemed reluctant to discuss *The Principles of Private Detection* unless pressed to do so, this *nice* man had gone right to the nub of the matter, and had done it effortlessly, as if he had hardly had to think about it at all.

She struggled to contain her excitement. 'I think you are right, Rra. That is the very question we should be asking ourselves.'

Clovis Andersen made a gesture with his hand – a turning movement that suggested the reframing of the question. 'Ask ourselves, or ask him?'

'You think we should speak to him, Rra?'

Clovis Andersen nodded. 'Yes. Let's go and talk to him about the building project. And while you're talking to him, I'll watch him.'

'You'll watch?'

'Yes. Because in my experience, Mma Ramotswe, people give themselves away. Even if he doesn't say anything, he'll tell us.'

They drank their tea. Mma Ramotswe felt almost euphoric. As far as she was concerned, the investigation was now in the hands of one who must, on any view of it, be one of the most highly regarded private detectives in the world. And he was here, in Botswana, with her, working on a case in which they were, without the slightest shadow of doubt, on the right side. If the last few days had been difficult ones, that was now almost completely forgotten. She now felt optimistic that they would come up with something that might bring about a reversal of Mma Potokwani's dismissal. And that had to happen, because if it did not, then there would be no justice left in the country – and that was a thought that Mma Ramotswe was not willing to entertain for anywhere, least of all for the place she loved so much, her Botswana.

It did not prove easy to track down Ditso Ditso, who was not listed under his own name in the telephone directory. It was Mma Makutsi who remembered the name of one of his companies and found a number for that. 'It is here,' she said proudly, pointing to an entry in the directory. 'DD Industries. That is what he calls himself. It is his initials, you see.'

They had gone back to the office, where Mma Makutsi, excited by the presence of Clovis Andersen, had made a great show of finding the telephone number. Mma Ramotswe complimented her, and had drawn their guest's attention to Mma Makutsi's framed certificate on the wall. 'The Botswana Secretarial College,' she had said. 'My assistant is one of their most distinguished graduates.'

'*The* most distinguished graduate,' corrected Mma Makutsi, smiling at Clovis Andersen as she spoke.

'Ninety-seven per cent,' said Mma Ramotswe hurriedly, before Mma Makutsi could say it. She did not want Clovis Andersen to think Mma Makutsi boastful.

Clovis Andersen glanced at the certificate. 'Very good, Mma

Makutsi. It is a very good training for detection, you know. I've come across several people who trained in office administration before they went into the profession. They did well. Very methodical.'

Mma Makutsi beamed with pleasure. 'Thank you, Rra. They always stressed method at the college. They said that if you follow a method, you'll never get lost. That is what they taught us.'

Clovis Andersen nodded his agreement. 'There's a lot to be said for that approach.'

'And they also taught us a great deal about filing,' Mma Makutsi continued. 'You see, if you have a good system for filing, then—'

Mma Ramotswe cut her short, looking apologetically at Clovis Andersen. 'That number, Mma. That Ditso number, if you don't mind.'

At first the number was busy, but at the third try Mma Ramotswe found herself talking to a secretary. 'This is not the right number of Rra Ditso,' she said. 'You will have to phone another number. I'm sorry, Mma. Goodbye.'

'But, Mma,' Mma Ramotswe blurted out. 'That is very sad. Very sad.'

There was a moment's silence at the other end of the line.

'I don't have another number for Rra Ditso, and he will be very sorry that we have not been able to speak.'

The hesitation was almost audible. 'Why so, Mma? What is this in connection with?'

'I cannot tell you, Mma,' said Mma Ramotswe. 'Other than to say that there is a very important visitor to this country who needs to speak to Mr Ditso.'

'Who is this visitor? I can take a message.'

Mma Ramotswe's tone now changed. 'Oh, sorry, Mma. This name is too important to give over the telephone. Thank you anyway, it doesn't matter all that much. Not to us.'

It was the *not to us* that worked.

'There is a number for his mobile phone,' said the secretary. 'You can try that.'

'Will he answer, though?' asked Mma Ramotswe. 'So often I have phoned those things and left a message, and nobody has ever listened to it. It is like talking to yourself. So maybe not, Mma. Some other time – but it's a bit of a pity for Rra Ditso.'

'There is another number,' said the secretary. 'I will give you a number that he will definitely answer, Mma.'

The number was provided and the call brought to an end.

'Who is this man?' said Clovis Andersen. 'Thinks he's the president, or something?'

'It is because he doesn't want to be asked for money,' pronounced Mma Makutsi. 'People are always asking other people for money in this country. It happens all the time. And if you're rich, as he is, then every day there must be people who say they are his cousins or something, and want help with doctors' bills or school fees or need new shoes. The cost of shoes these days—'

That's right, blame us! Blame the shoes!

Mma Makutsi stopped midstream. She looked down at her feet, furtively, as did Mma Ramotswe, who also thought she had heard something. It was not clear whether Clovis Andersen had heard anything, but Mma Ramotswe did notice that he frowned slightly and cocked his head, as if straining to pick up something indistinct.

Mma Ramotswe laughed nervously. 'Oh, there are many things that people want,' she said. 'And people try to help, but it is sometimes difficult. So maybe we should understand why he does not want people to be able to phone him up all the time.'

'That is what I just said,' chipped in Mma Makutsi.

You'd think that—

The small voice from down below – if it really was a voice rather

145

than a figment of the imagination – was cut short by Mma Ramotswe, who cleared her throat loudly and suggested that Mma Makutsi dial the number they had just been given and put her through to Mr Ditso. Mma Makutsi did this, and Mma Ramotswe soon found herself on the line to Mr Ditso Ditso himself.

The businessman was abrupt. 'Who are you, Mma?' he enquired.

Mma Ramotswe gave her name.

'So that is who you are,' said Ditso. 'I have seen your place. It's on the Tlokweng Road, isn't it?'

'That is me, Rra,' she said.

There was a brief silence at the other end of the line. Then he said, 'So, you want to investigate me. On whose behalf, Mma?'

Mma Ramotswe was momentarily taken aback. It was true that she had been trying to investigate him, but she had got nowhere. And since she was not calling him now as part of that abortive enquiry, then surely she could deny that she was investigating him. She did not have time, though, as Mr Ditso continued, 'If you'd like to see me, Mma, I'm in my office. You can come now, if you wish.'

This was even more surprising, but Mma Ramotswe accepted quickly. 'That will suit me very well, Rra. May I bring somebody with me? A visitor.'

'Yes,' said Mr Ditso. 'You can bring anybody you like. I do not mind.'

With that he rang off, and Mma Ramotswe turned to face Clovis Andersen. 'I had not expected it to be that easy.'

'Things that seem easy sometimes are not easy when you get up close to them,' chipped in Mma Makutsi. 'That is in Mr Andersen's book. Page 74.'

Clovis Andersen looked embarrassed. 'I'm not always right, you know,' he said mildly.

Mma Makutsi laughed. 'You are very modest, Rra. We have always found that you have been right, haven't we, Mma Ramotswe?'

Mma Ramotswe agreed that this was so, but did not press the matter. She had the impression that Clovis Andersen was beginning to feel awkward over these constant references to his book. She would try to avoid mentioning it in future – at least when he was with them – and she would have a quiet word to this effect with Mma Makutsi later on.

The offices of DD Industries proved easy enough to locate. Two large letters had been mounted on the side of an offshoot of the Lobatse Road. The first D was red, the second D a vivid green, and beneath them was a board on which a painted hand obligingly pointed in the direction of a large white building.

Seated on the passenger side of Mma Ramotswe's tiny white van, Clovis Andersen surveyed the sign. 'Ego,' he said.

'What was that, Rra?'

'I said *ego*, Mma Ramotswe. That man has a large ego. Why else would he choose his initials for the name of his business? And then put them up on great big cut-outs?'

Mma Ramotswe smiled. 'There are many businessmen who are a bit like that. They say *look at me*. I have often thought that would be a good name for a business: The Look at Me Company.'

Clovis Andersen agreed.

'What is your own business called, Rra?' Mma Ramotswe asked as she steered the van towards a patch of shade afforded by a couple of jacaranda trees.

Clovis Andersen stared out of the window. 'It is called Muncie Investigations.'

'That is a nice name, Rra. Who is this Muncie? Is he your colleague?'

'Muncie is a place,' Clovis Andersen explained. 'It is a place in the United States. In Indiana.'

'It sounds very nice, Rra. Muncie sounds like Gaborone. Is it like Gaborone at all?'

Clovis Andersen considered this as the van was parked. 'Maybe a bit. Some things are different, though. We have a river, and we make glass jars. We make some very famous glass jars for pickling fruit.'

'That is very useful,' said Mma Ramotswe, turning off the engine. 'Rra, I must tell you something. I am a bit nervous of this Ditso Ditso.'

'Why is that, Mma Ramotswe? Has he a reputation for violence?'

'No, not that I know of. It's just that these big men – they can make ordinary people seem very small.' She paused. 'And there is another thing: why was he so quick to suggest that I come and see him? Why would he do that, Rra?'

Clovis Andersen thought for a moment. 'Because he has something to hide,' he said. 'He knows that you're a detective, doesn't he? He has assumed, then, that you're looking into his affairs. And then he has decided, quite wisely, that the best way of dealing with somebody who is investigating you is to go out to meet them. Make the running yourself, and that will put them off. I've seen this sort of thing before.'

She sought reassurance. 'Do you think so, Rra?'

'I think so, Mma Ramotswe.'

She pointed to the glass door of the building behind which could be made out the figure of a guard slouched on a chair. 'We should go in,' she said. 'And I shall remember what you had to say.'

The guard, who was sitting somnolently staring out across the parched earth at the front of the building, seemed barely to register their arrival. 'That way,' he muttered, pointing down a corridor behind him. 'Second door on the right. That is where he is.'

Clovis Andersen exchanged a quizzical glance with Mma Ramotswe.

'That man is very lazy,' she whispered, as they made their way in the direction the guard had indicated. 'I have always found that guards are not very wide awake. I think it is a good job for a sleepy person.'

Clovis Andersen chuckled. 'It's probably better for them to be doing that job than driving buses or planes,' he said.

'That is very true, Rra,' said Mma Ramotswe.

They were now in front of Mr Ditso's door, which was simply labelled MANAGING DIRECTOR NO ADMISSION.

'No admissions, plural,' said Clovis Andersen.

Mma Ramotswe knocked, and they entered when a voice from within called out. Inside, seated behind a large expanse of desk, was Mr Ditso Ditso, his shirtsleeves rolled up, his left wrist dominated by what seemed an impossibly large wristwatch. A beam of sunlight, slanting in from the wide plate-glass window behind him, caught the dial of the watch and flashed rays back across the wall in dancing points of light.

It was the office of a wealthy man and a public citizen: anybody could see that immediately. On the wall to the side of Mr Ditso's desk there were several framed photographs and letters: Mr Ditso Ditso shaking hands with a former president; Mr Ditso Ditso at a charity function, handing over an outsized cheque; Mr Ditso Ditso presenting the prizes at Gaborone Secondary School. On a shelf there was a series of what looked like business awards: a trophy in the shape of a cash register, an engraved glass bowl.

Mma Ramotswe introduced Clovis Andersen. 'Mr Andersen is a visitor to Botswana,' she said. 'He is spending some time in my office, seeing how we work.'

Mr Ditso inclined his head politely in the direction of Clovis Andersen. 'You are very welcome, sir.' Then he turned to Mma Ramotswe. 'What is it, Mma? Who is wanting to investigate me? Is this to do with tax? Some people think I do not pay my taxes, but I do. Every *pula*.'

Mma Ramotswe shook her head. 'It's nothing to do with tax, Rra. I have come here to speak to you about a friend,' she said. 'A certain Mma Potokwani.'

The effect of this was immediate. Mr Ditso, who had been tense, appearing to want to be in command of the situation, now visibly relaxed. He had indicated to his visitors that they should sit down; now he stretched out in his own chair, his hands folded loosely on his lap. 'Oh, yes? That lady. You have come to ask me to give her her job back, I assume. You know her, Mma?'

Mma Ramotswe bit her lip. 'I know her, Rra. She is my old friend.'

Mr Ditso reached for a matchstick that was lying on the desk in front of him. Splitting the top with a fingernail, he began to use the stick as a toothpick; a gesture of calculated unconcern. Mma Ramotswe drew in her breath. She was as much embarrassed as angered by this display; what would Clovis Andersen think of people in Botswana if this was how they behaved?

She fixed Ditso with an intense stare. 'I am talking to you, Rra,' she said. 'And this man with me is a visitor.'

Mr Ditso's hand came away from his mouth. The toothpick was held up, as if it were a tiny baton. 'So, Mma? If I have something in between my teeth can I not remove it? In my own office. Or do I need your permission to do that?'

She looked down at her shoes. She knew that she should try to control herself; nothing was to be gained by falling out with the man who held Mma Potokwani's fate in his hands. But I have

150

already fallen out with him, she thought; I have already said too much.

She made a supreme effort. 'I beg you to reconsider your decision, Rra. Mma Potokwani has done a wonderful job as matron. Maybe they haven't told you about that. She is a very great lady.'

Mr Ditso lowered the toothpick. 'She has certainly done a very good job, Mma. Yes, that is quite true. But ... ' he paused, looking at Clovis Andersen as if for support. 'But there comes a time when things must move on. The same person shouldn't run a business for ever. That is not good business practice, Mma, as I'm sure our friend here will tell you.'

She tried to keep her voice even, but it rose in spite of her efforts. 'It is not a business, Rra. It is a home for children. That is not a business.'

Mr Ditso laughed. 'Mma Ramotswe, *everything* is a business these days. Even countries. They are businesses too. Churches. Look at how careful churches are with their money. They have accountants running them. Even the Pope – I have heard that he has trained as an accountant.'

Clovis Andersen could not let that pass. 'That is surely not true, sir,' he said.

Ditso Ditso did not look at him as he replied. 'What is true?' he said airily. 'Who can tell? One man says something is true; another says it is not. How can any of us tell?'

This comment brought silence. Clovis Andersen looked at Mma Ramotswe and frowned. She stared down at her hands. 'You won't reconsider, Rra?' she said quietly. 'There are many people who would be very happy if you did.'

Mr Ditso shook his head. 'Sorry, Mma, but the decision has been taken. I'm sure that Mma Potokwani will find something else. As you say, she has many talents, and there are these hotels looking for good housekeepers. How about that? She'd probably make much more money doing that.'

'It is not about money,' retorted Mma Ramotswe. 'She does not do what she does for money. The children need her.'

Mr Ditso smiled. 'The hotels have their needs too, Mma. It is good work. If there were not good hotels, then where would visitors sleep? They need people like Mma Potokwani.'

Mma Ramotswe sighed. 'It is such a small thing, Rra: to have an argument over a building. Why is a building that important?'

Mr Ditso stiffened.

'It is not about a building,' he said. 'It is not about that.' Then he added, 'The building contract has been awarded on tender. There is no reason for disagreement there.'

For a moment Mma Ramotswe said nothing, and sat quite still. Then she rose to her feet. 'What you are doing is wrong, Rra. You do know that, don't you?'

He held her gaze. 'That is your view, Mma. But you are the one who is wrong. And please do not be cross with me for saying this, but this has nothing to do with you. I do not wish to be rude to a lady like you, but I have to say that. This is not your business, Mma. That is all there is to it. It is not your business.'

The first part of their journey back to the office was completed in silence. Mma Ramotswe felt raw after the encounter with Ditso Ditso, and did not want to speak; but then, almost at the same moment, as Mma Ramotswe negotiated the traffic circle near the automotive trades training centre, they both poured out their feelings over what had happened.

'Who does he think he is?' Mma Ramotswe burst out. 'Sitting there and lecturing us on the needs of hotels!'

'I didn't like him,' said Clovis Andersen. 'Not one bit.'

'And what did I say about Mma Potokwani? There was so

much I could have said, but the words seemed to go from my head. I let my friend down.'

'You did not,' said Clovis Andersen. 'You put it very well, Mma.'

'It was a waste of time.'

Clovis Andersen disagreed. 'No, it wasn't a waste of time. Not at all.'

She glanced at him quizzically. 'How can that be?'

'We learned everything we needed to learn,' said Clovis Andersen. 'First, the reason why he agreed to see you so quickly was that he thought you were investigating him. That tells us something: there are grounds for investigation. And then, when he realised that it was all about Mma Potokwani, he changed. He realised the heat was off, you see.'

She saw that, but wondered where it led.

'And then,' Clovis Andersen continued, 'did you see how he reacted when you mentioned the building? He had been relaxed before that. Then suddenly he was worried. I could see it very clearly from where I was sitting. He clenched his fists – just a little, but I saw. It's the building, Mma. He said it's not about the building, but it is. That's where we have to look.'

'I do not see, Rra . . .'

'The obvious question is this, Mma: who is getting the contract for the building? And why? He volunteered the information that the contract had been put out to tender. Why did he say that? Because even if it's true, you can be sure it wasn't awarded on merit. No, he mentioned it because he has something to hide. He is very transparent, our Mr Ditso.'

'Yes . . .'

'Yes indeed, Mma Ramotswe. And as you know, I don't like to quote myself, but on this occasion may I be permitted to do so? Somewhere in the book – I forget where – I say that if you listen hard enough, people will give themselves away. They will always mention the things that are preying on their mind, the things that they have done wrong. All you have to do is listen: it always comes out.'

Mma Ramotswe took her eyes off the road to give Clovis Andersen a look of admiration.

'Be careful, Mma Ramotswe. There is a car coming.'

She swerved – just in time to avoid a car approaching from the other direction. The other driver waved; a friendly wave, for some reason, not an ill-tempered one.

'There certainly are nice people on the road in this country,' said Clovis Andersen.

'I think that driver was my cousin,' said Mma Ramotswe. 'It looked like her.'

Chapter Fourteen

Gold Inside, Not Just Outside

There was still a general sense that everything was going wrong. It was a strange feeling – shared not only by Mma Ramotswe and Mma Makutsi, but by Mr J. L. B. Matekoni as well – and it seemed to be there all the time, like ominous background music to some unsettling drama; always playing, filled with foreboding. Mma Ramotswe tried to get things in perspective, tried to project her usual optimism, and to an extent she succeeded – only to find that her efforts at cheering up herself and others would weaken after a while and the memory would return of the sheer bleakness of both Mma Potokwani's and Fanwell's positions: unemployment in Mma Potokwani's case, and the destruction of a world that goes with it, and criminal charges in Fanwell's, and all that such proceedings entail – although the less one thought about the consequences of that the better.

'I hear the food in prison is not too bad,' remarked Charlie over tea one morning. Fanwell was not present, having been sent by Mr J. L. B. Matekoni to collect a part from the spares depot. 'I have heard that from a friend who was sent to prison for hitting somebody too hard.'

Mma Ramotswe, Mma Makutsi and Mr J. L. B. Matekoni all looked at Charlie balefully.

'You should not talk about such things,' scolded Mma Makutsi. 'Fanwell will not go to prison.'

'He might,' said Charlie. 'I'm only talking about what could happen. What's wrong with that?'

'Sometimes it's better not to think about bad things that are not definitely going to happen,' Mma Ramotswe said mildly.

Mma Makutsi looked cross. 'And you said that this friend of yours hit somebody too hard. So that means that you can hit people just the right amount? Not too soft but not too hard?'

Charlie defended himself. 'I did not say that. I did not say that you could hit people. All I said is that he hit somebody too hard.'

Mma Ramotswe sought to end the argument. Mma Makutsi and Charlie rubbed each other up the wrong way even at the best of times; when there was tension in the air, as there was now, it was considerably worse. 'I think that we should not talk about prison,' she said. 'Nor about hitting people. We all know that Fanwell is innocent. What we must do now is hope that the lawyer will do a good job and make sure that the magistrate sees that.'

Charlie stared down into his tea. 'That is a very useless lawyer, Mma.'

Mma Ramotswe frowned. 'You should not say that, Charlie.'

'No, you shouldn't,' snapped Mma Makutsi. 'You don't know anything about it.'

Fanwell looked up. 'But I do, Mma. He is the lawyer who defended my friend who hit somebody too ... who hit somebody.'

For a few moments nobody said anything. Mma Ramotswe looked up at the ceiling, her attention seized by a small white gecko that was clinging upside down to the ceiling board. The gecko was stalking a fly that was only a leap away; and as she watched he leaped, bringing the little conflict to a rapid end. It was so unlike our own dramas, she thought: they can drag on and on, can take so long. Fanwell was forced to wait a long, nerve-racking time before he knew his fate; in the world of the fly and the gecko it was seconds. The lawyer ... She remembered the lawyer's attitude of resignation and the way she had felt about it; and here was Charlie, confirming the fears that she had tried to suppress within her.

She looked at Charlie. 'What happened, Charlie? What did your friend tell you?'

'He said that the lawyer came to court late. He said that—'

'Traffic,' said Mr J. L. B. Matekoni. 'The traffic can be very bad in the mornings, as we all know. You cannot blame a lawyer for being late at court just because there is too much traffic on the road.'

It was a valiant attempt to paint the lawyer in the best light, but Charlie simply shook his head. 'He was late because he had left the papers at the office,' he said. 'He had to go back to collect them. My friend told me that. He said that the magistrate was cross and this made him worried. It is not good to have an angry magistrate dealing with your case. "That is very bad news," he said.'

'And then?' Mma Makutsi prompted. If there was to be bad news, then she, at least, was in favour of facing it.

'And then he said that he – the lawyer, that is – stood up and my friend realised that he thought he was somebody else.'

'The lawyer thought he was somebody else?' asked Mr J. L. B. Matekoni. 'The lawyer didn't know who he was?' He looked at Mma Ramotswe in dismay. 'That doesn't sound like a very good lawyer, Mma.'

'No,' said Charlie. 'It was not like that, boss. The lawyer knew he was the lawyer. He thought that my friend—'

'The one who hit somebody too hard,' interjected Mma Makutsi.

Charlie glanced at her. 'Him, yes, him. He thought my friend was another person—'

'Who had not hit anybody at all?' asked Mma Makutsi.

Charlie showed his irritation. 'I'm trying to tell the story,' he complained. 'And she keeps interrupting me.'

Mma Ramotswe urged him to go on. 'Mma Makutsi is only trying to help,' she said. 'Carry on, Charlie.'

Finishing his tea, Charlie put his mug down on the filing cabinet. 'This lawyer – who is also going to be Fanwell's lawyer – had got his clients mixed up. So my friend had to whisper to him that he was not the person he thought he was, but another person. And the lawyer got all flustered and began to mumble all sorts of things. So the magistrate told him to sit down and drink a glass of water.'

Charlie paused.

'Go on,' said Mma Ramotswe faintly.

'Then he stood up again and asked some questions. My friend said they were stupid questions, and the magistrate eventually said to him that he was to shut up.'

'That cannot be true,' Mma Makutsi interjected. 'Magistrates don't tell people to shut up. It is not how they talk.'

'You weren't there, Mma,' snorted Charlie.

'Nor were you,' countered Mma Makutsi.

'My friend was. And he told me everything that happened. He

said that that was why he got three weeks in prison. It was all that lawyer's fault.'

Mma Makutsi was not prepared to let this pass. 'Excuse me, did the lawyer hit the person? Did I get something wrong? Maybe the lawyer should have gone to prison for hitting somebody too hard.'

Mr J. L. B. Matekoni looked at his watch. 'We should get back to work,' he said to Charlie. 'There are cars out there needing attention. They won't get fixed if we stay in here talking to the ladies.'

'You're right, boss,' said Charlie. 'Particularly talking to one lady ...' He glanced at Mma Makutsi, who smiled sweetly in response.

Mma Ramotswe sighed. 'All right,' she said, 'but this business with the lawyer, Charlie, I don't think you should say anything to Fanwell about that. I don't think it will help him to know. And just because the lawyer did not do a very good job with that friend of yours doesn't necessarily mean that he will not do a good job for Fanwell.'

'No,' said Mma Makutsi. 'So don't tell Fanwell about this, Charlie. I know how you talk. Just don't mention it to him. It's much better that he doesn't know.'

The door that linked the office of the No. 1 Ladies' Detective Agency to the courtyard of Tlokweng Road Speedy Motors had been slightly ajar during the tea break. Now it was suddenly pushed fully open, to reveal Fanwell standing on the step, holding in his left hand the car part that he had been sent to collect from the depot.

'Better for me not to know what?' he asked.

There are awkward moments from which one can retreat, and awkward moments from which there is no escape. This was one

159

of the latter, as Mma Makutsi explained to Phuti Radiphuti when she met him that lunchtime in his office at the Double Comfort Furniture Store.

'We couldn't lie to him,' she said. 'He had heard a bit of what was said and so we just had to tell him everything. He's got a no-good lawyer, you see, and Charlie said that . . . '

She narrated the story of Charlie's friend, of his inadequate defence and of the unfortunate consequences that followed. Phuti Radiphuti listened gravely. 'They should get another lawyer,' he said. 'Surely there are better people around. That man with the big nose – you know the one – they say that he's very good. The judges can't take their eyes off his nose, and so they always decide in his favour.'

Mma Makutsi wondered why a large nose should be an advantage in a lawyer, and decided that perhaps it had something to do with authority. Was it more difficult to argue with a large-nosed person? She had not considered the question before, but now it occurred to her that perhaps it was. But it was too late now to look for a lawyer with a more convincing nose, even if one were to be found. Money, she explained, had already been paid to the inadequate lawyer and Mma Ramotswe and Mr J. L. B. Matekoni, who were footing the bill for Fanwell's defence, could not afford to pay a second time.

'How did he take it?' asked Phuti.

'He was very worried,' she replied. 'Mr J. L. B. Matekoni tried to tell him that it would be all right; that he would speak to the lawyer and make sure that he handled it properly.'

'And was Fanwell reassured?'

'No.'

Phuti Radiphuti shook his head sadly. 'It is a very sad business. And if they send him to prison, you can imagine the men he will mix with there. He is just a young man, and they will corrupt him with their bad talk and their bad stories. It is very worrying.'

They looked at one another despairingly, but they had work to do that lunchtime, and life, as Phuti Radiphuti pointed out, had to go on. 'There are many sad things,' he said. 'They are all around us, but we have to get on with our lives, don't we? And that means that we must get on with choosing those things, Grace.'

Mma Makutsi agreed. The rapid progress with their new house meant that in a couple of months they would have to furnish it. At present Phuti had no furniture of his own, as the house they were occupying, which belonged to the wider Radiphuti family, was filled with family furniture: chairs that had been left in the house by various aunts, tables that had belonged to grandmothers and were now of uncertain ownership, beds that belonged to nobody in particular but had simply always been there.

Of course, to Mma Makutsi and Phuti the task of furnishing a house was considerably less daunting than it would be to most young couples. Not only was money not an issue in the same way that it was for average newly-weds, but Phuti's expertise when it came to choosing items would be invaluable. 'Everything we sell,' he said, 'is of the highest quality and built to last. But some things are of higher quality than others, and also built to last longer.'

Mma Makutsi considered this. 'That means that some of your things are better than others?'

'You could say that,' said Phuti. 'Although we do not say that ourselves, or people would then ask us which was the better furniture and they would buy that and leave the stuff that's not so good. That is always a big problem for people who have shops. So you have to say that everything's first class.'

'And this is true, isn't it?' asked Mma Makutsi.

'Yes,' said Phuti. 'Only some first-class items are *more* first class than others.'

'I see.'

That afternoon they were to look at sofas and beds. They had already identified a dining-room table and a set of eight matching chairs: these had been ordered from a trade catalogue and would arrive from over the border a few weeks later. The sofa and the bed would be chosen from the large stock that the Double Comfort Furniture Store, the largest furniture store in the country, already had in the showroom.

They left Phuti's office and made their way into the cavernous warehouse that was the Double Comfort Furniture Store. As they entered the store itself, they passed one of the employees, a middle-aged woman wearing a smock and carrying a bag of what looked like polishing equipment. The woman stopped, smiled at Phuti and then turned to Mma Makutsi.

'It is you, Mma,' she said. 'I'm very happy to see you.'

Phuti introduced her. 'This is Mma Rosemary. She has worked here for a long, long time.'

'Every day,' said Mma Rosemary. 'Same job.'

Mma Makutsi greeted her in the traditional way. She had noticed the courteous way in which Phuti dealt with his employees and had once mentioned the fact to Mma Ramotswe, who had commented that if that was so, then she could be sure that he would make a good husband. 'A man who is polite to the people he is in authority over will always be a good man,' she said. 'Look at Mr J. L. B. Matekoni; he is always polite to the apprentices. And he is a very fine husband, Mma.' She paused. 'He is even polite to Charlie, Mma – even when Charlie is being ... well, you know how Charlie can be.'

Mma Makutsi swallowed. She knew that she had to be kinder

162

to Charlie and she was trying, she really was. But how should a woman – any woman – react to a young man who said some of the things that Charlie said? Who had said, for example, that women could not fly aeroplanes because they would always be looking in the mirror to check that their lipstick was all right? Yes, Charlie had said that; those were his exact words, and she had exploded and said that he needed to wake up to the fact that women were flying aeroplanes right over his head at that very moment. Charlie had gone to the window and looked up at the sky and said that he could not see any aeroplanes being flown by women, and was this because they had perhaps already crashed? Mma Ramotswe had intervened then and politely taken Charlie to task, while Mma Makutsi calmed down. Those occasions were difficult. She knew Charlie would grow up eventually, but what if he grew up from a young man who held opinions like that into an older man who thought exactly the same way? That was the trouble with growing up: people did not always grow up in the way in which you might like them to grow up. And that, as Mma Ramotswe would put it, was a well-known fact.

Now Mma Rosemary reached out and took Mma Makutsi's hand in hers. It was an entirely natural gesture – one of acceptance, one of solidarity. 'You are now with us,' she said.

Mma Makutsi saw Phuti break into a smile, and she smiled too. 'It is very good,' she said.

'And you have chosen such a beautiful woman,' Mma Rosemary said to Phuti. 'You are a lucky man to have a beautiful wife like this. We are all very proud of you, Rra.'

Mma Makutsi felt her hands being gently squeezed as this compliment was paid; it showed, she thought, that it was meant. You did not squeeze hands when you lied; it could not be done.

'You are very kind to me, Mma Rosemary,' she said.

The other woman beamed up at her; she was considerably

shorter than Mma Makutsi. 'That is because you have made our Phuti so happy, Mma Radiphuti,' she said. 'And that has made us all happy.'

They moved off. Mma Makutsi thought: *Mma Radiphuti: that is me; I am Mma Radiphuti. I am the wife of this wonderful, kind man and I am not dreaming. This has happened. I am Mma Radiphuti.*

'She is the best polisher in all Botswana,' remarked Phuti as they continued on their way into the store. 'She can make tables glow like the sun. People come in, you see, and they touch the tables after they have been eating fat cakes or doughnuts. And so the tables have fingerprints all over them. Mma Rosemary sorts that out with her tins of polish and her rags.'

Mma Makutsi listened to this. 'People can be very dirty,' she said. 'They have dirty hands. Not all people, but quite a lot of people do.'

Phuti agreed with this. 'It must be very difficult if you are a person who has to shake hands with people all day. A president, maybe, or a big film star. All those people come up to you and say, *Please shake my hand*, and you want to ask them if they've washed their hands. But you can't do that, can you – not if you're one of these politicians or film stars. You have to shake hands first and then you must think afterwards: *have they washed their hands?*'

They passed one of the tables that had been freshly polished by Mma Rosemary. 'See that?' said Phuti, pointing at the gleaming hardwood surface. 'That is like a mirror. If you had a table like that you could use it to shave with in the morning. You could look at your face in the surface and shave.'

The sofas were next, and there they stopped. Mma Makutsi gazed out over the large array of highly stuffed, opulent-looking couches. Many of them were made of leather, most of it black, but in some cases cream or highly coloured reds and greens. She wondered what it would be like to have a red-leather sofa, and for a moment she saw herself seated on such a thing, fanned perhaps by one of those large electric fans, drinking tea and eating some rich morsel. If one had a sofa like that, one might sit on it all day, supported in the utmost comfort, reflecting on one's good fortune though not, she hoped, without a thought for those whose own sofas were less comfortable, or indeed for those who had no sofa at all.

She bent down to examine a large four-seater covered in a gold-coloured material to which a fringe had been attached. She hardly dared look at the price tag, but did so and recoiled in shock. Surely no single sofa could cost anything like that? How many cattle did that represent? She did a quick calculation. Were there people who would actually pay such a price, and if they did, would they not feel permanently uncomfortable knowing that they were sitting on so expensive a piece of furniture? Would one simply admire such an item and not sit on it? Could one perhaps leave the price tag on it after purchase, so that visitors to the house could see what you had paid for it and marvel? An ostentatious person would probably do that, but she, Mma Makutsi, would never want to flaunt her wealth. Or Phuti's wealth, she reminded herself; for I am still Mma Makutsi from Bobonong, and I shall never – *never* – indulge myself in a sofa like that when there are people in villages in the country for whom even a chair, a modest wooden chair, is a luxury, well nigh unaffordable.

Phuti noticed her examining the gold-coloured sofa. 'Do you like that one, Grace?' he said. 'Why don't you try sitting on it? See if it's comfortable.'

Mma Makutsi hesitated. 'Oh, I was just looking, Phuti. We do not need a gold-coloured sofa ...'

'Try it out,' he said. 'Sit on it.'

She moved round to the front of the sofa and very slowly lowered herself on to it. She felt the cushion beneath her, at once firm and soft, supportive but yielding. She leaned back, and it was like giving oneself into the arms of a gentle, comforting lover. 'Oh,' she muttered, and then, 'oh,' again.

'You look very good on that,' said Phuti. 'That sofa is the right colour for you. Gold. That is your colour, Grace.'

She felt the fabric with her fingers. It was as smooth as satin. Gold? Was that really her colour? She had always thought that red suited her very well, but perhaps gold was also suitable for people who looked good in red. If they bought this sofa, which of course they would not – not at that price – then she might perhaps buy a pair of gold-coloured shoes that she could wear when she was sitting on her sofa. She had seen a pair in the shoe shop at Riverwalk, and she could go back and see whether they were still available.

'Would you like that one?' Phuti asked. 'We can get it if you like.'

She sat up and propelled herself off the sofa. 'No,' she said. 'It is very nice, Phuti, but it is not right for us.'

He frowned. 'Are you sure? You looked so comfortable.'

'I am sure. And I can already see one over there – that brown one – that I think might be right for us.'

They made their way over to the brown sofa – a much more low-key affair – and she sat down on it. It was considerably less physically comfortable than the gold-coloured sofa, but correspondingly more mentally comfortable. This was a sofa on which one might sit in casual clothes, on which one might eat a doughnut or drink a cup of tea without worrying about crumbs or splashes. This was a sofa *entirely free of guilt*.

'I think that this will be a very good sofa,' she said to Phuti. 'You try it.'

Phuti sat down. 'It is well made,' he said. 'I know the people who make these sofas. They are honest people.'

'Then I would like this one,' said Mma Makutsi.

Phuti leaned across and whispered in her ear. 'I am very happy, Grace. I am very happy that you have chosen this one rather than the gold one. That shows me that you are not one who is impressed with flashy things. You are gold inside, Grace, not just outside.'

She turned and kissed him lightly. 'That is the kindest thing anybody has ever said to me.' *Gold inside, not just outside.*

Phuti called over the floor manager, who had been hovering in the background, and arrangements were made to transfer the sofa to the storage warehouse. Then they returned to the office before Phuti drove Mma Makutsi back to the agency. On the way, they stopped at a petrol station, and Phuti set about filling the car. As he instructed the attendant, a van drew up alongside the neighbouring pump and a man in blue overalls stepped out.

Mma Makutsi watched. Phuti looked up and saw the man, whom he obviously recognised. For a moment or two they looked at one another before Phuti gave a nod of greeting. The other man turned away. Now he hesitated, looked over his shoulder and then busied himself with the cap of the van's fuel tank. It struck her as strange that the man should have so pointedly failed to respond to Phuti's friendly overture; even a smile would have been polite – a smile or a nod of acknowledgement.

'Who is that rude man?' she asked Phuti as they drove off a few minutes later.

'He is one of the builder's men,' he said. 'I met him when I went to look at the house. Now he doesn't seem to want to know me.'

Mma Makutsi frowned. 'Why?'

'I have no idea,' replied Phuti. 'There are some people who are very shy. Maybe he is one of those.'

Mma Makutsi thought for a moment. 'Shy, or rude, maybe. Rude like his boss,' she said. 'He is rude too. Rude boss; rude men. Sometimes that is the way it happens.'

That was possible, he said. His own father had drummed into him the lesson that the way you treat your staff is the way they will treat you. 'That is something that some employers just do not understand,' Mr Radiphuti Senior had said. 'But in the Double Comfort Furniture Store we will never forget that, will we, Phuti?'

He had not. He had remembered it.

Mma Makutsi was silent for the rest of the brief journey back to the office. Silent; thinking.

Chapter Fifteen

How Many Cups of Tea . . .

The following day, Mma Ramotswe received a telephone call from the secretary at the orphan farm. This was a woman she knew only slightly – a woman who had been brought up in Lobatse and whose son was a promising athlete, a barefoot runner, whose prowess on the track was occasionally featured in the *Botswana Daily News*. They exchanged the customary greetings and then Mma Ramotswe, vaguely remembering that there had been something in the papers about the son – what was his nickname? – had asked after the young man.

'I'm sorry, Mma,' she said, 'I cannot remember your son's name, but I saw something in the papers and I wondered how he's doing. You must be very proud of him.'

The woman laughed. 'Nobody remembers his real name. That is because they all call him by his nickname. They call him

Lightning now, and we even use that at home. Yes, I am proud of him, Mma; I am very proud.'

'Lightning is a good name, Mma. Very good.'

'As long as it doesn't go to his head,' said the secretary. 'I heard him call one of the other runners Tortoise the other day. I told him that was very unkind and that one day his own legs would get slow – like mine.'

Mma Ramotswe made a sympathetic noise. 'Everybody's legs get slow, Mma. That is well known. But it doesn't matter, as long as one can get about a little bit. That is all that is needed.'

There was a moment of silence; the point of the call had not yet been revealed, but that was not so unusual. People often took some time to say what they needed to say – to rush a conversation could be considered rude, especially among old-fashioned people, and Mma Ramotswe remembered that the secretary was indeed a somewhat old-fashioned person.

Then the silence was broken. 'I am phoning about Mma Potokwani,' said the secretary.

Mma Ramotswe felt a momentary stab of alarm. Was Mma Potokwani not well? 'Is she ill . . . ?' Mma Ramotswe stuttered.

'I do not know whether or not she is sick,' said the secretary. 'She never complains about herself, as you know. But I cannot tell because she is not here. She has gone.'

'Where has she gone?'

'She has gone somewhere else. I do not know where. All she did was leave a note to say that her deputy, Mma Paloi, is in charge now until the end of the month when Mma Potokwani is due to go anyway. That is all she said.' The secretary paused, allowing this information to be absorbed. 'I wondered if she was with you, Mma. You are her great friend. But obviously she is not.'

'No, she is not here. And I am very shocked, Mma, to hear this news. Mma Potokwani would normally never leave her post. Never. You know what she's like.'

The secretary was quick to agree. 'If she was on one of those big ships and it was going down, she would be the last one to jump off, Mma. That is very true.'

Mma Ramotswe could not help but picture it: Mma Potokwani standing on the deck of a ship waiting for everybody else to clamber into lifeboats and cast off. And perhaps Mma Makutsi would be beside her, clinging on to her certificate from the Botswana Secretarial College, anxious to save that from the encroaching waters. And then Mma Potokwani would jump into the last lifeboat and ... and it would tilt precariously because of her weight and perhaps begin to sink, and again she would make sure that she was the last one to abandon ship, or she would even go down with the lifeboat, dutiful to the last; and the waters would swirl around with odd bits of detritus – spars of broken wood, unoccupied lifebelts, the framed certificate from the Botswana Secretarial College ...

'Have you spoken to her husband?' she asked.

The secretary explained that Rra Potokwani had gone to spend some time with a cousin who needed help with his cattle. 'He has no phone with him,' she went on, 'and I cannot find the name of the cousin. I do not know how to contact him.'

Mma Ramotswe thought out loud. 'I do not think she will have gone up to her husband. I do not think so.'

'No?'

'No, I do not think that she would do that. She does not like that cousin of her husband's – she has spoken to me about that. She says he is a drunkard.'

'I have heard her say that too,' said the secretary. 'She says that he eats too much as well. She told me that that cousin eats all the

171

meat in the household and leaves none for his wife. That is what she said, Mma: I am only repeating what she said.'

Yes, she thought, there are men like that; men with fat bellies and thin wives and children.

'I have an idea, Mma.'

The secretary sounded relieved. 'I knew that you would come up with something, Mma. I knew that you would know. You are the detective, you see ...'

This was not a time for flattery. 'Thank you, Mma, but it is only an idea. There is a big difference between an idea and a solution.'

'Oh, Mma, that is absolutely true. There is a very big difference.' The secretary cleared her throat. 'And what is this idea, Mma?'

'The lands,' said Mma Ramotswe. 'I think that she will be out at her fields.'

'Why do you think that, Mma?'

'Because that is where she went once before.'

Mma Ramotswe explained how there had been an occasion – not as serious as the current one – when Mma Potokwani had felt rather overburdened by her duties and had arranged to take a short break out at her fields, or lands, as they were called. 'It was only for a weekend, but she said that it was the best place to go if one was feeling exhausted. So I think we could see if she's there now.'

The conversation came to an end, with Mma Ramotswe promising to contact the secretary as soon as she had any news. She would go out there herself, she said; she knew the way – roughly – and it was a journey of no more than four hours.

The secretary was concerned. 'That is a long way, Mma. And I don't think you should go out into the bush by yourself.'

Mma Makutsi, on the other side of the room, overheard this. 'Tell her you will not be going by yourself,' she interjected. 'You will be going with me.'

Mma Ramotswe relayed this information. She was not sure that it was the best of ideas but it was a generous offer, and no more than one would expect from Mma Makutsi who, for all her faults – and they were not very big ones – was loyal and supportive through thick and thin . . . She paused for thought: would all this be described as thick, or was it thin? She was not at all sure, but whatever it was, it would be good to have Mma Makutsi at her side.

Of course there were preparations to be made. A journey out into the Botswana bush was not something that could be undertaken lightly. Those tracks, pitted by use and eroded by rains, were a trial for any vehicle, even one accustomed to such roads, as was the tiny white van. You had to be careful: if you broke down, it could be many miles from help, and so you had to know where you were. You also needed to take water – there would be no supplies of that along the road – and enough fuel to get you to your destination and back, with a little bit left over for emergencies.

At first, Mr J. L. B. Matekoni was unwilling to allow her to go. 'It is the middle of nowhere, that place,' he said. 'And what if she isn't there? You will have wasted a lot of time looking for somebody who may be at the opposite end of the country, for all you know.'

'If she isn't there,' countered Mma Ramotswe, 'then at least we will have found out that she isn't there. It will not be wasted.'

He shook his head in exasperation. 'That is no answer, Mma. And what if the van breaks down? That is a very old van, that one, and its engine—'

'Its engine is very good,' said Mma Ramotswe. 'You serviced it two weeks ago, Rra, and you said that it was in good condition. Have things changed so quickly?'

He sighed. 'It is in good condition for a van of its age. But you cannot take an old vehicle like that into the bush without running some risk. I have known many cars that have died ...' He lowered his eyes as he spoke, as if in respect for the souls of departed cars. 'I have known many cars that have died out in the bush. And that has meant a very long walk for their drivers.'

'That is a risk we shall take,' said Mma Ramotswe. 'It is the same with people. People can become late at any time – just like that. But that does not mean that we should not do anything and not go anywhere just because there is a possibility that we may suddenly become late.'

Mr J. L. B. Matekoni sensed that there was no point in his arguing any further; he would never persuade Mma Ramotswe to act otherwise when a friend was in need. And in spite of his anxiety over this trip, he shared her concern for Mma Potokwani, whom he had always admired in spite of her tendency to ask him to fix something whenever she saw him. She had to do that, he understood; it was her job, and the children in her care had benefited a great deal over the years precisely because she took her job so seriously. Rather than waste his energy on trying to stop the expedition, he expended it on making sure that the van was as ready as it could be for the journey. He placed spare cans of fuel in the back and lashed them down for the bumpy ride, and stowed two plastic demi-johns of water beside them. Then the oil was checked, the battery tested and a coil of rope tucked underneath one of the seats. 'You never know,' said Mr J. L. B. Matekoni. 'You never know, do you?'

'I shall be very careful, Rra,' said Mma Ramotswe, adding, 'I always am, you know.'

And as she said this, she gave him a look that implied that any

174

dangers about which he was concerned were ones that she would be very careful about – whatever they were.

The lands to which Mma Potokwani was suspected of retreating lay to the west of Gaborone, some distance beyond Molepolole, hard against the edge of the Kalahari, the great semi-desert that made up the heart of the country. This was dry land at the limits of the inhabitable, and fields here, if they could be called fields, grew very little: a few melons and patches of sorghum – not much more than that. Yet the families who tilled them, scratching at the parched soil to coax growth out of what sometimes seemed little more than powdered stone, did so by ancient right. This is where their people had been as far back as anybody could remember, and they maintained this link with the land even after they had moved to towns and villages. Each year the women and children would trek off to their lands for weeks at a time, to plant and tend the crops. It was a ritual that survived growing prosperity, even when there was no real need to harvest these small crops; it was a way of showing children who they were and reminding adults of the same thing.

'You do know the way, don't you?' asked Mma Makutsi as they left Molepolole behind them and began to follow the smaller road west.

Mma Ramotswe sounded confident. 'Yes,' she said. 'We follow this road to Takatokwane and then after that we go that way.' She pointed vaguely towards the north.

Mma Makutsi glanced at her nervously. 'That way, Mma?'

'Yes. There is a road that goes like this . . .' She made a winding gesture. 'We don't follow that one.'

'No?'

'No. We follow the one that goes like *this*.' The gesture now was more up-and-down. 'That's the road we need to look out for.

175

Then, after a while – quite a long time, because you have to go very slowly – there is a place where the road splits in two, or maybe three.'

'Which is it, Mma? Two or three?'

Mma Ramotswe shrugged. 'I cannot remember everything, Mma. But I will know which way to go, I promise you. I have been taught these things.'

Mma Makutsi remained silent while she digested this information. Then she asked what exactly Mma Ramotswe had been taught. The road system of Botswana?

Mma Ramotswe smiled. 'You cannot learn all the roads of Botswana, Mma. That would be a lifetime's work because they are always changing roads and adding to them. They look at a map, those people in the Roads Department, and then they draw a line across it and say that is the best place for a new road. Let us build a new road soon. That is what they say.'

'And then they have tea,' added Mma Makutsi.

They both laughed. 'Yes, Mma Makutsi, that is absolutely right. They are always drinking tea in those government offices. When you think of how much the Government must spend on tea ...' She shook her head in disbelief at the unimaginable figures.

'We spend quite a lot on tea,' mused Mma Makutsi. 'If you add it up, Mma. You have ... how many cups of tea do you have, Mma Ramotswe? Ten? Twelve?'

'I haven't counted, Mma Makutsi. And you yourself—'

Mma Makutsi did not let her finish. 'Well, let's think, Mma. You have tea when you wake up, don't you? You have told me about that.'

'Of course I have tea when I wake up,' retorted Mma Ramotswe. 'Is there anybody who *doesn't* have tea when they wake up?'

She received no answer to this question, and so she continued, 'I sometimes have two cups of tea before breakfast. It depends. There are some days when I seem to drink my tea more quickly than others. Then there are days when I just sip my tea and it takes a bit longer. One cup will do on those days. One cup to start with, that is: there is more tea later on.'

'And then?' asked Mma Makutsi.

'And then there is the tea that goes with breakfast. I make that in a pot and put it on the table and drink maybe two cups of tea . . .'

Mma Makutsi looked at her sideways, and Mma Ramotswe revised her account. 'Maybe three, Mma. In fact, three. Always.'

Mma Makutsi nodded at the admission. 'And then, Mma, there is the office tea. We must not forget that.'

'That is correct,' said Mma Ramotswe. 'Morning tea – one cup only, though, Mma. You have seen that. Then at lunch there are two cups, and then there is afternoon tea.' She paused. 'How many does that make, Mma?'

'I think that makes eight,' said Mma Makutsi. 'Call it ten.'

'Ten cups,' said Mma Ramotswe thoughtfully. 'And we haven't counted the evening tea. That must be added. So maybe fourteen cups of tea in all.'

'Fourteen cups,' intoned Mma Makutsi, making a rapid calculation before continuing. 'That means seventy cups between Monday and Friday. What about the weekend?'

'I do not think it is much different over the weekend,' said Mma Ramotswe. 'I drink that office tea at home over the weekend.'

Again Mma Makutsi performed a calculation. 'Ninety-eight cups,' she said. 'Call that one hundred. There is something called reporting error, Mma. I have read about it. It is all over the place. There are many, many reporting errors.' She looked out of the

177

window on her side of the van, as if to scan the passing bush, the acacia trees, for reporting errors.

'One hundred cups,' repeated Mma Ramotswe. 'That will be doing me a lot of good. One hundred cups of redbush tea, Mma. That bush tea is full of good things. It will be making me very strong.' She paused. 'I am not ashamed of all that tea, Mma.'

'Of course not,' said Mma Makutsi. 'There is nothing to be ashamed of in drinking one hundred cups of tea a week, Mma. Which is . . . ' She paused again. 'More than five thousand cups of tea a year, Mma. That is very impressive.'

'Well, there you are, Mma Makutsi. Those are the figures. You cannot argue with figures, can you?'

Mma Makutsi looked thoughtful. 'And ours is just a small business. We use all that redbush tea for you and all that ordinary tea for me, and we are just a tiny business. Imagine how much tea the Standard Bank drinks. Imagine all their tea, Mma. Just think of it. Or the Government. All those government people in their offices drinking tea.'

'It is a miracle that there is any tea left for us, Mma,' said Mma Ramotswe. 'After the Government and the banks and people like that have taken all the tea they need, it is a miracle that there is any tea left for people like you and me, Mma, the tea-drinking public.'

'You're right, Mma Ramotswe. It is a miracle. The miracle of the tea.'

'A good miracle, Mma Makutsi.'

'A very good miracle, Mma Ramotswe.'

Chapter Sixteen

The Habits of Lions

Mma Ramotswe seemed to find the turning without any difficulty. 'I remember that tree,' she said to Mma Makutsi as she swung the van off on to the pitted dirt track. 'When I came here with Mma Potokwani four years ago, we turned off at that tree. This is definitely the right place.'

Mma Makutsi was impressed. 'I could never remember a tree after four years,' she said. 'Or after four days, really. You are very good at these things, Mma.'

'Of course there was the signpost too,' said Mma Ramotswe. 'That helped. Did you not see it, Mma? There was a small sign that gave the name of the village that we pass through on this track.'

Mma Makutsi had missed that. Looking out of the window, she gazed at the featureless bush. 'It all looks the same to me,' she said. 'All these trees. All the same. And the bushes. Also the same.'

Mma Ramotswe gingerly but skilfully manoeuvred the van round a large pothole in the track ahead. 'I would not like to drive on this road at night,' she said. 'All these holes.'

'And lions,' said Mma Makutsi, shivering at the thought. 'We are very close to the Kalahari now, Mma, and there could be lions.'

'The lions will keep their distance from Mma Potokwani,' said Mma Ramotswe. 'It would be a very foolish lion who tried to eat her.'

Mma Makutsi smiled. 'A very brave lion, perhaps, Mma. But we should not talk about lions like this. It is very bad luck. Talk about lions brings lions – that is what I always say.'

Mma Ramotswe considered this. It was true; the contemplation of misfortune undoubtedly attracted misfortune. Why this should be so, she was not sure; perhaps it had something to do with noticing things. If you thought of something, then you noticed it; if you did not think of it, then it might be there but you did not notice it. That was possible, but . . .

She did not finish the thought. They had been travelling painfully slowly but had, for the last couple of hundred yards or so, been on a slightly better section of track, one that did not seem as badly potholed and eroded. Without intending to speed up, she had nonetheless done so, with the result that the tiny white van was now travelling almost at the pace it would have travelled on a much better, official road. That was safe enough, except for the sand, which had slowly been becoming deeper and had begun to encroach on the track itself. Now, with a fair degree of speed behind it, the van hit a section of track in which the sand covered the entire surface. For a four-wheel drive vehicle, that would not perhaps have presented too much of a challenge; for the van, however, it was too much, and the front wheels, engaging only with sand that shifted and collapsed as the tyres tried to gain a hold, veered sharply and brought the van into a deep bank of fine white earth at the edge of the road.

'We have stopped,' said Mma Makutsi, as they shuddered to a halt.

'So it seems,' muttered Mma Ramotswe.

'Maybe you can reverse out of this,' said Mma Makutsi. 'If you reverse, then you can get back on the road. What do you think, Mma?'

'It is the only thing to do,' said Mma Ramotswe, through clenched teeth. Sometimes Mma Makutsi's advice was ... how might one put it? Obvious.

She put in the clutch and engaged reverse gear. The engine responded, but the wheels merely spun in the fine sand, sending up a cloud of dust on either side of the van.

'It's digging in, Mma,' said Mma Ramotswe. 'The wheels are turning, but they have nothing to grip.'

Mma Makutsi sighed. 'I think we are stuck in the sand, Mma.'

'I think you're right, Mma Makutsi.'

Mma Ramotswe turned off the engine. 'We should get out and see what has happened,' she said. 'I was stuck in sand once before. But I got out.'

'Oh yes, Mma? How did you do that?'

'I put two sacks under each front wheel. That gave the tyres a surface they could hold on to.'

Mma Makutsi clapped her hands together. 'That is a very clever idea, Mma. Sacks. We can put sacks under the tyres.'

'If we had sacks ...'

'You don't have any, Mma?'

Mma Ramotswe shook her head. 'I thought about it, Mma. I even made a mental note to get some. Mr J. L. B. Matekoni has a pile of old sacks back at Zebra Drive. If only I had remembered.'

They climbed out of the van to inspect the situation, which was worse than Mma Ramotswe had feared. The two front wheels of the van had spun energetically into the sand, effectively burrowing deeper with each revolution. Now the sand came three-quarters of the way up each wheel, and any further movement would undoubtedly sink them further.

'This is very bad,' said Mma Makutsi.

Mma Ramotswe looked down the track. 'How long will it take us to walk back to the main road, Mma? You are good at calculations.'

Mma Makutsi stared in the direction from which they had come. 'We've been travelling along here for about thirty minutes,' she said. 'And we've been doing about fifteen kilometres an hour. That means we have come about seven kilometres. How fast do you think we walk, Mma?'

Mma Ramotswe scratched her head. 'Three kilometres an hour?' she ventured. 'Maybe less in places where it is very sandy.'

'Then we are at least two hours from that road,' said Mma Makutsi. She looked at her watch. 'And now, Mma, it is almost four o'clock. We would get back to the road at about six o'clock, just as it is becoming dark.'

Neither of them said anything. There had been a conversation about lions only a short time ago, and they were both thinking the same thing. Mma Ramotswe looked at Mma Makutsi, who looked first at the ground and then at the sky.

Mma Ramotswe cleared her throat. 'People say that you should never leave your vehicle when it breaks down,' she said. 'If you do, then when the search party arrives, the searchers find the car but they don't find you.'

182

'If there is a search party,' said Mma Makutsi.

Mma Ramotswe looked around them. It was often the case that a landscape that appeared to be empty was not; human habitation could be found in unexpected places – a single hut tucked away here, a collection of dwellings there; and there were paths between such places, bringing life to the landscape as arteries do to the body.

'Somebody may come along,' she said. 'I think that we should stay in case that happens.'

Mma Makutsi shook her head. 'There will be nobody, Mma. Who is going to come along here this close to sunset? No, we will not see anybody for a long time. Maybe days, Mma.'

As Mma Makutsi spoke, her voice faltered slightly, and Mma Ramotswe realised that her assistant was frightened.

'Don't be afraid, Mma Makutsi,' she said. 'There is nothing that can harm us out here. All we shall have to do is to wait until help comes along.' She tried to sound cheerful. 'And even if we spend the night out here, we shall be fine. We have water, and we also have food. And we shall be quite safe in the van. Lions cannot open doors, you know. They are not that clever.'

Mma Makutsi did not appreciate this mention of lions. 'Oh, please don't talk about lions, Mma. I am trying not to think about lions, and you keep talking about them.'

Mma Ramotswe laid a calming hand on Mma Makutsi's arm. 'I'm sorry, Mma, I should not have mentioned lions. I do not think that there are any lions round here. I shall not mention lions again.' She paused. 'We could make a fire, Mma. I have some newspaper and some matches. We could get a fire going and then we could have tea. That would help, I think.'

'Tea is always a big help,' said Mma Makutsi. 'I'll get some twigs and some wood and then we can make a fire. Maybe the smoke will attract attention and somebody will come.'

'That is a real possibility,' said Mma Ramotswe, pleased that Mma Makutsi seemed to be cheering up.

Mma Makutsi wandered off to retrieve a small branch that had fallen off an acacia tree. Part of the wood had been covered by a mud casing painstakingly put in place by termites; this she brushed off as she carried it back to the van. And it was while she was doing this that they heard the creaking sound of an approaching donkey cart.

'You see!' shouted Mma Makutsi. 'I told you that somebody would come.'

Mma Ramotswe was on the point of reminding her that she had said exactly the opposite, but decided not to spoil the moment. 'Well, there we are, Mma. We are no longer alone.'

The donkey cart was a rickety affair, cobbled together with ancient painted boards and a chassis that had once belonged to a motor vehicle of some sort – an incongruous union of wood and metal, but serviceable enough. This cart was twenty or thirty years old, and could be expected to last another few decades at least. Out here, where the rainfall was so slight and inconstant, rust was not a problem. More dangerous were the ants, with their appetite for wood, but these could be watched for and dealt with easily enough.

Riding in the cart, on a battered old red-leather seat saved from a car somewhere, was an elderly man. At the end of the reins he held were two donkeys, yoked side by side, pulling the cart with that somnolent acceptance – resignation, even – that marks their breed. Their steps, taken on small black hooves, were sure enough, but slow; they would be faster on the return journey, with the smell of home in their nostrils, but for the moment there was no rush.

Mma Ramotswe stepped out onto the track and raised her hand in greeting. The man riding the cart pulled on the reins, took off his hat and wiped his brow. She caught her breath: the hat was so like the hat that her father, the late Obed Ramotswe, had worn every day of his life after he had returned from Mochudi – or so it had seemed to her. The hat that they had tucked into his coffin to accompany him on that final journey to the grave; the hat that he had once lost on the road and that had been rescued by some stranger and placed on a wall where its owner might see it; that same shapeless hat that she had felt embarrassed about as a small girl – other girls' fathers having more modern hats – but that she had come to love as standing for everything that he, and indeed Botswana, stood for – decency, quiet, courtesy – the things that were slipping away in the world but that were remembered and pined for.

The man replaced his hat, tied up the reins of the cart and got down from his seat.

'I think you're stuck, Mma,' he said to Mma Ramotswe. 'This bit of sand is well known for this. Every time anybody comes along here they find that this sand wants them to stay and talk.'

Mma Ramotswe laughed. 'Maybe it is lonely, Rra.'

The man nodded. 'That could be, Mma. But maybe it is just thinking that it will remind people that four-wheel-drive trucks are the only way to travel out here – four-wheeled or ...' and here he pointed to the donkeys, which were eyeing Mma Ramotswe lugubriously, 'four-legged.'

Mma Ramotswe accepted the implicit censure graciously. 'You're right, Rra. My husband would agree with you. But my friend over here and I were very anxious to see Mma Potok-wani, and we came anyway. Now I have plenty of time to regret it.'

'We always have plenty of time to regret things,' said the man. 'I have been regretting everything for years and years.'

Mma Makutsi, who had been standing to the side, now came

forward and introduced herself. 'I am this lady's assistant ... associate. Could you help us, Rra? Soon it will be dark and—'

'My friend here is worried about lions,' interjected Mma Ramotswe.

'Lions?' The man chuckled. 'There are no lions here, Mma. You ask my donkeys – if they get a smell of a lion, even if the lion is far, far away, they run. No, there are no lions any more – not here. A day's walk over that way – over towards the Kalahari, yes, you get one or two lions. But not here.'

'A day or two's walk for us, or for a lion?' asked Mma Makutsi.

Mma Ramotswe made light of the question. 'It doesn't matter, Mma. He says there are no lions.'

'For us,' said the man, turning to Mma Makutsi. 'For a lion, two hours, maybe. Lions are very fast runners. Have you seen them running, Mma?'

Mma Makutsi thought for a moment. She had never seen a lion doing anything, not ever having come across one, but somehow she felt she knew how they ran.

'I know how they go,' she said. 'They lie down on their stomachs and creep along.'

The man frowned. 'No, that is only when they are stalking their prey, Mma. And that is a lioness. If you are walking through the bush, say, and a lioness sees you and decides that she will eat you, then she goes down like this and she walks on bended legs. That is so that her head doesn't stick up over the top of the grass. It means that nobody can see her. That is what lions like.' He paused, and gestured to the bush that stretched out behind the van. 'Over there, you see, that is a good place for a lioness to creep. Those little bushes would cover her and we wouldn't know that she was there, while all the time she's getting closer, closer.'

He turned back to face Mma Ramotswe. 'You said you were here to see Mma Potokwani, Mma?'

Mma Ramotswe smiled. 'That is so, Rra. She is our old friend, and she has her lands along there.'

'Oh, I know that,' said the man. 'She is my old friend too. In fact, she is the cousin of my brother's cousin, by a different mother. I have known her all my life.'

'Is she here, Rra?' asked Mma Makutsi.

The man pointed down the track. 'Yes, she is here. She came out yesterday. Nobody had been expecting her, but there she was. There is something wrong, I think, but she won't speak to the other ladies about it. My wife has asked her and she says that everything is all right. But it isn't.'

'No, Rra, you're right,' Mma Ramotswe. 'There is something very wrong. It's to do with her work.'

The man absorbed this. 'She can come back here. She has good fields. She could stay. She has many relatives out here, and they will look after her.' He turned to look at the van. 'But you cannot get to her place in that van, Mma. You will have to leave it here and walk. It is not far to her place now – just half an hour or so along that way.'

'But we can't leave the van stuck in the sand,' objected Mma Makutsi. 'How will we get back to Gaborone? We cannot walk.'

'We won't leave it in the sand,' said the man. 'I will help you pull it out, and then we will leave it here. You can collect it when you have finished visiting Mma Potokwani. It will be perfectly safe.'

Mma Ramotswe and Mma Makutsi looked at the donkeys. One of them, clearly older than the other, grey about the muzzle and the eyes, appeared to be asleep on his feet, his head drooping, indifferent to the flies that buzzed about what looked like an open sore on one of his ears.

'They are very strong,' said the man, intercepting the glance. 'They have pulled bigger vans out of there. You needn't worry, Mma.'

'I have some rope,' said Mma Ramotswe. 'Under the seat there is some rope that my husband put in there. We could use that, Rra.'

The man shook his head. 'I have my own, Mma. I always carry it because I know that I need it. We can use mine.'

He walked round to the back of the cart and extracted a length of rope from a box nailed to the boards. Then he detached the yoke from the front of the cart and began to cajole the two donkeys into position in front of the tilting nose of the tiny white van. Mma Ramotswe was impressed by his businesslike manner – this was a man, she decided, who knew what he was doing. 'You get in and steer, Mma,' he said to her. 'Otherwise the wheels will point in the wrong direction and you'll go further into the sand. Steer back into the middle of the road.'

Mma Ramotswe returned to the van and eased herself into the driver's seat. The man now addressed Mma Makutsi, suggesting that she push at the back of the van while he pulled on the yoke at the front and persuaded the donkeys to take the strain. Then they both got into position and the man started to shout at the donkeys.

Inside the cab, Mma Ramotswe felt the van move – but only slightly. Then, as the man gave a resounding smack to one of the donkeys, it moved again, rolling forwards as the wheels were dragged through the sand; only to stop and then roll back the few precious inches it had just achieved.

'Stop,' called out the man, both to the donkeys and to Mma Makutsi.

'I have stopped,' shouted Mma Makutsi from the back. 'It's too heavy, Rra.'

The man was perplexed. 'They are very strong ...' He trailed off. He looked at Mma Ramotswe. 'Perhaps, Mma, it might be better if we asked the other lady ...' He gave a toss of the head in the direction of Mma Makutsi. 'Perhaps we could ask that lady to steer while you pushed. It's just that she's quite a bit less ...'

Mma Ramotswe was polite but firm. 'Traditionally built.'

'That is right,' said the man. 'She is a bit thinner, and you are ...'

'Traditionally built,' prompted Mma Ramotswe again. 'Don't worry, Rra. I am not ashamed of being who I am.'

The man made an elaborate show of rejecting the very thought. 'Of course, Mma, of course. It's just that the donkeys are a bit old – that one in particular – and they are finding it a bit difficult to drag a van *and* a ... a traditionally built lady. With the other lady at the wheel, I think we can do it.'

Mma Makutsi, who had been following this exchange, smiled as she made her way round to the door. But she said nothing; that would have been rude, of course, and would have demonstrated a complete lack of feminine loyalty. Men, she knew, did not understand these matters.

'You must be careful not to get *too* thin, Mma,' muttered Mma Ramotswe, as she yielded her place in the van.

Mma Makutsi smiled. 'Mma, I am already becoming a bit traditionally built. I do not think there is any danger of that.'

The man now returned to his position with the donkeys while Mma Ramotswe leaned up against the back of the van, digging her feet into the sand and preparing to apply her weight in the hoped-for direction of travel. Already, as she did so, the van moved slightly, even before the donkeys had engaged.

'I'll count to three,' called the man. 'Then we'll pull and you push, Mma. One, two, three!'

This time the reaction of the van was immediate, and Mma Ramotswe had to act quickly to avoid falling over backwards.

'That's it!' shouted the man from the front. '*Pula, pula, pula!*'

Pula, pula, pula! was the cry of triumph, of joy, that was universal in Botswana. It meant *rain, rain, rain* – just the right cry for a dry country that lived for the day that the first life-giving rains arrived – that day of ominous purple skies, and heat, and the wind that precedes the first drops of water splattering and dancing on the baked ground. *Pula, pula, pula!*

With the van free of the sand, Mma Makutsi decided to start the engine. She did this with her foot pressed down hard on the accelerator pedal – she was no driver, really – and the engine raced in response. For the donkeys, yoked so closely to this unusual burden, this was a source of sudden alarm, and they responded by backing sharply against their restraining straps. One of them, the older one, stumbled, attempted to regain its footing, failed to do so and then collapsed.

The man gave a shout. 'Turn the engine off, Mma! Turn it off!'

Mma Makutsi complied, her hands shooting up to her mouth in a gesture of horrified realisation. 'Oh, Rra,' she cried. 'I have killed your donkey.'

The man struggled with the straps that held the fallen donkey in the yoke. As he did so, the other donkey brayed suddenly, a mournful, broken sound. It took a few moments, but when the straps were released, the donkey sagged back into the sand, its chest heaving. It moved its head as if trying to get up, but then lowered it again and fixed the sky with a stare of reproach. Mma Makutsi, distraught over what she had done, was now joined by Mma Ramotswe. The donkey's eyes, Mma Ramotswe found herself thinking, were so beautiful; flecked, almost golden, and rimmed with delicate black eyelashes. It was an incongruous thought – this admiration of the beauty of a creature that seemed to be on the point of death.

Mma Makutsi was now in tears. 'Oh, Mma, what have I done?'

'It was an accident,' said Mma Ramotswe gently. 'It was not your fault, Mma. You were not to know.'

The man, who had been bending over the donkey, now rose and walked over to his cart. He seemed to be curiously unconcerned by what had happened, simply saying, 'He will get up. He will know we are going home now.'

He was right. The donkey now suddenly heaved a sigh and staggered to his feet.

'See, Mma,' said Mma Ramotswe. 'No harm done.'

'He is very lazy,' snapped the man. 'He is always doing this.'

'Maybe he is tired,' said Mma Ramotswe.

'Maybe,' said the man. 'But I'm tired too, Mma. We are all tired.' He looked about him. 'There is so much sand.'

She thought about what he said. Perhaps Mma Potokwani was tired too. Perhaps there were just too many orphans, just as there was too much sand. Perhaps she had had enough of helping. If that were true, then she wondered whether she should be seeking her out here, or whether she should leave her in peace. It would be easy to go back now and leave Mma Potokwani at her lands, but then she reminded herself that Mma Potokwani had never once spoken in the past about retiring or giving up. No, the defeatist Mma Potokwani was not the real Mma Potokwani. The real Mma Potokwani was a fighter.

With the donkeys back in harness, Mma Ramotswe reached into her bag to retrieve a fifty-*pula* note. 'You have been very good, Rra. This is a present for you.'

The man looked at the money. 'You do not have to pay me, Mma. I wouldn't leave anybody here. But since you are so kind ...' He reached out and took the money, which he quickly tucked into the breast pocket of his shirt. 'Since you are so kind, I will take you and this other lady to Mma Potokwani's place. You should leave the van here because it gets even sandier later on. You can come back for it when you want to go home.'

They collected a few necessities from the van, which Mma Ramotswe had driven on to a piece of firm ground beside the track. Then, climbing on to the back of the cart, they started the journey down the track, the same journey that people had made countless times over the years, back in the time of their parents, their grandparents; in the same way, in the same quiet, at the same pace, closer to the world than in the metal cocoons in which we now travel. There was birdsong, and the gentlest of breezes; and they heard the donkeys, the noise made by their hooves against the ground, the sound of their breathing, their sighs.

Chapter Seventeen

Have You Had Any Injections Recently?

With Mma Makutsi away, Phuti Radiphuti felt at a loose end. He had very rapidly become accustomed to marriage – so rapidly, in fact, that on this first occasion on which he had been left alone, he found himself unable to settle. Mma Makutsi had left him a stew for his dinner and this required only to be warmed up, but Phuti felt disinclined to eat by himself in a kitchen that he now associated with the presence of his new wife. On impulse rather than on any serious reflection, he telephoned the aunt with whom he had stayed during his recent convalescence. This aunt, who had done her best to discourage his marriage, believing that Mma Makutsi was unworthy of her nephew and motivated, too, by a jealousy that would have prevented her from approving of any prospective wife for Phuti, had not attended the wedding. She had observed it from afar, though, sitting in the brown car with its mean-spirited narrow windows and watching the reception tents through a pair of binoculars. Phuti had seen her car and had started over towards it in the hope of persuading his aunt to bring hostilities to an end and join them at the wedding party; he had not succeeded in speaking to her, though, as she had seen him approaching and had driven off at speed.

This had not prevented him from sending her a piece of wedding cake and a photograph of himself in his wedding suit, inscribed *To my dear aunt, from your faithful nephew, Phuti.* With a more forgiving woman, this might have resulted in a letter of thanks, or at least a message, but neither had been forthcoming. Phuti did not take offence – it was not in his nature to do so – and now, ignoring her previous bad behaviour, he called his aunt and asked her whether he could possibly come for dinner that evening. 'Just me,' he said quickly. 'I shall be alone.'

The aunt had been quick to agree to this self-invitation. She had been hoping to see him but had been unable to swallow her pride sufficiently to make the first move. And this reference to being on his own intrigued her: was it too much to hope that he had tired of the whole business of being married to Mma Makutsi and was keen to revert to bachelor status, preferably living with her and occupying the bedroom in which he had stayed on his last visit? She could feed him up again – as she had done during his convalescence – and make him happy. It would be better, far better, for him to be away from that dreadful woman with her large round glasses and her Bobonong ways.

It was not without trepidation that Phuti parked his car at the aunt's front gate that evening and began his way up the short path to her front door. The last time I was here, he thought, I was a single man. And now I am a married man with a talented and attractive wife. I was a boy back then; now I am a man.

He glanced at the garden in the fading light of evening.

There were the paw-paw trees from which his aunt had picked the heavy yellow fruit she had served to him with lumpy custard. There was the tree that he had climbed when he visited his aunt as a twelve-year-old; the branch on which he had strung a swing that had broken at a crucial moment and sent another boy, a friend from school, sailing through the air to a broken leg and three days in hospital. And there, parked beside the house, in the position it had occupied for so many years, was the unfriendly brown car with its pinched windows and its sign that said *Don't Waste Water*. That sign had always been there, although his aunt, as far as he could make out, had never been particularly abstemious when it came to water. The patch of grass outside her house was always liberally irrigated, and he had noticed that the baths she ran for herself almost reached the rim of the tub.

He knocked at the door and called out, *'Ko, ko,* Auntie!' From somewhere within the house he heard her footsteps approaching and then the door opened. Seeing Phuti on the doorstep, the aunt opened her arms to embrace him. *I am forgiven*, he thought.

'Phuti!' exclaimed the aunt. 'Now you have come back to see your auntie.'

He stepped into the house and allowed her to give him a hug.

'Let me see you,' she said, standing back. 'You're looking so handsome, Phuti! Such a waste, such a waste.'

He recoiled momentarily at the words. In what way was it a waste for him to look handsome, not that he thought he looked handsome at all?

'You are well, Auntie?'

She made a non-committal gesture. 'I am well, and then I am not well.'

He looked concerned. 'You have been ill?'

'Not exactly ill, Phuti. But then, not well either. It is not easy,

195

being alive these days, what with everything changing. But we must not talk about me, we must talk about you. You are the important one now, not me. Tell me what has happened.'

As she asked this question, she led him into the sitting room. In the middle of the room several large armchairs were positioned around a table on which a dictionary, a world atlas and an arrangement of red plastic flowers had been placed. There was a stale smell in the air.

'Sit down, Phuti.' It was more of a command than an invitation, but Phuti was used to his aunt's adopting this tone and he obeyed without murmur.

She fixed him with a concerned stare. 'You are looking very thin,' she began. 'Here and here.' She pointed to her neck and stomach. 'Those are the places where it always shows, Phuti.' She narrowed her eyes. 'You're not getting enough food, are you?'

Phuti held up his hands in denial. 'No, no, Auntie. I am getting too much food, really. I am putting on weight, I think.'

She shook her head. 'That cannot be, Phuti. Your neck is very thin, now, and look at your trousers: they are hanging on you like an empty sack. You are very thin.'

Phuti struggled with his feelings of annoyance. It was quite obvious to him what the implication of these comments was: his new wife was no cook – or at least, that is what his aunt was trying to suggest without actually saying it.

'I am eating very well, Auntie,' he said. 'Grace is a very good cook, and she is giving me plenty to eat.'

The aunt affected surprise that she should have thought that Mma Makutsi was anything but an expert cook. 'Of course she is,' she said. 'Of course she . . . ' She struggled, as if finding it difficult to remember the name.

'Grace. Grace Makutsi.'

'Of course, Grace . . . Grace Ma . . . '

'Makutsi.'

'Yes, that woman.' She looked down at the floor and frowned. 'Makutsi? Where is that name from, I wonder? It is not from any-where near here, I think. Perhaps it is South African. They have some very odd names over there.'

'She is a Motswana, Auntie. She comes from Bobonong.'

The aunt transferred her gaze to the window, looking out into the distance in the direction, perhaps, of Bobonong. 'That is far away. I do not know any people up there. Maybe they are nice people, but how can you tell when you don't know any of them? There are many people in China, but I cannot say whether they are nice people or not because I do not know any of them.'

Phuti felt his cheeks burning. He always felt like that when his aunt said such things. And he knew that if he closed his eyes and counted slowly, he worried less about it. But now he could not do that; Bobonong and China? What had China got to do with it? Nothing, he thought. Nothing at all.

'Bobonong is in Botswana,' he said. 'The people who live there are all Batswana – same as you and me, Auntie. They are no dif-ferent.'

'I did not say they were,' said the aunt. 'All I said is that I do not know any of those people, apart from Gracious . . .'

'Grace.'

'Yes, apart from her.'

The aunt sniffed. 'You must eat more,' she said. 'It is not good for a man to become too thin.'

'I am eating very well, Auntie. You mustn't worry about me.'

The aunt looked pained. 'How can I stop worrying about you, when you are my own nephew? How can I stop worrying about you when you go off and marry somebody I don't know and whose people we've never heard about?'

197

Phuti did not answer, and the aunt continued. 'And now where is she? Gone away, I believe, and you have nothing to eat. Well, you always have a home to come back to. There is that same room you stayed in – I have changed nothing. And you will get fatter and stronger if you stay here – where you belong.'

'But Grace is only away for one night,' said Phuti mildly. 'She is on business with Mma Ramotswe. They have gone—'

'Oh, that Mma Ramotswe! That fat lady who calls herself a private detective but who sits in her office all day eating doughnuts! That is what they say, you know. You'll have to be careful, Phuti, if Gracious eats doughnuts with that woman all day then your bed will break. You just remember that.'

Phuti closed his eyes. It was easier to talk to his aunt with his eyes closed, he had decided. Not only did this help him to say what he wanted to say, but it also had the effect of disconcerting her, which, he found, was of some help.

'We mustn't talk about Grace too much,' he said. 'She is a good wife to me and I am very happy. That is what I want you to know, Auntie: I am very happy.'

The aunt sniffed. 'I'm glad to hear that. But if you ever are unhappy, you know where to come. That is all I will say for the time being.' She sniffed again. 'And why are your eyes closed, Phuti? Did you not sleep enough last night?'

Phuti opened his eyes. 'I slept well, Auntie. But now I'm hungry, and the thought of your delicious cooking is making my stomach jump up and down.'

The aunt smiled coquettishly. 'You're right to remind me, Phuti. I have some very good stew that I am going to give you.' There was a pause – the slightest pause. Then: 'Far better than anything you get at your place, I think, but let's not talk too much about that . . .'

The stew, when it was served, proved to be every bit as good as the aunt had claimed. Over the dinner table, watching Phuti tackle his second helping, she seemed to mellow, and the conversation moved on to less controversial subjects. The aunt had been to Lobatse to visit a relative who had been ill; she had found a new pair of shoes in a shop and had bought them because they had been reduced in price by sixty per cent. She had received a telephone call that morning from somebody who had got the wrong number; her neighbour had been bitten by a dog and had been obliged to have anti-rabies injections – 'just in case' – but knowing the neighbour as she did, it was almost certainly the neighbour's fault rather than the dog's. 'They should give that dog a course of injections, if you ask me, Phuti. You know what that woman is like – I've told you, haven't I?' And then, 'Have you had any injections recently, Phuti? I must go to the doctor myself some day and get an injection.'

They finished the meal and the aunt made a pot of tea. She served this on the veranda, where it was cooler, and from where they had a good view of the neighbour's house, now a dark shape in the night. 'You never know what you're going to see going on in there,' said the aunt. 'Sometimes they leave a light on and forget that it is on. I have seen some things that I cannot speak about, you know. Even if you ask me, I cannot speak about them.'

There was an expectant silence, as if she was waiting for Phuti to ask her. But he did not, and the conversation moved on to the new house.

'I hear that you have that Mr Putumelo building you a house,' said the aunt. 'I know his wife. She is a big lady in the church, although you never see him there.'

'Maybe that is because he is very busy,' said Phuti. 'Some people are too busy to go to church.'

'That's true,' said the aunt. 'I myself cannot go every Sunday, because I am so busy.' She reached out to refill Phuti's cup. 'He is building his own house, you know. It's very close to my butcher's house. The butcher says it is a very fine house.'

'That's what you'd expect of a builder,' observed Phuti. 'I have never known a builder who lived in a not-so-good house. They know what makes a good place. They know those things, Auntie.'

The aunt nodded. 'That's very true. Yes, they know. The butcher told me that this house is made of very high-class bricks. They are imported, he says.'

Phuti was not surprised by this. 'He likes bricks, that builder. He recommended that we use bricks, too.'

'Mind you,' the aunt continued, 'I do not know where he finds the money. The butcher says that he has a big bill run up with him, and when he talked to him about it he told him that he is finding things very difficult at the moment. He says that there is not very much work, and that he has a big overdraft with the bank.'

This did not sound unfamiliar to Phuti. 'People often say that,' he remarked. 'They say that their business is not doing well when it really is. They do not want to make other people jealous.'

The aunt considered this. 'Maybe, but not in this case. The reverend at the church said something about them. He said that they were in financial difficulties and we should pray that the Lord brings them some money. The wife must have told him that.'

Phuti closed his eyes. Financial difficulties. Bricks. The Lord. Houses. There was so much to think about, and the thoughts came crowding in on him. Then one line of thought, in particular, emerged from the rest. *How could the builder be building a house for himself when he had no money? How did one do that? With the Lord's help?*

*

While Phuti was wrestling with the question of Mr Clarkson Putumelo's new house, Mma Makutsi, along with Mma Ramotswe and Mma Potokwani, was sitting around an open fire, under the stars. They had finished the meal Mma Potokwani had prepared for them – a stew of beans, carrots and tomato soup, all poured over a base of freshly cooked pap. Mma Ramotswe had pronounced it delicious, and Mma Makutsi had enthusiastically concurred. Mma Potokwani had accepted their compliments, but had added a remark to the effect that she would have more time to cook now that 'nobody had any use for her'. This had been vigorously refuted by Mma Ramotswe, who had insisted that of all the citizens of Botswana – all two million of them – Mma Potokwani was without question one of the most useful. Mma Makutsi, without prompting from Mma Ramotswe, had agreed. 'Nobody is useless,' she said heatedly, 'and you are less useless than nobody else, Mma. Definitely.'

This remark was greeted with silence while Mma Ramotswe and Mma Potokwani had tried to work out what it meant. The spirit in which it was made, though, was clear enough, and Mma Potokwani simply thanked her. 'You have always been very kind to me, Mma,' she said. 'Always.'

'And you to me,' said Mma Makutsi.

Mma Ramotswe knew that this was not entirely true – indeed it was completely false – but was pleased that such good spirit was abroad, and said nothing to contradict what had been expressed. New friendships can be every bit as strong as old friendships, and of course became old friendships in due course. She thought of this in silence, watching the flickering light of the fire play across the faces of the other two women; three friends sitting out in the darkness in the immensity of the surrounding bush, with the Kalahari a stone's throw away and the stars, silver-white fields of them, hanging high above, so dizzying, so humbling to look at.

'No,' said Mma Potokwani after a while. 'I have made up my mind, you see. I have stopped working, and I am going to do some things for myself – things I've always wanted to do.'

Mma Ramotswe understood this. She knew a number of people who had stopped working with the same thing in mind, and they had told her that the decision had been the best decision of their lives. One had opened a poultry farm and now supplied eggs and chickens to many of the major shops in Gaborone; another, a mechanic friend of Mr J. L. B. Matekoni's, had taken to restoring old cars and had already sold a 1956 Pontiac to a collector over the border. There were so many things that you could do if you simply had the time, but most of us left it too late.

'I can see that,' she said. 'What will you do, Mma?'

There was a silence. Mma Makutsi looked at Mma Potokwani with interest, as did Mma Ramotswe.

'Well . . .' Mma Potokwani began. 'Well . . .'

'You will be very busy,' Mma Makutsi suggested helpfully. 'All those things . . .'

Mma Potokwani pursed her lips. 'Many things,' she began. 'There are many things.'

They waited. Mma Potokwani poked a stick into the fire, making a few short-lived sparks fly heavenwards. Yes, thought Mma Ramotswe; yes, there are so many other things that might come to mind, but not if you have given your life to orphaned children; not if you have spent every waking hour working out how to advance their interests, how to procure some little benefit, some little treat that would make each of them feel loved, special; not if you had given to those same children all the love that a large – traditionally built – frame could muster; not then, not then was there anything that you wanted to do but to continue with what you had always been doing, which was to look after those children.

Mma Ramotswe decided to break the silence. 'But the most important thing to you, Mma, is running the orphan farm. That's what you really like doing, isn't it?'

Mma Potokwani did not answer: she did not need to, as her expression said everything that needed to be said.

'I thought so,' said Mma Ramotswe. 'And that's why I think you should come back with us.'

Mma Potokwani looked up sharply. 'No. I have left now. My deputy will run the place until they get somebody else.'

'Then he will have won,' muttered Mma Makutsi. 'That man will have won. Bullies often do.'

Mma Potokwani turned to look at her. 'Why do you say that, Mma?'

'Because it's true, isn't it? Bullies often win. They know that people are not prepared to stand up to them, and so they win.' She looked at Mma Ramotswe for confirmation. 'And there are many men who bully women. You agree with that, don't you, Mma Ramotswe.'

Mma Ramotswe's reply was cautious. 'Well, sometimes . . . But remember, Mma, there are many men who are not bullies.'

'Of course,' said Mma Makutsi. 'Phuti is not like that. Mr J. L. B. Matekoni is not like that. And your husband, Mma Potokwani, I have heard he is not like that either . . . '

'He is certainly not like that,' said Mma Potokwani. 'Rra Potokwani is very kind. He does not go around pushing people about.'

No, said a small voice, *you do all the pushing, don't you?*

Mma Makutsi shot a glance down in the direction of her shoes. *Sorry, boss, we couldn't resist that.*

She looked at the other two women: had they heard too? Mma Ramotswe had a slightly puzzled expression on her face – it was possible that she might have heard – but Mma Potokwani seemed

203

unaffected. Of course she would not have heard, Mma Makutsi reminded herself: there was nothing to hear. These apparent interventions by her shoes were nothing but her own imagination: a sort of conversation with herself – that was all.

So you think, boss!

Mma Ramotswe now continued. 'But even if not all men are like that, at least some are. They insist on getting their way on everything, even on the question of whether children should eat at home or in big rooms ...'

'Horrible big rooms,' said Mma Potokwani.

'Yes, horrible big rooms,' agreed Mma Ramotswe. 'And how will they get to know each other and their house-mother if they do not eat together, in a kitchen? How will they do that?'

Mma Potokwani became animated. 'That's just what I said! And it's just what the house-mothers themselves said. All of them. They said: we want to feed the children in the houses. We want to do the cooking ourselves, in our own kitchen, with our own pots.'

'Of course they said that, Mma. And they said that because they knew what they were talking about. And then some man comes along – a man who probably has never cooked so much as a potato in his life – this man comes along and says, *I know best.*'

'Not one potato,' fumed Mma Potokwani.

Mma Ramotswe glanced at Mma Makutsi, who was smiling. 'Of course, if people – if women – let men like that get away with it, then they'll do it again, and again, and again. Soon they'll have all of us eating in big halls from big kitchens – just to save money.'

'That will not be possible,' said Mma Makutsi. 'People would never agree ...'

'I do not mean that exactly,' said Mma Ramotswe patiently. 'I am just pointing out how things could get worse.' She turned to

Mma Potokwani. 'So it's quite important, Mma, that we don't give up too early. Not while there's still a chance.'

Mma Potokwani gave Mma Ramotswe a searching look. 'Do you think there's still a chance, Mma? Do you really think so?'

Mma Ramotswe had not been able to come up with anything about Mr Ditso Ditso that could be used to get him off the board, and she was not sure that she would. But of course there was a chance, and there was something that told her that she had already found what it was but just did not realise it. It was a curious feeling, but it was there, and it was enough to make her want to persist.

'I think so,' she said.

Mma Potokwani sighed. 'So you want me to go back?'

Mma Ramotswe nodded. 'Yes, that's what we want, Mma.'

Mma Potokwani hesitated before she gave her reply. 'If that's what you want, Mma, then . . . then I'll do it.'

'Good,' said Mma Ramotswe.

'Yes,' said Mma Makutsi firmly. 'Good.'

They sat in silence after that. Later, though, shortly before they retired to bed in Mma Potokwani's large sleeping hut, shared with two young Potokwani nieces who had been helping in the fields, Mma Ramotswe whispered to Mma Makutsi, 'She's still not herself, Mma. She says she hasn't given up, but I think she has.'

Mma Makutsi was dismayed to hear this; she had been more optimistic. 'But she said that she's coming back. She said that . . . '

'People say things,' said Mma Ramotswe. 'But when they're in that frame of mind, they don't mean them. The lips say one thing, the heart says another. Or says nothing.'

The lips say one thing, the heart says another. Those words echoed in Mma Makutsi's mind as she drifted off to sleep that night. Outside, in the night, a dog barked at some shadow, some creature in the night. *The lips say one thing, the heart says another.* She wondered whether that was true, or whether it just *sounded* true. And what did it mean to say that the heart said nothing? Were there people whose heart really did say nothing? And if there were, who exactly were they? The dog gave another bark, followed by a yelp. Then there was silence. She opened her eyes in the darkness. Nothing.

Chapter Eighteen

A Lawyer Spills Tea Over His Shirt

They returned the next day, a Saturday, arriving back in Gaborone in the middle of the afternoon. On Sunday Mma Ramotswe went to church at the Anglican Cathedral, as she always did, and helped with the tea afterwards, an opportunity for people to chat, to inspect at closer quarters what others were wearing and to discuss – and if necessary criticise – the day's sermon. One of the members of the congregation, an Indian accountant from Kerala who had lived in Botswana for twenty years or so, was going home to India for a daughter's wedding. He told Mma Ramotswe about the wedding plans, which involved, he revealed with a modicum of pride, several hundred people travelling from all over India, all wanting hotels and feasts and special treatment. She listened to this with sympathy – weddings were rarely simple, and Indian weddings, it seemed to her, were even more complicated and fraught with difficulty than their Botswana counterparts – but she was not really concentrating. Nor did she pay attention when Bishop Mwamba himself came up to speak to her and told her about a book he had been reading that he thought she might enjoy, if she had the time.

'But I know how busy you are, Mma Ramotswe,' the Bishop said, 'what with your business and all those investigations, and so on.'

She nodded politely. He was right, but it was the *so on* that was the trouble now, and in particular that bit of the *so on* that was made up of Mma Potokwani's troubles. And then there was Fanwell, whose trial was due to take place the following day.

'Yes, Bishop. There are many things to worry about in this life. Many things.'

The Bishop smiled. 'But we must not let those overwhelm us,' he said. The smile faded, to be replaced by a look of concern. 'You are all right, aren't you, Mma Ramotswe?'

She looked up at the sky. The man to whom she was talking, she reminded herself, had major concerns to think about. He knew the issues of Africa, its sorrows. He knew all about the burdens and difficulties of those who struggled to get by in countries where there was cruelty and oppression. It was all very well for her to stand here drinking tea in a peaceful and well-ordered country, but what about those who did not have that luxury? And should she then worry him with her petty concerns – very small ones, really – when there were many weightier things occupying his attention? No, she thought. No. 'Everything is all right, Bishop,' she said.

The Bishop was tapped on the shoulder by one of the members of the choir and detached himself from Mma Ramotswe. She helped a few people to tea, poured another cup for herself, and then looked around the group of people who were still talking to one another in the church courtyard. Mma Ramotswe felt that she needed to catch up on local news. There were always the newspapers, of course, but the *real* news, a complete picture of what was really happening, could only be gleaned from actual conversation with people. It was ordinary people who knew what ___ the editors of news- ___ roots, the nearer one ___ ced the effect of what ___ them, the more com-

___ ation. These were all ___ that hour on a Sunday ___ it more difficult still ___ more difficult when ___ e all human, just as she was, and the real issue was whether they were doing their best. Mma Ramotswe felt that as long as you did your best, then it was not too important if you fell below the standards that others might expect of you. What mattered was doing your best and then, if your best turned out to be not very good, at least admitting it and trying a bit harder next time.

There were some people, of course, who clearly had no intention of doing their best – Violet Sephotho, for instance, but that was another matter . . . Fanwell's trial: that was the thing she would have to think about now. Poor Fanwell – how would he be feeling now? She imagined that he would not sleep that night – how could one be expected to sleep, knowing that at nine o'clock the next morning one would be standing in the dock facing the full force of the law of Botswana?

She looked down into her cup. If only she could speak to the magistrate, whoever he was, and tell him what sort of young man

Fanwell was; of course he would be reading the letter that Mr J. L. B. Matekoni had so painstakingly drafted that would say much about Fanwell's character – and she had drafted one too – but it was one thing to receive a letter, quite another to have somebody express her feelings to you in person. If she were to be given five minutes – only five minutes – with the magistrate, she would explain to him that it was simply impossible that Fanwell would knowingly fix a stolen car. He was not like that; it was just not in his character. She would say, 'Rra, I beg you. Rra, I beg you: listen to what I am saying. I have met many wicked people in my work, Rra – just as you have – and I'm telling you, Rra, from the bottom of my heart I do not think this young man could have done what they say he has done.'

She sighed, and took a sip of her tea. Magistrates must hear that sort of thing day in, day out. They could be forgiven if their eyes glazed over, or if they looked out of the window in the face of such pleas. Everyone has a mother who believes in them; everyone has somebody who says that they would never do anything wrong; of course they have. And the job of a magistrate was not to let everybody off just because their mother, or their aunt, or their employer spoke highly of them.

Again her eyes moved over the members of the group. It was interesting, she thought, to see how different people held their teacups: that woman over there, for example – the woman who sometimes arranged the flowers and whose daughter had married that man whose brother was a pilot with Air Botswana – that woman held her cup round the rim, ignoring the handle. And the man she was talking to was balancing the saucer on his palm as if his hand were a table; it was very strange. And the man next to him, the one in the dark suit ... he was a lawyer. She stopped; a possibility had occurred to her. He was a lawyer.

Putting down her empty teacup, Mma Ramotswe negotiated

her way past the milling members of the congregation until she was standing beside the lawyer. He was in the process of bidding farewell to the woman to whom he was talking; having done so, he turned to Mma Ramotswe.

'So, Mma, how are you?'

She might have replied that her world, in various respects, was falling down about her head, but she did not. 'Everything is fine, Rra, and you?'

Everything was fine in his world too, he said; indeed, it could not be better – he had recently won a major case and his client had given him a large Brahmin bull as a present. 'Your late father would have approved of this bull, Mma Ramotswe. He is a very fine beast, and we will breed many good cattle from him.'

Mma Ramotswe expressed her satisfaction at this. 'A good bull is better than—'

'A bad bull,' the lawyer chipped in, and laughed. 'There is no doubt, Mma Ramotswe, that it's worth paying for the best.'

She smiled at this, but ruefully. This man was a good lawyer – everybody said that – and his clients obviously paid well for his services. Fanwell's lawyer, by contrast, was reputedly hopeless, and yet Mr J. L. B. Matekoni had already paid handsomely for him.

'My husband has a young mechanic,' she said. 'He works in the garage – a very good young man. But unfortunately he has got into a bit of trouble.'

The lawyer shook his head. 'Young men and trouble – those two things go together, Mma.'

'Yes, Rra.'

The lawyer gave her a searching look. 'Are you wanting me to help him, Mma?'

She looked at him hopefully. 'He has a lawyer,' she began. 'But I am not sure about him.'

'Well, in that case there won't be anything I can do, Mma. Lawyers are not allowed to steal clients from other lawyers. I'd get into big trouble if I did that.' He took a sip of his tea. 'I imagine it's the same with private detectives. You cannot take another detective's clients, can you?'

She wanted to explain to him that there were no other private detectives in Botswana, but he had more to say.

'That can be a good thing, I suppose, but it can also be a bad thing. Particularly if you get a bad lawyer. But I'm sure this person you have is fine. Tell me, who is he? Or she?'

Mma Ramotswe gave him the name just as he was taking another sip of his tea. She was not prepared for his reaction, which was to splutter, almost to choke, sending a spurt of tea down his chin and on to his shirt-front.

'Oh, Rra, I'm sorry. Please let me.' She fished for her handkerchief to wipe at the tea stain.

'I'm all right, Mma Ramotswe. Don't worry. It's just that ... well, it's just that that man is absolutely useless. I know I shouldn't speak about a fellow member of my profession like that, but I can think of nothing else to say. He knows no law at all, Mma – none. In fact, none of us knows how he ever managed to get his LLB in the first place. Maybe they're putting law degrees in cornflakes boxes these days.'

There was little comfort in this conversation. She had been hoping that somehow this man might offer to help, yet he seemed to have precluded the possibility. But then he lowered his voice and said, 'Don't tell anybody this, but the young man could fire him. Then, once he has no lawyer, he could contact me and I could see what I could do.'

Mma Ramotswe reached for his hand and squeezed it. 'Oh, Rra, that is such good news.'

'When is he due to appear in court?'

212

'Tomorrow. Nine o'clock.'

The lawyer recoiled. 'Tomorrow? Oh dear, Mma, that will not be possible then. He cannot dismiss his lawyer at the last moment, because I won't have time to read the papers in the case, and anyway, I am busy for the next three weeks. I have a big case for the Government.'

'So he'll have to stick with the lawyer he has?'

'I'm afraid so, Mma. And maybe it won't be too bad. You never know with the law. It's a bit of a lottery, as they say: you win some and you lose some.' His tone was sympathetic. 'This young man, of course, might be one of the losers.'

She thanked him. 'You have been very kind, Rra.'

'I'm sorry I couldn't do anything, Mma, but I hope all goes well . . . if he's innocent. If he's guilty, well, then he's guilty.'

She felt she could not argue with that. Perhaps that was why this lawyer had the reputation he did: because he put things succinctly, in a way that anybody could understand.

Mr J. L. B. Matekoni drove Fanwell to court the next day in his garage truck, with Mma Ramotswe and Mma Makutsi following in the white van. The magistrate's court was in a handsome new building of an open disposition that in no way spoke of the distressing events which it witnessed daily: the accounts of petty crime, the tears and protests of litigants, the outrage and the untruths – in short, the business of the average court. This court stood on the road to the jail, a fact that both Mma Ramotswe and Mma Makutsi could not help thinking about as they drove there that morning but also secretly hoped would not be relevant to Fanwell.

From behind the wheel of the truck, Mr J. L. B. Matekoni dispensed a few final bits of advice. 'When you speak,' he said, 'look at the magistrate as you give the answers. Don't look at him cheekily – don't stare – but look at him as you would look at a priest or a headmaster: with respect.'

Fanwell nodded miserably. 'I will, boss.'

'And here's another thing. The person who's going to be asking you questions is called the prosecutor. He may try to make it look as if you're lying.'

'But I'm not lying,' protested Fanwell.

'I know that,' said Mr J. L. B. Matekoni. 'But you have to remember that the people in the court don't know that. So what I was going to say to you is this: you mustn't lose your temper with that person, whatever he asks you. You just reply very calmly and say, "I am telling the truth, Rra." That is what you must say. Understand?'

Mr J. L. B. Matekoni glanced at his young employee. His heart went out to him – it really did; sitting there in that ill-fitting suit with a white collar and tie, and all the time inside he must be shaking and trembling. Poor, poor boy – and he really was just a boy, this young man; he may have been in his early twenties, but at that moment he looked not much more than fifteen. And he had worked so hard and been so good to his demanding family.

'I want you to know something, Fanwell,' he said. 'Whatever happens today – whether they listen to you or not – Mma Ramotswe and I both believe you. And we will never lose our faith in you. We will not. You remember that.'

Fanwell said nothing.

'Did you hear that, Fanwell?'

The young man nodded. 'I'm scared, boss.' His voice was small and timid.

'Of course you're scared. Who wouldn't be? But you be brave now, Fanwell. You do that for me. You be brave. And remember what I said.'

They drew up in front of the court, where Mr J. L. B.

214

Matekoni parked the truck. Mma Ramotswe's van drew up next to the truck, and the four of them walked into the court.

'Charlie's already there,' whispered Mma Makutsi as they approached the public seats. 'He said he would be here early.'

They slid into one of the bench seats, with Mr J. L. B. Matekoni sitting next to Charlie. Fanwell had reported to the office and was now in the custody of the police, along with a handful of others awaiting trial. They glimpsed him as he was led away and Mma Ramotswe's heart lurched. *He's too young for this*, she thought. *He's far too young.*

The next to arrive was the lawyer, who was wearing a black gown over his suit and was carrying a pile of dishevelled papers. Mma Makutsi looked at these papers critically, and Mma Ramotswe, noticing this, realised what lay behind this critical look: it was a filing issue. She closed her eyes. *Cornflakes*, she thought.

The lawyer greeted them absentmindedly. 'They have found his fellow-accused,' he said, reading a name from the paper at the top of his pile. 'One Mr Chombie.'

'Chobie,' hissed Mma Makutsi. 'You should get the name of your clients right, Rra.'

The lawyer looked up in surprise. 'But he's not my client, Mma. They have very different interests, you see.'

Mma Ramotswe leaned forward to ask the lawyer a question. 'Is this Chobie going to tell them that Fanwell did not know that the vehicle was stolen?'

The lawyer looked at his papers. 'Not according to his statement,' he said. 'He is going to say that Fanwell knew that it was stolen and that he, Chombie, did not.'

Mma Makutsi exploded. 'But that's a lie, Rra! That's a big, big lie.'

The lawyer shrugged. 'These fellows are always telling lies,' he said. 'You know, Mma, if this building were a cinema and they had a big board outside saying what was showing, they would have to put LIES in big letters. Then they might add, EVERY DAY ADMISSION FREE.' He laughed at his joke, which was greeted with silence from the others.

'This is very serious . . . ' Mma Ramotswe began, but could not finish, as Fanwell and Chobie were now being led into the dock and the court had gone quiet.

'The trial is about to begin,' whispered the lawyer helpfully. 'You must stop talking now.'

The lawyer representing Chobie had now arrived – a small man with a bustling sense of energy. He seemed to be much more in command of the situation than Fanwell's lawyer, whom he acknowledged with only a curt nod of the head.

'That is a real lawyer,' whispered Mma Makutsi. 'See how different he looks.'

It was now the turn of the magistrate to enter, which he did through a door at the back of the court. A policeman indicated that everybody should stand up, and there was shuffling and murmuring as people got to their feet. Unfortunately Fanwell had been looking down at the floor when this happened, and did not see either the policeman's gesture or the figure of the magistrate entering the court. He remained seated.

'Fanwell!' hissed Mma Ramotswe. 'Fanwell, stand up, stand up!'

It was too late. Fanwell heard his name, but being unaware of where the voice came from he looked in the wrong direction. And by that time the magistrate had taken his seat and everybody in the court had sat down too.

The magistrate had noticed. Frowning, he nodded to the policeman who was standing immediately behind Fanwell. The policeman leaned forward and seized Fanwell's arm, pulling him to his feet. Fanwell looked completely dismayed; he had now realised what was going on and glanced desperately in the direction of the lawyer. But the lawyer simply shook a finger at him.

'Young man,' the magistrate said. 'Do you know what contempt of court is?'

Fanwell looked blank.

The lawyer now rose to his feet. 'I represent this man,' he said.

'I know you do,' snapped the magistrate. 'Can your client speak?'

The lawyer nodded. 'He can speak, sir.'

'Then tell him to answer me. Does he know what contempt of court is?'

The lawyer looked at Fanwell. 'Do you know what contempt of court is?'

Fanwell shook his head.

'Well,' said the magistrate, 'let me tell you. It is the offence that is committed by a person who fails to show proper respect for the court. So not standing up when the magistrate or judge enters is contempt of court, and it can be punished there and then with a fine or imprisonment.'

Fanwell groaned. 'I'm sorry, sir. I did not hear.'

The magistrate looked at him in silence. 'Well, remember what I said to you.' He looked down at his papers. 'Pleas?'

Fanwell's lawyer stood up. 'My client is not guilty, sir.'

The magistrate looked at him incredulously. 'That is not for you to say, don't you think?'

The lawyer looked flustered. 'He is not guilty, sir.'

The magistrate sighed. 'Listen, Mr . . .' He consulted a piece of paper in front of him. 'Listen Mr Mapoeli, the point I'm making is this: whether or not your client is guilty is a matter for the court to decide – it is not for you to say. What I want from you is his plea. Is he pleading guilty or not guilty?'

217

The lawyer smoothed the front of his jacket. 'He is pleading guilty, sir.'

The magistrate nodded. 'Very well. Guilty.'

Mma Ramotswe gripped Mr J. L. B. Matekoni's arm. 'He's got it wrong,' she whispered. 'He's pleading not guilty.'

Fanwell was now tugging at his lawyer's sleeve. The lawyer, however, was attempting to brush him off. 'Not now, Fanwell. You can speak later.'

Witnessing this, Mma Ramotswe could not contain herself. 'He's pleading not guilty,' she said in a loud voice.

The magistrate looked up sharply. 'Who is that? Who's speaking?'

Mma Ramotswe raised a hand. 'Me, sir.'

'The public is not to address the court,' said the magistrate. 'I will not tolerate any disturbances. Is that quite clear?'

Fanwell's lawyer cleared his throat. 'For the avoidance of doubt, your honour, my client is pleading not guilty to the charge.'

The magistrate took off his spectacles and polished them with his handkerchief. 'He's changing his plea, is he?'

'Not changing it, your honour,' said the lawyer. 'That is what he is pleading.'

'Do you mean that was his original plea?'

'No, sir.'

The magistrate's irritation was now very evident. 'You mean that he originally pleaded guilty?'

'No. He has always said he is not guilty.'

The magistrate tapped his pen on his desk. 'So the position is this: your client is pleading not guilty and always has.'

'Has what?' asked the lawyer.

'Has always pleaded not guilty.'

The lawyer nodded. 'Only in this case, your honour. He has not pleaded not guilty any other time. Nor has he pleaded guilty.'

The magistrate ignored this. 'Not guilty,' he said tersely.

The lawyer seemed surprised. Turning to Fanwell, he made a gesture to suggest that it was all over. 'Not guilty,' he said. 'The charges are being dismissed.'

The prosecutor now sprang to his feet. 'I think the defence misunderstands the situation,' he said.

The magistrate stared at Fanwell's lawyer. 'What is this about the dismissal of charges, Mr Mapoeli? Who said anything about that?'

The lawyer started to shake. 'You said it, your honour. You said my client was not guilty.'

The magistrate grinned. 'Did I? I don't think I did, Mr Mapoeli. I merely said that his plea is one of not guilty. That's what I said.'

'Oh,' said the lawyer lamely. 'I see.'

'I hope you do, Mr Mapoeli,' said the magistrate. 'Now the other accused? Accused No. 1, Chobie?'

Chobie's lawyer rose to his feet. 'He is pleading not guilty, sir.'

It was at this point, while the magistrate was making a note of the plea, that Mma Ramotswe noticed that Charlie was staring at Chobie. For his part, the young man in the dock initially seemed to avoid the stare, but then returned it. Charlie had made a gesture, not a very obvious one, but a gesture nonetheless. Chobie watched, and shifted in his seat. Charlie then made another gesture – a small movement of the hand that seemed, to Mma Ramotswe's surprise, to be pointing towards her. Or was it something else altogether?

The magistrate cleared his throat and invited the prosecutor to begin. Chobie and Fanwell were prodded to stand up by the two policemen seated one on either side of them. The charges were then read out. A section of the Botswana Penal Code was mentioned, and there was reference to something having been done *knowingly and willingly* and then there was silence.

219

Mma Ramotswe was watching Charlie, who was still looking at Chobie. Again there was a surreptitious gesture. Mma Ramotswe shifted her gaze to Chobie and noticed, rather to her surprise, that he was staring at her.

The prosecutor mentioned a police witness, but before he could finish what he was saying, Chobie stood up. 'I am guilty, sir.'

His lawyer spun round. 'He has entered a plea of not guilty, sir.'

'No,' said Chobie. 'I am saying I am guilty now.'

The magistrate adjusted his spectacles. 'That sounds like a guilty plea,' he said.

Chobie, still standing, spoke again, ignoring the policeman who was tugging at his shirt, urging him to sit down. 'This one here' – he gestured to Fanwell – 'this one didn't know the car was stolen, Rra. I am the one who did it. I am very sorry.'

The magistrate sighed. He looked at the prosecutor, who was busily conferring with Chobie's lawyer. 'It seems that this is going to need a bit of sorting out,' he said. 'I shall adjourn the court for fifteen minutes while the State decides what to do. But it seems to me as if it might be an idea to dismiss the charges against accused No. 2.' He paused. 'A cursory examination of the papers seems to point that way. And if accused No. 1 is saying that accused No. 2 had no knowledge of the fact that the car was stolen, then that rather changes things, doesn't it, Mr Prosecutor?' He then answered his own question. 'Frankly, this is a bit of a mess, and I propose to dismiss the charges against accused No. 2. We can come back to deal with accused No. 1's revised plea in a quarter of an hour. No. 2 is discharged. You can go, young man. You, No. 1, you stay.'

They went outside. As she left the building, Mma Makutsi ran out into the sun and uttered the traditional ululation of delight that women contribute to any great Botswana occasion. Mma Ramotswe would have joined her, had she not been busy explaining to a shocked and shivering Fanwell that his ordeal was over.

'I cannot believe it,' stuttered Fanwell. 'What has happened?'

Fanwell's lawyer shuffled his papers about officiously. 'A very satisfactory result,' he said. 'I am very pleased with this case.'

'But what happened, Rra?' asked Fanwell. 'How did you get me off?'

Mma Ramotswe watched the lawyer, who hesitated momentarily. She realised that he had no idea, but she did not want to spoil his moment of victory. This, she thought, was probably the first case he had won for a long time – if ever.

'You just thank your lawyer,' she said to Fanwell. 'The important thing is that he has won your case for you. That is what counts.'

'Yes,' said Mr J. L. B. Matekoni, reaching out to shake the lawyer's hand. 'Well done, Rra.'

The lawyer beamed. 'Thank you, Rra. These cases can be difficult, but I am very glad that this young man can return to his work without a spot on his reputation.'

They made their way to the vehicles. Mr J. L. B. Matekoni, Charlie and Fanwell drove back in the truck, followed by Mma Ramotswe and Mma Makutsi in the tiny white van. It was a small procession, but no great march, no Roman triumph could have matched it for sheer joy, or relief.

Once back at the No. 1 Ladies' Detective Agency and Tlokweng Road Speedy Motors, they tried to get back to work, but it was hard, and eventually Mma Ramotswe simply brought forward the tea break so that they could all calm down and get back to normal.

'One thing I cannot work out,' she said, looking at Charlie, 'is

221

why Chobie suddenly changed his story. Why would he decide to take the blame?'

'Because he did it,' blurted out Mma Makutsi. 'He said he was guilty, and he was.'

'But he had been planning to try to shift everything on to Fanwell,' said Mr J. L. B. Matekoni. 'And then it all changed.'

Mma Ramotswe was still staring at Charlie. 'I wonder whether he was frightened of something,' she mused. 'What do you think, Charlie?'

Charlie shrugged. 'I don't know.'

She watched him. There was the slightest hint of a smile playing about his lips. Of course he knew. Of course he did.

'I think that he might have been frightened of *you*, Charlie. I don't know why I think that, but I think that's what happened.'

Charlie was now clearly struggling not to laugh.

'It's not funny, Charlie,' reprimanded Mma Makutsi.

Suddenly Charlie put down his mug of tea and pulled a piece of paper out of the pocket of his overalls. Now smiling broadly, he passed the paper to Mr J. L. B. Matekoni.

'What's this, Charlie?'

'It's a newspaper cutting, Rra. Or rather it's a piece of paper that I had somebody make up as a newspaper cutting. You know that printing place at Riverwalk? I have a friend there who can print anything from his computer. Driving licence? No problem. Birth certificate? No problem too. And in this case, an article from a newspaper over in Johannesburg.'

Mr J. L. B. Matekoni, who used reading glasses, took these out of his pocket and unfolded the piece of paper and read out loud. '"Police search for dangerous hit-woman. The public is warned that the convicted murderess, Bella Dlamini, is on the loose and may be looking for further contracts. This woman is dangerous and has been known to carry out contract killings for as little as one thousand rand."' He looked up from the paper. 'What is all this, Charlie?' He looked down again. 'And this . . . ' He stopped, and held up the paper. 'My goodness, this Bella Dlamini looks exactly like you, Mma Ramotswe.'

Charlie let out a hoot of laughter. 'But it *is* Mma Ramotswe. It's her photograph.'

'Why have you made that rubbish?' asked Mma Makutsi. 'This is not funny, Charlie.'

Mma Ramotswe, though, was looking at Charlie through narrowed eyes. 'Charlie,' she said. 'Did you show that to Chobie?'

He beamed with self-satisfaction. 'Yes. Two days ago. I found him and I showed it to him.'

'And?'

'And I told him . . . ' Charlie looked about him, as if for support. They were all staring at him intently. 'I told him that we had arranged something. If he didn't tell the truth in court, then . . . ' He pointed to the cutting. 'Then he would be seeing this lady.'

There was complete silence.

'And she was there in court,' Charlie continued. 'So he decided to tell the truth after all. And who wouldn't?'

She took Charlie outside.

'Come for a little walk with me, Charlie.'

'I don't see what the fuss is about, Mma Ramotswe.'

'Just come with me, Charlie, so we can talk.'

He went reluctantly, dragging his heels in the sand like a surly schoolboy. Mma Ramotswe took his arm. She would not be cross with him; she knew that this never worked with Charlie. You had to try to reason with Charlie; you had to be gentle.

'You do know how serious it is?' she asked.

'What?'

223

'How serious it is to threaten a witness. Especially to threaten to have them killed.'

He said nothing.

'You could go to jail if the police found out. You know that, don't you?'

Charlie defended himself. 'He wasn't a witness, Mma. He was the one who did it. I just told him to tell the truth.'

She increased the pressure on his arm. 'You threatened him, Charlie. And you brought me into it. You made him think I was that lady, that . . .'

'Bella Dlamini,' he prompted. 'It's a good name, isn't it, Mma Ramotswe?'

'Charlie, you have to take this seriously. You have done a very bad thing.'

'With a good result.'

She had to admit that this was the case. Truth, it seemed, had triumphed – by means of a lie.

'Yes,' she said carefully. 'It may be a good result, but never forget, Charlie, that you should not try to get good results by doing bad things.'

'Why not?'

'Because . . .' She looked up at the sky. She was not sure how she could explain it to this young man, and then she decided that she could not. Not just yet.

'Because it's not right, Charlie. Sometimes we have to see bad things happen because we can't do another bad thing to stop them. Do you see that?'

'No,' he said. 'I don't.'

Mma Ramotswe sighed. 'I'm very pleased that Fanwell is back with us, of course.'

'So am I. He is like a brother to me, Mma.'

'I know, Charlie.'

'And you have to help your brother, Mma.'

'I understand that, Charlie, but ... but be careful what you do.'

Charlie looked at his watch. 'We should get back to work, Mma.'

She nodded. 'All right, Charlie, let's get back to work.'

They retraced their steps, as friends now, or at least as those who have established an understanding, even if the understanding is about just what one of them understands and the other does not.

Chapter Nineteen

You Are a Visitor to Our Country

With the removal of the threat hanging over Fanwell, Mma Ramotswe found herself with more energy to help Mma Potokwani. Clovis Andersen had at least given a lead in suggesting that the contract for the building of the new hall should be investigated, and she felt that this could now be tackled. The great authority had offered to accompany her to Mma Potokwani's office to see what could be uncovered, and now they were approaching the gates and the large, shady tree under which Mma Ramotswe habitually parked her van on these visits.

'This is a very fine place,' commented Clovis Andersen, looking about him as the van came to a halt. 'We had an orphanage in Muncie, Indiana back when I was a boy.'

'Your place in America, Rra?'

'Yes. Muncie. The orphans' home was a place made of a curious yellow brick and its windows were painted red round the edges. It's odd how you remember these little details years later.'

'We all do that,' said Mma Ramotswe. *I remember*, she thought. *I remember my late daddy, and how he took me on his shoulders and we walked along the road outside our house and I was proud, so proud that I thought my heart would burst.*

'The boys and girls from the orphanage went to school – same as us. We had three or four in my class. There was a boy called Lance. He had freckles and ginger hair. I remember asking him what had happened to his parents, and he told me that they had been Arctic explorers and had drifted off on an ice floe. He said that there had been an article about them in the *National Geographic*. He said that he used to have the issue the article was in, but another boy in the orphanage had stolen it.'

They were standing outside the van now; standing in the morning sun, which was gentle on them. It seemed to Mma Ramotswe that they were in no particular hurry and that they could talk, if that was what Clovis Andersen wanted. 'That is very sad, Rra,' she said. 'That is stealing that boy's past.'

He smiled at the memory. 'Of course it wasn't true. A couple of years later I was told by some other kid that his parents had committed suicide together and that the story of the ice floe was all invention. I asked my own parents about that. They never lied to me, and so they had to admit that it was true: the suicide had taken place in the dry-goods store that the boy's parents used to run. The father had shot his wife and then himself.'

Mma Ramotswe gasped. 'And left that little boy . . . '

'Yes. But they probably weren't thinking straight, poor people. They were in debt, I imagine – a lot of those small storekeepers got into terrible debt.'

'And the boy?' asked Mma Ramotswe. 'What happened to the boy?'

'He went to college in Bloomington. As I did. He was a great football player. He taught high school, I think. Things went well for him.'

'I am pleased to hear that ending,' said Mma Ramotswe. 'It would have been a very sad story otherwise.'

'There are plenty of sad stories, Mma Ramotswe.'

'Of course there are.' She pointed to the scattered cottages in which the children lived with their house-mothers. 'Every one of those houses has sad stories in it.'

'I guess that's right,' said Clovis Andersen.

'But Mma Potokwani tries to write a happy ending for them,' Mma Ramotswe went on. 'That is what she does.'

She held Clovis Andersen's gaze as she said this, and he knew immediately what she meant: this was not an idle enquiry they were about to embark upon – there was a great deal at stake here.

'I think we should go in,' he said softly. 'Is that the office over there?'

'Yes. That is where she works.'

Mma Potokwani was briefly out of her office, her secretary explained, but she would be back soon; one of the house-mothers had sprained an ankle and she was attending to that. In the meantime they were welcome to sit down in the office, where it was cool.

They had talked in the van earlier about what they should do, and now Mma Ramotswe tackled the secretary. 'Are you the secretary, Mma, to the board as well as to Mma Potokwani?'

The secretary nodded. 'I do both, Mma. When the board has its meetings I am always there to bring papers and do things like that.'

Mma Ramotswe looked about the room, at the array of filing cabinets. 'You keep the board papers here, Mma?'

The secretary confirmed that this was the case.

'So that means you have the tenders for the new hall?'

228

The secretary glanced in the direction of one of the filing cabinets. 'They are all there,' she said.

'Could you show me something, Mma?'

The reply came quickly. 'Certainly not, Mma. The board's papers are confidential. They have that typed on the top of them. I cannot show them even to you, Mma Ramotswe. It would be improper.'

'Of course it would be,' said Mma Ramotswe hurriedly. 'It would be improper. But it's a pity, really.'

The secretary looked at her suspiciously. 'Why, Mma?'

'I take it that you are fond of Mma Potokwani, Mma?' asked Mma Ramotswe.

'Of course I am, Mma. She is the best matron this place has ever had. She is the best boss I am ever likely to get.'

'So you'll miss her?'

'Of course I'll miss her, Mma.'

'And I can imagine how the children will miss her,' said Mma Ramotswe. 'Oh, they'll be so sad, those children. First they lose their parents, and then they lose Mma Potokwani. They will be very sad, I think.'

'Yes, they will be.'

'And there will be a lot of crying.'

The secretary lowered her gaze. 'We shall all cry, Mma. All of us.'

Mma Ramotswe waited a moment or two. Clovis Andersen, who felt as if he were an intruder into a private family moment, studied his hands.

'Then I take it that you would be very pleased to have her dismissal set aside?'

The secretary's reply was vehement. 'I would do anything to make that happen, Mma.'

'Anything?' probed Mma Ramotswe.

'Yes, anything at all.'

Mma Ramotswe glanced at Clovis Andersen before she next spoke. 'Then please show us the tender documents that the board received for the new hall,' she said.

The secretary hesitated. 'They are confidential,' she said.

'Then we can do nothing for Mma Potokwani.'

'However, if it is in the interests of the children,' went on the secretary, 'then I shall overlook the confidentiality issue.'

She rose from her chair and unlocked one of the filing cabinets. Thereafter it took a few minutes before she found what she was looking for: a brown manila file on which *Hall* had been inscribed in thick black lettering. She turned to face Mma Ramotswe.

'This has the quotes received from the builders,' she said. 'And it also has the report that went back from the tender committee to the main board.'

Mma Ramotswe was intrigued. 'The tender committee?'

The secretary explained. 'That was the committee that decided who should get the job of building the hall.'

'And who was on that?'

'Only two people, I think,' came the reply. 'Mr Ditso Ditso – you know him, Mma? – and that lady from the Ministry, I am always forgetting her name. But she never went to the meetings, I believe. She is a very lazy woman – everybody knows that.'

'So the meetings of the tender committee just consisted of Mr Ditso Ditso?'

'Yes. And he said something to me about it once. He joked that it was very pleasant being on a committee where nobody disagreed with you because there were no other members. He said he wished all committees were like that.'

Clovis Andersen now intervened. 'I'll bet he does!' he said.

The secretary handed the file to Mma Ramotswe, who put it on the table in front of her and began to look through the documents it contained. 'Here,' she said, passing four stapled pages to Clovis Andersen. 'Those are the estimates from the builders.'

Clovis Andersen looked at the papers. 'They aren't too far apart,' he said. 'It means that the builders wanted this job. If you get one that's much higher, then it usually means that the builder who put it in didn't really want the job but would take it if his excessive price got it.'

'And here's Mr Ditso's letter of recommendation to the board saying that the job should be awarded to . . . ' She looked up. 'Kalahari Forward Construction.'

Clovis Andersen consulted the papers in front of him and frowned. 'They're not on the tender list,' he said.

'That is the firm,' said the secretary. 'They are the ones who are going to do the job. You will find a copy of the letter of appointment from the board in there.' She gestured to the file. 'I copied it myself. It is all in order.'

'All in order, not in order,' muttered Clovis Andersen. 'Can you find that one, Mma Ramotswe?'

Mma Ramotswe paged through the remaining papers in the file. 'Here,' she said. 'This is the one.' She examined it more closely. 'It is an agreement to build the hall and kitchen for three million and six hundred thousand *pula*.'

'That's right,' said the secretary. 'That is a lot of money, Mma.'

Clovis Andersen took the letter from Mma Ramotswe and read through it quickly. 'Interesting,' he said at last. 'The highest tender from the list was just over two million.'

'So the contract was not awarded to the lowest bid,' said Mma Ramotswe.

'No,' said Clovis Andersen. 'Of course that sometimes happens. There may be some reason why a more expensive contractor is preferred. For example, he may do better quality work. Or . . . or he may be a relative.' His tone became more ominous. 'Or the

231

contractor may be paying a kickback to the person awarding the contract. There are many possible reasons.'

The secretary drew in her breath. 'That is very bad,' she hissed. 'I did not know anything about it, Mma Ramotswe.'

Mma Ramotswe reassured her. 'Of course you didn't, Mma. Nobody is blaming you.'

The secretary looked satisfied. 'I know about those people,' she said. 'They came round to look at the site.'

'Kalahari Forward Construction?' asked Mma Ramotswe. 'They came here?'

'Yes, they came here, Mma. Their boss came. My brother knows who he is. He used to drive a taxi for him when he was in the taxi business. Then he became a builder and did quite well. My brother did not like him.'

Mma Ramotswe looked interested. 'And what was this man's name, Mma? Do you remember?'

'He is called Sephotho,' said the secretary. 'He is a tall man who has lost a finger on his left hand. It looks like this.' She held up a hand with one digit tucked back.

Mma Ramotswe felt her heart pound within her. 'Sephotho?' she said. 'And has he got a sister, this man?'

'Yes. My brother says she is not a very nice woman . . .'

'Called Violet?'

'I think so,' said the secretary. 'Violet, or Rose. Something like that. He said that she should really have a name like Thorn or Cabbage.'

Mma Ramotswe shuffled the papers back into the file and handed it to the secretary. 'I think we are going to go and look for Mma Potokwani,' she said, indicating to Clovis Andersen that he should follow her. 'We have some very interesting news to give her.'

*

They told Mma Potokwani about what they had discovered. She listened carefully, then rushed forward and threw her arms around an astonished Clovis Andersen. 'Oh, thank you, Rra! Thank you, thank you!' If, over the last few days, there had been signs of depression in her demeanour, these now disappeared with extraordinary rapidity.

Clovis Andersen extracted himself from the embrace. 'It wasn't me, Mma. You should thank Mma Ramotswe. She found this out.'

'You did,' said Mma Ramotswe. 'It was your idea.'

He refused to accept the credit. 'No, Mma, it was you.'

'Does it matter?' said Mma Potokwani. 'Maybe it was the two of you.'

'It was definitely her,' said Clovis Andersen, pointing at Mma Ramotswe. 'It was not me.'

They returned to Mma Potokwani's office, where tea was poured and accompanied by liberal slices of fruit cake. Then Mma Ramotswe and Clovis Andersen travelled back to the agency.

'Paper,' said Clovis Andersen as they turned on to the Tlokweng Road. 'You'd be surprised, Mma Ramotswe, by how often people leave a paper trail. It's the undoing of so many malefactors – so many.'

Mma Ramotswe repeated the word *malefactors*. 'That is a very interesting word, Rra. We do not use it very much here in Botswana. What exactly does it mean?'

Clovis Andersen explained. 'It means people who do wrong – any sort of wrong.'

Mma Ramotswe repeated the word several times. 'It is a good word,' she said. 'I shall use it more often. Malefactors. Malefactors. There are many malefactors.'

'There are,' agreed Clovis Andersen.

'Are there many malefactors in Munchie?' asked Mma Ramotswe.

'Muncie. No, no more than anywhere else. In fact, maybe fewer. Muncie, Indiana is not a bad place.'

'Like Gaborone?'

He smiled. 'Yes, a bit like Gaborone. The human heart, you see, Mma Ramotswe, is pretty much the same wherever one goes.'

She nodded her agreement. 'Yes, Rra, that is certainly true. All human hearts are the same, no matter how different we are on the outside.'

They travelled in silence for a short while. Then Clovis Andersen turned to Mma Ramotswe and said, 'What now, Mma?'

'I have an idea,' she said. 'I have an idea why Mr Ditso gave the contract to that firm.'

'And why is that?'

She smiled. 'Would you mind, Rra, if I didn't tell you just yet? I think I'm right, but I'm not absolutely certain.'

'Not one hundred per cent certain?'

'No, not one hundred per cent. More like . . . more like ninety-seven per cent, I think.'

Clovis Andersen frowned. 'Where have I heard that figure before? Where has ninety-seven per cent cropped up before?'

'It is just a guess, Rra. Ninety-seven per cent is a figure that I have also heard before. So it just came into my mind.'

Mma Makutsi was sitting at her desk drinking a cup of tea when they arrived back at the office. She glanced up at Mma Ramotswe and knew immediately that something important had happened.

'You have found something?' she asked. 'You look very happy.'

'We sure do,' said Clovis Andersen. 'We are feeling very happy, Mma Makutsi.'

Mma Makutsi gave him an encouraging smile. *Star-struck*, thought Mma Ramotswe. *You are still star-struck.*

'Mr Ditso Ditso has not been behaving very well,' said Mma Ramotswe. 'And this means, I hope, that we shall be able to persuade him to drop his plans.'

Mma Makutsi clapped her hands together. 'That is very good news, Mma – very good news.'

There was still a further step, though, and Mma Ramotswe now made the request that would make it possible for that step to be taken. 'Mma Makutsi,' she began, 'am I right in remembering that you have a picture of your graduation from the Botswana Secretarial College?'

Mma Makutsi seemed surprised, but was obviously pleased by the question. 'As it happens, Mma, I do have that photograph in my drawer here. Would you like to see it?'

'It would be very useful, Mma.'

Mma Makutsi opened a drawer in her desk and took out a photograph that had been pasted on to a piece of stiff cardboard. 'Here it is,' she said, dusting it reverentially. 'There were fifteen ladies who graduated in my group. Here we all are, sitting with the Principal. And there, you see, is the college crest and the motto.' She turned to Clovis Andersen. 'Ninety-seven per cent, Rra. That is what I got in the final examinations.'

'Ninety-seven per cent!' he said. 'That's almost impossible. Virtually flawless.'

She bobbed her head. 'That is what some people said. I am very lucky.'

'Not luck, Mma Makutsi,' he said. 'Talent.'

Mma Ramotswe took the proffered photograph and examined it. 'Yes,' she said. 'This is what I need.' She looked up. 'May I borrow this photograph, Mma? Not for very long, and I will take very good care of it, I promise you.'

Mma Makutsi sounded puzzled. 'Of course you may, Mma. But why do you need it?'

'I need a photograph of Violet Sephotho,' said Mma Ramotswe. 'And this is the only one we have, I think. This is her in the middle row, isn't it?'

Mma Makutsi wrinkled her nose. 'She looked the same then as she looks today. Look at all that lipstick. Look at it.'

'And the nails,' mused Mma Ramotswe. 'Those nails. They have a lot to do with this.'

'With what?'

'With this enquiry,' said Mma Ramotswe.

'Nails, Mma?'

'I shall explain everything very soon, Mma Makutsi. In the meantime, Mr Andersen and I need to go into town.'

There was something in Mma Makutsi's look that made Mma Ramotswe hesitate. It was a look of disappointment, coupled, perhaps, with yearning.

'Unless you would like to come with us, Mma Makutsi?' she said.

Mma Makutsi blurted out her answer. 'I think I would, Mma. Thank you very much.'

Mma Ramotswe picked up the keys to the van. 'Of course, there is a bit of a problem about seats. The van only has two seats in the cab, which means that somebody will need to sit in the back. That will not be very comfortable.'

'Me,' said Clovis Andersen.

'No,' snapped Mma Makutsi. 'I will sit in the back, Mma.'

'I won't hear of that,' said Clovis Andersen.

'But we cannot let you do that, Rra. You are a visitor to our country.'

'I insist,' said Clovis Andersen.

Mma Ramotswe drew Mma Makutsi aside. 'You must let him,' she said. 'Mr Andersen is a gentleman, and he is thinking of the comfort of ladies. You must let him.'

Mma Makutsi yielded. It was a small thing, she knew, but a small thing that was, in its way, a big thing. And in the van, on the way into town, with Clovis Andersen bumping around in the back and unable to hear them, she said to Mma Ramotswe: 'It is good that there are still gentlemen, Mma. Mr Andersen, Mr J. L. B. Matekoni and Phuti. All gentlemen.'

'Yes, all of those are gentlemen,' said Mma Ramotswe. 'And it is good that they are still there. Not only for ladies who want to ride in the front, but for all sorts of other reasons as well.'

Mma Makutsi pondered this. 'Why are there fewer and fewer gentlemen, Mma Ramotswe?'

'It is our fault, Mma. It is the fault of ladies.'

'Why is that?'

'Because we have allowed men to stop behaving as gentlemen, and when you allow people to do what they wish, then that is what they do. They stop doing the things they need to do.' She looked at Mma Makutsi across the steering wheel. 'That is well known, I think, Mma. That is well known.'

Chapter Twenty

Better Nails, Better Life

'I never worry about my nails,' said Mma Makutsi as they passed the Princess Marina Hospital. 'We were taught at the Botswana Secretarial College that long nails were not a good thing if you have to do typing. We were told some very alarming stories.'

Mma Ramotswe was intrigued. 'Alarming stories about nails?'

'Yes, Mma. There was one case, in the days of electric type-writers, of a secretary who got a shock when one of her nails went through the space between the keys. She became late as a result.'

Mma Ramotswe swerved the van slightly at the thought. But could you get a shock through a nail? A finger, certainly, but a nail? 'Are you sure, Mma? Would electricity go through a finger-nail?'

Mma Makutsi pursed her lips before answering. 'It is true,

Mma. Electricity can go through many things, not just wires. And there's another thing – you can get long nails stuck in a filing cabinet when you close it. I have seen that happen, Mma.'

They negotiated the traffic circle at the end of the central square before parking behind the President Hotel. Clovis Andersen appeared to have enjoyed his ride in the back of the van, and jumped down with a smile. 'The best way to see a town,' he said. 'With the sun on your face.' He patted down his dishevelled hair. 'Now then, Mma Ramotswe, where are you taking us?'

'To a nail parlour,' said Mma Ramotswe, leading them past the entrance to the hotel and into the busy open marketplace beyond.

Clovis Andersen laughed. 'I'm not sure whether I need—'

'Not as clients,' Mma Ramotswe interrupted.

'These people are always good sources of information,' said Mma Makutsi. 'Hairdressers, barmen, nail ladies – they always know what's going on. As you say, Rra, in your own book: always ask the people who know.'

Clovis Andersen looked pensive. 'I said that, did I? Well, it sounds reasonable enough to me.'

It was a short walk to the Better Nails, Better Life nail parlour. This was a hole-in-the-wall shop advertising its presence with a large picture of a hand sporting long nails painted in various bright colours.

'If you tried to type with a hand like that you wouldn't get very far,' said Mma Makutsi dismissively.

'I don't think it would be much good trying to do *anything* with a hand like that,' said Clovis Andersen.

'People who have nails like that usually don't want to do anything,' said Mma Makutsi. 'That is not a working hand. That is the hand of an idle, useless person.'

'I don't think it's meant to be a real hand,' suggested Mma Ramotswe. 'I think it's intended just to give you an idea of what they can do.'

'A bad idea of what they can do,' snorted Mma Makutsi.

They entered the shop. In front of them was a table with a box covered in some soft material. That, thought Mma Ramotswe, was were you rested your hand while your nails were being painted. It looked rather comfortable, she decided. There were several chairs, a stack of well-thumbed magazines and a shelf along which numerous bottles of nail varnish were lined. As they came in, a curtain at the back of the room was pulled aside and a well-dressed young woman came out to greet them.

'Have you made an appointment?' she asked. Her voice was friendly.

Mma Ramotswe greeted her in the traditional way before asking: 'Are you Mma Soleti's sister, Mma?'

The woman smiled warmly. 'Yes, we are sisters, Mma. I am called Soleti too. They call her Mma Soleti (Face) and me Mma Soleti (Nails). You know her?'

Mma Ramotswe explained that she had only visited the Minor Adjustment Beauty Salon once, but that she had enjoyed a long conversation with Mma Soleti. 'I am a private detective, Mma,' she went on. 'I am looking into a troubling matter and I need some information. It will be very confidential and nobody else will know about it.'

Mma Soleti (Nails) looked at Mma Makutsi and Clovis Andersen. 'And these people, Mma? What about them? Are they nobody?'

Mma Ramotswe was quick to explain. 'Mma Makutsi here is my assistant—'

'Associate,' corrected Mma Makutsi.

'Associate,' said Mma Ramotswe. 'And this is Rra Clovis

Andersen, who is one of the most famous detectives in the United States of America. They are both very good at keeping secrets, Mma. Their lips are permanently closed.'

'For ever,' confirmed Mma Makutsi.

Mma Soleti seemed reassured. 'In that case, Mma, what is it you wish to know?'

Mma Ramotswe took the photograph out of the brown envelope in which she placed it. 'There is somebody in this picture who you may know, Mma. Please will you look at it.'

Mma Soleti (Nails) took the photograph and examined it. She looked up at Mma Makutsi. 'Her. Your assistant—'

'Associate,' said Mma Makutsi.

'Yes, your associate. It is you, Mma, standing in the centre.'

'I was standing in the centre because I had the highest mark, Mma. That is why.'

Mma Soleti (Nails) looked at the photograph again. 'And . . .' She looked up, a glint in her eye. 'And this lady here. Oh, yes! There she is. There she is.'

'So that is the lady who comes here, is it, Mma?' coaxed Mma Ramotswe. 'The lady who is the mistress of a certain man called Ditso Ditso who also has a wife who comes here to have her nails done?'

'Ow!' exclaimed Mma Soleti (Nails). 'You know everything, Mma. No wonder you're a detective. Yes, that is all true.'

'Her name is Violet Sephotho,' said Mma Ramotswe.

There was a silence as the name was mentioned, and it seemed that it hung in the air for some time, a chilling presence in the room. Violet Sephotho.

Eventually Mma Soleti (Nails) spoke. 'I shall remember that,' she said. 'She is a very rude woman. She speaks on her telephone while I am doing her nails and she never says anything to me. She thinks I am just a . . . a nail lady of no importance.'

Mma Ramotswe reached forward and touched her gently on the arm. 'The work you do is good work, Mma. You help people to feel good about themselves. That is good work, my sister.'

Mma Soleti (Nails) patted Mma Ramotswe's hand, casting an eye on her nails as she did so. 'Thank you, Mma. And if there's anything I can do ...' She looked down at Mma Ramotswe's nails again. 'I would be very happy to help, Mma.'

Intercepting the glance, Mma Ramotswe laughed. 'It would be wasted on me, Mma. I am always washing up and doing things like that. Fancy nails would not suit me, I'm afraid.'

'Nor me,' said Clovis Andersen. 'I don't think much about my nails.'

Mma Soleti (Nails) looked disapproving. 'But that's a great pity, Rra. These days it is quite all right for men to look after their nails. We are living in an equal society, you see, and that means that nails are equal too.' She paused. 'So I think we could do something with your nails, Rra. In fact, I am sure we can.'

'We now have all the information we need,' said Mma Ramotswe.

They were standing about the tiny white van, ready to embark on the next stage of the investigation, which was to confront Mr Ditso Ditso with the truth.

'This is always the best stage of a case,' said Clovis Andersen. 'I call it the denouement. It's when you reveal who is responsible for whatever it is you're investigating.'

'But we know that already,' said Mma Makutsi.

Clovis Andersen raised a finger. 'But Mr Ditso doesn't know that we know. Now we tell him. This is the good part.'

Mma Ramotswe looked doubtful. 'You have to be careful not to count on anything,' she said.

Clovis Andersen agreed. 'Of course. A case is not closed until it's closed.'

They considered the force of this. It was most impressive to both Mma Ramotswe and Mma Makutsi how Clovis Andersen spoke in short, pithy aphorisms – just like his book. It was, they thought, a great gift.

'I look forward to seeing his face,' said Mma Makutsi. 'Big Mr Ditso shown to be a corrupt bully. Should we invite Mma Potokwani to come with us?'

Mma Ramotswe did not think this a good idea. 'You should not rub a person's nose in it, Mma. Let him think about what he has done. Let him reach his own conclusion – it is always better that way.'

'As long as he reinstates Mma Potokwani,' cautioned Clovis Andersen.

'Of course,' said Mma Ramotswe. 'That is the most important thing of all.'

They had not notified Mr Ditso Ditso of their arrival, but encountered no obstruction at the offices of DD Industries. Yes, Mr Ditso would see them if they did not mind waiting for ten minutes or so. Would they like tea?

Eventually an assistant showed them into the office of the man himself. He stood up politely as they entered and gestured for them to sit down. 'Last time there were two of you,' he said. 'Now there are three. Am I becoming more important all of a sudden?'

They laughed at the pleasantry. Then Ditso Ditso looked at his watch. 'I'm afraid I only have five minutes, Mma Ramotswe. So what is it, Mma?'

'I've come about Mma Potokwani—'

He raised a hand to interrupt her. 'Look, Mma, we've discussed that, and I've told you already. Do I need to spell it out again? Mma Potokwani has resigned, and that's the end of that.'

'She did not resign,' said Mma Ramotswe. 'She was dismissed.'

Ditso Ditso shrugged. 'What's in a word, Mma? Resigned, dismissed, retired; jumped, pushed, shoved out? All the same at the end of the day.'

'You can add to that list of words, Rra,' said Mma Ramotswe quietly. 'Add: betrayed, destroyed, tricked.'

Ditso Ditso's manner changed abruptly; gone was the earlier joviality. 'Be careful what you say, Mma.'

'You be careful what you write, sir,' said Clovis Andersen.

Ditso Ditso spun his chair round. 'You said something, Rra?'

'I said: be careful what you write. For instance, when you make a list of contractors' estimates, make sure that you put on that list the name of the firm you eventually give the work to – otherwise it looks odd.' He paused. 'More than that, Rra. It looks criminal.'

Ditso Ditso froze.

'So,' Clovis Andersen continued. 'So you should be careful when you give a contract to your mistress's brother. Especially if there's one million *pula* difference between the prices. That looks like corruption, I'm afraid.'

'Yes,' chipped in Mma Makutsi. 'That looks very like corruption, and corruption is something we don't like in Botswana. Have you noticed that, Rra? Have you read in the papers about what happens to people who practise corruption? There are not many of them around because they are mostly in another place. And that is that place at the edge of the Village. You know that place, Rra? The place with the big fence around it?'

For a few moments Ditso Ditso was silent. He had now shrunk back in his chair and was looking down at his desktop. When he spoke, his voice was barely audible. 'What do you want me to do, Mma Ramotswe?'

'I want you to look at me, Rra.'

He raised his eyes. It was clearly difficult for him to look directly at her, but she waited until he did so.

'Now, Rra, you have to call a meeting of the board. You have to tell them that you have let them down and you are resigning. You will say that you will be making a generous gift to the orphan farm to mark your time with them. Then you will withdraw your support for the hall project and tell them that it must be cancelled. You will then ask them to reinstate Mma Potokwani with immediate effect.'

He nodded. 'I will do all that, Mma.'

'And there's another thing,' Mma Ramotswe went on. 'You will also say sorry, Rra. And don't forget to do that – maybe it is the biggest thing of all.'

That evening, Clovis Andersen was invited for dinner with Mma Makutsi and Phuti Radiphuti. Mma Makutsi left the office early to complete the preparations. She could barely believe that she would be actually entertaining, at her own table, the author of *The Principles of Private Detection*; such a thing was almost inconceivable, and yet it was happening. Phuti, too, was aware of the significance of the evening, and had bought a new shirt and tie for the occasion.

'You don't have to be too formal,' said Mma Makutsi as they prepared for the arrival of their guest. 'He's very natural – just like an ordinary person. You'd never know he had written an important book like that. You'd never know that he was world famous.'

Phuti struggled with his new tie. 'There are very few world-famous people in Botswana,' he said. 'There is President Khama and the two former presidents. They are world famous. But who else is there? Can you think of anybody, Grace?'

'I cannot,' she said. 'So that makes four world-famous people altogether – and one of them, Phuti, is going to be in our place tonight.'

The thought made him fumble more. 'You'll have to help me with my tie, Grace. I get very nervous when I think of a world-famous person coming to our house.'

She helped him with the knot; she held his hand as she did so; his hand warm against hers, loving flesh on loving flesh.

'I am so proud of you, Grace,' he said. 'I am so proud.'

'And I am very proud of you, Phuti.'

There was nothing more to be said, but a great deal to be done, in the kitchen at least, where one of Mma Makutsi's tried-and-tested stews was gently simmering on the stove. She had purchased the best cut of meat available – of fine Botswana beef – and the largest, most succulent vegetables. It would be a meal that Clovis Andersen remembered; or that was what she hoped.

He arrived on time and they sat down at the table almost immediately. Mma Makutsi said grace before they began, invoking blessings on the stew, the vegetables, the house, the Double Comfort Furniture Store, the No. 1 Ladies' Detective Agency and, at the end of this rather full list, on 'our famous guest who has come from so far away but whom we have known as a friend for many years, even if we had never met him'. Phuti reached for his fork, but quickly realised that Mma Makutsi had not yet finished. 'And as we sample these good things,' she continued, 'we remember those who do not have these good things on their table or do not have a guest to share their meal with them.' Phuti nodded his agreement and reached once more for his fork, but again it was premature. 'And may our guest take back to America,' Mma Makutsi went on, 'memories of this country that are good. May he remember us when he has gone home, and may he remember too that our door is always open for him if he wants to come back. Amen.'

The *amen* was taken as a safe enough indication that the grace

246

had come to an end and the meal could begin. Clovis Andersen was delighted with the stew and had three helpings, while Phuti had two, and Mma Makutsi had a single helping – although that was a substantial one.

The conversation flowed easily. Mma Makutsi told Phuti of the events of the day, with certain details being filled in by Clovis Andersen as her narrative unfolded. Then the discussion shifted to talk of Muncie, Indiana and its charms. Phuti Radiphuti was interested to hear about any woodworking industries in the vicinity and whether they made furniture, and, if so, what that furniture was like. Mma Makutsi was keen to hear details of Clovis Andersen's cases: had he ever been to Los Angeles? Had he had any cases in Hollywood? Were there any colleges in the United States that taught both private detection and secretarial skills? For his part, Clovis Andersen wanted to know when the rains would arrive, how long they would last and how the water table held up during the dry season. He wanted to find out, too, about the old steam trains that he heard used to come down from Bulawayo; also, had all the diamonds been discovered, or was there a good chance that more would be found?

Then, when a brief silence had descended, Mma Makutsi made her suggestion. 'Wouldn't it be a wonderful idea to have an academy, Rra Andersen – to have a school of private detection? We could set it up here, and you could be one of the directors. We could call it . . . ' She turned to Phuti for inspiration.

'How about the Limpopo Academy of Private Detection?'

Mma Makutsi looked at Phuti admiringly. She was the creative one in the marriage, of course – Phuti's concerns being furniture and cattle and things of that nature – but this demonstrated an imaginative ability that might perhaps be coaxed out further. But not too far. 'That would be a very good name,' she said. 'I could be the Principal, and you could be in charge of the courses. Mma Ramotswe could be in charge of making tea. And we'd use your book as the set book.'

Clovis Andersen looked wistful. 'That would be very good, Mma. But I'm afraid . . . '

It would be so easy to stay. After all, there was nothing to take him back, and he could spend the rest of his days with these agreeable people, listening to Mma Ramotswe, doing the same small, everyday things that he filled his days with at home, but doing them here, in this place that he was gradually discovering he loved. Could one fall in love with a whole country – just like that? He wondered about that.

'We can think about it,' said Mma Makutsi. 'It's best to think about these things.'

'Yes,' said Clovis Andersen, a bit reluctantly. Things you thought about – wild, irresponsible things like setting up the Limpopo Academy of Private Detection – and never did. Good sense intervened; good sense and responsibility and perhaps also sheer inertia. Yet you could dream about them; you could keep an idea alive, filed away with all those other wonderful, foolish ideas.

At the end of the meal, Phuti ran Clovis Andersen back to his friend's house. Mma Makutsi came to keep Phuti company on the way home, and it was on this journey, after they had dropped off their guest, that she and Phuti discussed him.

'I like him very much,' said Phuti. 'He is a kind man, Mma.'

'Yes,' said Mma Makutsi. 'But there is something sad about him, isn't there? He became sadder as the evening wore on, I think.'

'Perhaps it is because he writes books,' offered Phuti. 'There are very sad-looking photographs of authors on the covers of their books. Perhaps they are all sad.'

'He is a widower, isn't he?' asked Phuti Radiphuti. 'Perhaps he's missing his late wife.' He almost said, *As I would miss you, Grace, if you became late*. But he did not say this. They were just starting their life together, and it was premature to reflect on how it would feel if one of them were to go. And he was sure that it would not happen; not for a long time, until they had been married for years and years and their children were married too and they were ready to go. That is what he hoped, as all of us who have found somebody to ease the pain of the world must hope, for ourselves, and for others.

Chapter Twenty-one

Mma Ramotswe, I Have a Confession to Make

Following, as he did, the progress of his new house with some interest, Phuti Radiphuti had now taken to visiting the site every day on his way home from work at the Double Comfort Furniture Store. Mma Makutsi sometimes accompanied him on these visits, although she was less interested in the technical details than he was. She wanted to see the walls plastered and painted; she wanted to see the tiles in position in the bathroom; she wanted to stand in her new, finished kitchen and savour the cooking smell coming from the oven. That was the prospect to which she looked forward and that she had heard would be achieved on time, just as Mr Clarkson Putumelo had promised.

Clarkson Putumelo himself was rarely on site when Phuti or Mma Makutsi visited, which was a relief from her point of view. Most of the time, building operations seemed to be under the control of a foreman, a thickset man with a moustache who had set up a table on which the house plans were spread out and from which he directed operations. This man was pleasant enough, and seemed to take the trouble to explain what was happening in a way that could be appreciated by those to whom building was a closed book.

Thomas, the builder whom Phuti had met at the beginning of the project and whom he had glimpsed briefly at the petrol station, was still working on the site, though he barely acknowledged Phuti when he saw him. Mma Makutsi had tried to engage him in conversation on one or two occasions, and although he had answered her, he had seemed embarrassed by the contact.

'It is probably because he is working illegally,' said Phuti. 'Poor man. He will have a big family back at his place and no work permit. It's probably life and death for him.'

'He's a hard worker,' said Mma Makutsi. 'Have you seen him? He never sits about when the others are having their breaks – he carries on with what he's doing.'

Phuti had seen that. 'I feel very sorry for him,' he said. 'It cannot be easy, being him.'

The day after the dinner with Clovis Andersen, Phuti Radiphuti and Mma Makutsi both paid a visit to the building site. The large wooden beams that would bear the roof were now installed on the already completed walls, and in many of the rooms the window frames had been placed in position.

'It is looking very much like a house now,' said Mma Makutsi. 'It will make all the difference having a roof.'

They inspected the bathroom, where a large white bath was already in position. Mma Makutsi stood and admired this for several minutes, dreaming of the almost inconceivable luxury of lying in the embrace of hot water and scented bath salts. She had always had to rely on showers – and weak and dribbling ones at that; she had never owned nor had the use of a bath, let alone a bath as beautiful and enticing as this. And it was such a large bath, too – enough room for two ... She turned away, her ears burning with embarrassment.

'What were you thinking about, Grace?' asked Phuti.

The question caught her unawares. She could not possibly tell him that she had entertained the thought that they might both use the bath; and yet she could hardly lie to him.

'I was thinking of how big the bath is,' she said softly.

He stared at the bath. 'Room for two,' he whispered.

They both laughed, and her embarrassment faded. 'It's also a very suitable bath for a traditionally built person,' she said. 'Even Mma Ramotswe would fit in that bath.'

'She will be very welcome to come round to our place and take a bath,' said Phuti. 'From time to time, that is. You wouldn't want people coming to use your bath every day.'

They moved through to the kitchen, where the carpentry was already at an advanced stage. Mma Makutsi thought that she had never seen so many cupboards and shelves, and said as much to Phuti. He smiled and said, 'We shall have a lot of food to put in them, Grace.' She examined one of the cupboards; the door had been well constructed and opened smoothly, closing again to make a perfect seal.

'There will be no mice in this kitchen,' she said. 'There are no holes for them to run in and out of.'

It was while Phuti was laughing at this observation that Thomas walked into the room. He had been working elsewhere on the site and had clearly not seen them, as he strode in whistling, with a saw in his hand and a large piece of insulation board tucked under his arm. His whistling stopped, and he stood stock-still.

'Well, Thomas,' said Phuti. 'This is all looking very good. And my wife thinks so too, don't you, Grace?'

Mma Makutsi smiled at the builder. 'You have been doing a very good job. Thank you for all your hard work.'

For a moment or two it seemed that Thomas was uncertain what to do. Then he put the piece of board down on the floor, at the same time looking over his shoulder.

Phuti was puzzled. 'Is there anything wrong, Rra?'

Thomas shook his head. He had been avoiding Phuti's gaze; now he met it directly. 'I want to talk to you, Rra. I will be finished in ten minutes. I will meet you down the road. You go first, and I will follow.'

'Can we not talk here?' asked Phuti. 'If you want to talk in private, my wife can go and look at the outside.'

'No, I don't mind talking to the lady too. But not here.'

They left the site and drove a short distance down the road before stopping.

'I'm not surprised by this,' said Mma Makutsi. 'Something has been going on. I noticed how strangely he behaved when we saw him at the petrol station. Remember? He pretended not to know you.'

'I thought he was shy,' said Phuti. 'There are some people like that. And there's that business with his being illegal.'

'No, it was more than that. There was something else.'

Phuti drummed his fingers on the steering wheel. He looked in the driving mirror. 'We'll soon see,' he said. 'He is coming now. He's walking down the road.'

Phuti got out of the car to greet the builder.

Thomas spoke tersely. 'Can I show you something, Rra? Can we go in the car?'

Phuti agreed, and Thomas got into the back seat. Mma Makutsi turned round to smile at him, to set him at his ease. 'We can take you wherever you want,' she said brightly. 'We are not in a hurry.'

'I'll show you,' he said. 'It isn't all that far. If you go down to the bottom of this road and turn right it will take us about fifteen minutes.'

They set off in silence. Mma Makutsi exchanged glances with Phuti, and then turned to engage Thomas in conversation.

'We are very happy with the work, Thomas. We are very happy.'

He nodded. 'It is a well-built house, Mma. It is very solid.'

She decided to press him. 'But you are unhappy about something? Do you want to speak to us about it? We know how difficult it can be for you people, being so far from home. That cannot be easy, Rra.'

He looked at her with his bloodshot eyes; it was the dust, she realised – a building site was not easy on the eyes. 'Please do not tell anybody that I have shown you this thing,' he said. 'Please do not say it was me.'

'Of course not. We won't say, will we, Phuti?'

Phuti Radiphuti assured him that he would keep the whole matter confidential – whatever it was. But what was it? Could he tell them now?

'I will show you,' said Thomas simply. 'Then you will understand.'

Thomas said nothing else on the brief journey other than to tell them which turning to take. They arrived at a side road off a residential street, and there, at the end of the road, was another building site.

'We can go in,' Thomas said. 'There is nobody working here today, and Mr Putumelo is up in Francistown this week.'

They left the car at the entrance and manoeuvred their way past a pile of building equipment – a cement mixer, a cache of planks covered with a tarpaulin, an upturned wheelbarrow.

'This is another fine-looking house,' observed Phuti. 'It is a bit bigger than ours, I think.'

'This is going to be Mr Putumelo's own house,' said Thomas. 'We are working on this one at the same time as we are working on yours.'

'Builders often do two jobs at the same time,' said Mma Makutsi. 'I have heard that ...'

She did not finish.

'Yes,' said Thomas, 'we are building Mr Putumelo's house at the same time as we are building yours.' He paused. They waited. 'And with your bricks.'

He pointed at the front wall of the house. 'See,' he said. 'Those good bricks there. Do you see them?'

Phuti looked confused. 'They are ...'

'Yes,' said Thomas. 'They are the same bricks. But you paid for them, Rra. He has been ordering double quantities for your house and then using half of them to build his own house.' He stared at Phuti. 'You have been paying all the bills he gives you, Rra?'

Phuti nodded. 'I always pay promptly.'

Thomas sighed. 'Come with me, please.'

He took them up to the wall and pointed to one of the bricks. 'Look at that brick, Rra. Just look closely at it.'

Phuti bent down to examine the surface of the brick. 'It has something scratched on it,' he said. 'I cannot quite make it out.'

'It is the letters PR,' said Thomas. 'Look. That is the P and that is the R. That stands for Phuti Radiphuti. I scratched those letters myself on a few of your bricks to make sure, and here is one of them. There is another one round the side there. There is no doubt: these bricks are yours, Rra. They come from the pile of bricks he ordered for you – I have made quite sure of that.'

Phuti straightened up. He was remembering his conversation with his aunt. She had talked about Mr Putumelo's financial problems; she had commented on how strange it was that in his straitened circumstances he should still be building himself a house. Of course; of course. 'We are being cheated,' he said.

'Yes,' said Thomas. 'Mr Putumelo is a very good builder. He is quick and he has very high standards. But he is a cheat. That is the problem.'

Phuti reached out to put a hand on Thomas's shoulder. 'You have been very brave, Rra.'

Thomas shook his head. 'I am not brave ... '

'Yes, you are,' said Mma Makutsi. 'You are very brave. It is hard to tell the truth about the person who gives you your job – and who can take it away again.'

Thomas sighed. 'I have been feeling very bad about this because I know that you are good people. I felt ashamed.'

'But it was not your fault, Rra,' said Phuti reassuringly. 'You just did your job. It is that Mr Putumelo.' He turned to Grace. 'We will have to do something.'

'Yes,' she said. 'We'll have to do something.' She had no idea, though, of what to do. Perhaps Mma Ramotswe might suggest something.

But it was Thomas who made the suggestion. 'I think that it would be best not to do anything just yet,' he said. 'If you went to the police you would not have any real proof, and even if they charged him, then what would happen to all of us – the men who work for him? Let us finish your house. If you have a row with him now, then he will pull all the men off the site and you will have a house with no roof.'

'That would not be good,' said Mma Makutsi.

Thomas smiled. It was the first time they had seen him do this. 'No. You need a roof.'

'And then?'

'You will have a final bill to pay at the end. Cut it in half and say that this is for the bricks that he borrowed from you. Tell him that you can easily see how he forgot to take that into account with the bill, and so you have corrected the error. Tell him that you have seen the bricks in his new house – you were just passing by – and you realised that this had happened when you saw your initials on one of them. Say that you had put the initials there when you had called in at his yard and he was not there. Tell him that you were keen that the bricks should not be stolen by some passer-by. Tell him where to look for the bricks with the initials.'

Phuti listened to this gravely. 'I think I shall do all that, Rra,' he said. 'You know, I'm remembering something. When we first agreed to do this job, he said that my house had his name written all over it. Well . . .'

'His house has *your* name written all over it,' said Grace.

The builder reflected on this for a few moments. 'That is true,' he said.

They walked back to the car. 'I'm very grateful to you, Thomas,' said Phuti. 'You didn't have to do this.'

'I did,' said Thomas. 'I did have to do it, Rra.'

Phuti looked thoughtful. 'You're a carpenter, aren't you?'

'That, and other things,' said Thomas. 'But that is my first trade.'

Phuti looked at Mma Makutsi, who was watching him with interest. 'We have a small workshop,' he said slowly. 'We have it for repairs and for some contract work. We have been able to get work permits for one or two men we take on because we make quite a lot of furniture for schools. Desks and things like that. We could get you one if you came to work for us.'

Thomas stood quite still. 'That is not why I did this, Rra.'

'I know,' said Phuti. 'And that is why I want to offer you that job.'

'You will like working for my husband,' said Mma Makutsi.

'I will,' said Thomas. 'Yes, Mma, I will.'

They got into the car and drove off down the road.

Clovis Andersen came to see Mma Ramotswe on the day before his departure. It was early on a Saturday morning, and she was at home, walking about her garden, when he called. She offered him a cup of tea, which she said they could drink as she showed him her plants and Mr J. L. B. Matekoni's vegetables. He had expressed an interest in hearing the Setswana names of some of the plants, and she had promised to tell him these – or at least to try to. 'The trouble is that we are losing many of those words, Rra. We're forgetting what these plants are called. They are lovely names, but we are losing them.'

'We're losing words too,' he said. 'People are forgetting about the land.'

'Even in your place, Rra?'

'Yes,' he said. 'Even in my place.'

Mma Ramotswe looked up into the branches of her favourite acacia tree. 'So, we'll all soon be living in towns and cities and will forget where we came from. We'll forget who feeds us. That is the earth, I think. And yet we'll forget her.'

'I hope not,' said Clovis Andersen. 'At least I won't forget it. Nor you, Mma . . . '

'No, I won't forget it.'

'I meant: I won't forget you, Mma Ramotswe.'

She smiled at him. It was a kind thing for him to say, but of course he would forget her. He was an important, busy man from far away: why should he remember a woman who lived in a place that was small by comparison with his own country; a woman who had only a tiny business and not very important things to do? Why should he remember?

She made tea and brought it out to him, and together they

started to walk about the garden. She showed him her mopipi tree, which had been making good progress but had to be protected from the ravages of ants. She showed him her bed of aloes that were producing intense red flowers on spiky shafts. She showed him the beans that Mr J. L. B. Matekoni irrigated in the dry-land way, with drips of precious water tracking down a suspended thread.

And then, quite suddenly, he turned to her and said, 'Mma Ramotswe, I have a confession to make. I cannot leave without saying something to you.'

She looked up at him; he was much taller than she was. 'What is it, Rra?'

'You have been so kind to me, Mma Ramotswe. You and Mma Makutsi. You have made my stay such a good one.'

'But we have enjoyed it, Rra, and you have helped us so much. We've been honoured to have you. Mma Makutsi in particular. Your visit has been a very, very big thing for her. She comes from Bobonong, you see, and—'

'It's not that,' Clovis Andersen interrupted. 'It's just that . . . well, I'm not who you think I am.'

She looked him with astonishment. 'You're not Clovis Andersen?'

'No, of course I'm Clovis Andersen. But Clovis Andersen is not the great detective you think he is. He's a failed detective from Muncie, Indiana. He's a man who has hardly any clients and never really solves any cases. He's a nobody, Mma Ramotswe.'

She laughed. 'But that is nonsense, Rra. You are the author of that great book, *The Principles of Private Detection*. That book is world famous. It's very important.'

He shook his head – sadly. 'No, Mma Ramotswe. The book's not well known at all. I wrote it, yes, but I couldn't even get it properly published. So I had it printed privately – just two hundred copies. Eighty of those are still in boxes in my garage. We sold about thirty copies, that's all. I gave away the rest, but somehow one of those seems to have got into your hands. I have no idea how it happened, but it did. The book's nothing, Mma. Nothing.'

She stood in front of him, the sun in her eyes now, preventing her from seeing him properly. She lifted a hand to shade her brow. She saw his face, which seemed to her to be racked with pain, with regret.

'Rra,' she said. 'You mustn't say that. You must never, never say that. Even if you had printed only ten copies – five copies, maybe – it would still be a very important book. It has helped us so much, Rra, and in turn we've been able to help so many people in our work. Every one of those people, Rra, is happier now because of what you did. Think of that – just think of that.'

He stared at her. 'Do you think . . .' he began.

'Of course I think that, Rra. I *know* it, and Mma Makutsi knows it too. And Mr J. L. B. Matekoni. We all know it.'

He was at a loss for words. Mma Ramotswe could see that, and so she continued. 'I could tell, Rra Andersen, that you were unhappy when you came here. I could tell that it was because you were thinking of your late wife.'

'I was. Yes.'

'Of course you were. We must think of late people because I believe they're still with us – in a way. And so a late person can stay with you all your life, until it is your turn to become late too. And the late person doesn't want you to be miserable. A late person doesn't want you to think that your work is no use. A late person wants you to get on with life, to do things, to make good use of your time. That is well known, Rra. It is very well known.'

He said nothing, but she knew that he had heard her words.

'So, let's finish our tea, Rra. Then we can look at that tree over there. Its leaves are very fine, Rra, and I want to show them to you.'

They walked to the far side of her garden. 'We have a lot to be grateful for, Rra,' Mma Ramotswe said. She gestured to the small patch of her country that made up her garden. Her gesture took in her fence, and beyond that the road, and beyond that all Botswana and the world. 'All that,' she said. 'That is what we have to be grateful for.'

She did not look at him, because she sensed that he needed privacy, and a man may be embarrassed by his tears. So she simply touched him lightly on the arm and waited until he was ready to walk back.

He thought: *The Limpopo Academy of Private Detection*. Then he thought: *Not really*. But he smiled nonetheless.

Alexander McCall Smith is the author of over eighty books on a wide array of subjects. For many years he was Professor of Medical Law at the University of Edinburgh and served on national and international bioethics bodies. Then in 1999 he achieved global recognition for his award-winning series The No. 1 Ladies' Detective Agency, and thereafter has devoted his time to the writing of fiction, including the 44 Scotland Street and Corduroy Mansions series. His books have been translated into forty-five languages. He lives in Edinburgh with his wife, Elizabeth, a doctor.